WHO NEEDS A HERO

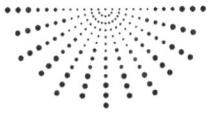

JENNIFER L. HART

ELEMENTS UNLEASHED

❀ Created with Vellum

A NOTE TO MY READER:

Who Needs A Hero, originally titled *The Story of Maggie and Neil*, started out as backstory I developed while working on the *Misadventures of the Laundry Hag* series. When creating the first mystery I found myself asking questions about the two of them. How did they meet and become the dynamite couple I'd grown to love? What happened to Maggie's parents, and Josh's and Kenny's biological mother? Why is Maggie terrified of hospitals and so indulgent with her mooch of a brother? And just what the hell goes on in Neil's head, is he really that perfect?

Yes, yes he is. Best. Hero. Ever.

So anyhow, there I was, saddled with all of these damn questions that just would not leave me in peace. So I started writing and while I'd like to say I blazed through this book, sadly that's not how it happened. I'd wander off, get distracted on another project, come back and poke. It wasn't until I hooked up with my amazing critique partner that this story really started to take shape. Original scenes were cut, some altogether, others added to make a more cohesive whole. There were times it felt more like piecing together a patchwork quilt than a book.

This book is unique in many regards. It is set ten years before the first Laundry Hag book, approximately 1996. You'll notice for the most part the use of pagers instead of cell phones, and no one is on Facebook or Twitter. Film cameras, instead of digital, stuff like that.

Neil's been given his own first-person point of view. I took a whole lot of grief over this peculiarity. That sort of thing "just isn't done".

Well, it is now. I pride myself on being a trendsetter. Remember where you saw it first, folks! This book is also the first one of my own that reduced me to tears. Laughter and tears in one story. It's my love letter to them and to you. Enjoy the ride and as always happy reading,

~ *Jennifer L. Hart, 2011*

An updated note to my reader:

It's never fun to go back to a work you held in such high esteem after a decade and realize what a horrific train wreck it really was. ***Heard from outside my office*** "What, are you trying to use every SAT word in one book?" and "For the love of grief, woman, learn how to use a hyphen!"

Despite my early career growing pains, or maybe because of them, Who Needs A Hero? *still hold a special place in my heart. It was a women's fiction book masquerading as a military romance, that grew out of a not so cozy mystery series. It's a tribute to my years of being a Navy wife. It's a visible marker on the trailhead of my career pointing me to the place I would eventually end up.*

Right back to where I started. Writing dirty books full of laughter, cussing, and getting naked.

Happy reading!

Jen

WHO NEEDS A HERO

Who Needs A Hero
Hart/ Jennifer L.

1.Women's—Fiction 2. Virginia Beach—Fiction 3. Military—
Fiction 4. Navy SEALs—Fiction 5. Family Life—Fiction 6.
Humor—Fiction 7. Military Towns—Fiction 8. Parenthood
—Fiction 9. American Humorous—Fiction 10. Beach Living
—Fiction 11. Divorce— Fiction 12. BBW—Fiction I. Title

ISBN: 978-1-951215-80-4

WHO NEEDS A HERO

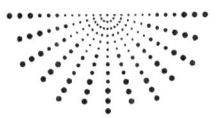

CHAPTER ONE

"Seriously Maggie, why does he want to marry you?" my younger brother asked with a mouthful of pizza, one eye on the Redskins game playing on the television. My family believed in multitasking. "You're his secretary for God's sake."

"Don't talk with your mouth full, you're going to choke. And I'm his *assistant*, you weenie. We're getting married because he loves me." I replied with the utmost confidence. Sure, he hadn't said the words, but why else would he want to spend the rest of his life with me?

"I'm moving in with Gloria next week and I don't love her. How come this guy who supposedly loves you won't let you live with him?" Marty raised one eyebrow, a skill I'd never mastered.

"He's old-fashioned. He wants to wait until after we're married."

Marty snorted and some root beer shot out of his nose. "Old-fashioned guys don't get it on in the backseat of a Camaro."

I winced at the memory. "I never should have told you

about that. It was a long time ago and how was I supposed to know the rocking car meant he was boffing his girlfriend? Can I help it if my warped little prepubescent mind thought a vagrant was stealing his car? I was only ten, for the love of grief!"

"Well, you're being naïve again, Maggie. Something isn't right."

I wiped up the root beer with a napkin. "Maybe I am naïve, but I'm happy. Can't you be happy for me, too?"

Washington scored a touchdown and Marty yeah baby-ed the team before he answered my question. "I want to be happy for you Sis, but I still think you should ask him about the money again. Get it before the two of you are married. Go over there now and ask him for it." Marty pointed his pizza crust at the door.

"If it'll make you happy, Sprout, I will." With a spring in my step, I went.

My fiancé only lived a few blocks to the southwest of my sublet condo. The Jetta—or the pee-pee mobile as Marty was fond of calling my ride—was on its last legs so I decided to walk. The leaves on the deciduous trees had a jaundiced look, pale yellow or light orange with brown flecks as they often did this time of year. Richmond didn't boast the glorious fall foliage that some other parts of Virginia were known for. My one-point-five caret diamond sparkled with the colors of the setting sun and an early October breeze lifted my hair back from my shoulders. Life was good.

I reached his apartment building as the light faded and the doorman recognized me right away. "Good evening, Miss Maggie." He greeted me with a slight bow of his stooped, arthritic shoulders.

"Hi Eddie, how are you feeling?"

"Can't complain." The dour-faced doorman offered me one of his rare half-smiles. "You look very nice this evening."

"Thank you. Is he in?" I chucked my thumb at the second floor.

Eddie's expression clouded over—he didn't care for my fiancé. "I believe so, Ma'am."

My spirits soared so high I didn't even mind the Ma'am-ing. I thanked him and continued on my way into the lobby.

Wanting to burn off my second slice of pizza, I skipped the elevator and headed for the stairs. An elderly couple with a pair of wiener dogs made their way down and we exchanged pleasantries as I held the door for them.

The second-floor hallway was empty, as most of the building's inhabitants were the upwardly mobile sort who spent every evening out being seen. Upwardly mobile types, much like my boss.

Whose door I'd reached. Mentally calling up the office schedule, I gnawed on my lip and wondered if he was even home. Well if not, I'd wait, maybe call his mother and talk wedding details. All those colors and fabrics to choose from, all the time I needed to invest—never mind the money for something I'd wear once. Ick, not a chore made for a woman like me. Might as well get it over with, since I lacked female relatives to run interference and his sister, Justine, had emailed me from college to say my future mother-in-law wanted to talk turkey. I put the key in the lock, turned the doorknob, and was about to announce my arrival when I saw it.

The tract lights over the entryway were dim and it took a moment for me to absorb the significance of the lacy black bra draped over the barstool. I picked it up between shaking fingers and turned toward the cracked bedroom door, where Barry White crooned in dulcet sensuality. I stopped outside the door, fighting the urge to hurl when his voice greeted me.

"That was great, baby." The Jackass sounded out of breath. I closed my eyes in revulsion, knowing *exactly* how he looked as he said those words. After all, it had been my bra on the barstool often enough.

"You never answered me. When are you gonna ditch her?" The female voice sounded catty and I had no doubt I was the 'her' in question.

I heard a distinctly male grunt. "These things take time, sweetheart. You need to be patient."

"I've been patient for over four years now, you jerk! You promised me you were going to tell her you lost all of her money and send her packing! Then the next day, you tell me you're engaged to her!"

"Well, I couldn't tell her I was paying for your breast implants with their inheritance! Really Darcy, how do you suppose—"

Darcy. I knew that name. The rat bastard had me cancel engagements with Darcy for him regularly about six months before I'd started shtupping my boss. I had only seen her in person once and I could clearly picture her silky long blond hair and trim figure. Must have been before the breast augmentation.

"Besides, it's just a phony engagement." My heart ripped in two at his callous words.

"Watch your tone with me, Mr. High-and-Mighty! You were the one who wanted me to get that surgery! Besides, you told me you made nearly a million dollars with her investment. Where did it all go?"

I needed to sit down. Good question, Darcy. "Darcy, honey, calm down. You know I've had problems with the IRS —they froze my assets. I needed the money to keep me afloat while I straightened everything out."

A million dollars. I had owned a million dollars and I never even knew it. Now the money from my father's hard-ware store and the insurance capital from my childhood home was gone, used to support the yuppie lifestyle of a scamming, no good rat bastard.

"I want her out of my condo. You told me it was only temporary, yet she's still there, her fat ass leaving imprints on my sofa!"

That. Was. It.

I pushed open the door. "Don't worry, Darcy. I'll be out of your condo by morning." I looked at The Jackass. "And I'll be calling your good friends at the IRS to let them know what a considerate taxpayer you've been." I spun on my heel and marched out of the apartment with my dignity in shreds, held together with spit and phony pride.

"Maggie, wait!" The Jackass chased me down the hall, twig, and berries bared for all to see. He grabbed my arm and spun me around to face him, but I didn't think before I brought my knee up with all the force of a woman scorned. His face took on a deathly pallor before he crumpled like a sack of shit to the beige carpet. I didn't bother to stick around to see if he would retch—though the thought held a certain grim appeal— just swung my ass out the door without a backward glance.

My brother was gone when I returned to the condo to pack my belongings. With shaking hands I called Marty's girlfriend's cell phone and left a voice mail to inform my brother I was packing up his stuff and I would get him a room at the Holiday Inn until he moved in with Gloria. I jogged down to the super's door and asked him if I could borrow a Phillips Head. Then I took some tuna steaks out of the freezer and used the screwdriver to remove the vent covers on the heating system. I dropped the fish in, reattached the covers, and cranked the thermostat to eighty-five. Welcome home, Darcy.

I returned the screwdriver on my way out to the car and

bags loaded, drove over to the nearest motel, where I rented a room under Marty's name. I could have stayed there, but I was wound up and needed to move. Put some distance between my body and my sham of a life. I dropped off the bags and headed east on I-64. The pee-pee mobile took a crap in the form of a busted alternator right at the 264 interchange. It was a struggle but the downhill momentum helped me guide it to the shoulder of the road. Without a moment's hesitation, I left my bags in the car and started to walk. I hoofed it the next ten miles to the resort area of Virginia Beach fueled by indignation. Every step drove the point home.

Stupid, stupid, STUPID!!!!

Fury burned through my system like acid. I was furious at The Jackass, at my parents for dying, my brother for being an ungrateful burden, but most of all with myself for being so gullible. Somewhere in my brain, a voice shouted that I could be accosted, mugged, raped, left for dead in a gutter, but the rage blotted out fear and rational thought. At that point, I had truly hit emotional rock bottom.

Only when the sun rose directly in front of me, due east from my current location at Atlantic Avenue at Seventeenth Street, did I realize I'd been walking all night. Gulls cried out, eager to find a tasty treat in the churning ocean below. I broke into a jog when I saw the first waves and inhaled the salty tang of low tide. At least it was the end of October and there was nary a tourist to be seen. I really didn't want witnesses to my meltdown. So focused on my goal. I crashed into a girl out for some early morning roller-blading on the boardwalk. Murmuring a very insincere apology, I helped her to her feet. She surveyed me for a second, eyes wide, mouth agog, and took off in the direction she had come from at an unnecessarily fast clip.

I trudged through the sand and went to the water's edge to remove my ring. It bounced in my palm a few times before

I pulled back my arm and hurled it with all of my strength into the sea. My purpose was achieved. I felt...empty. My legs wobbled as I staggered back a few feet and collapsed into a fetal ball, crying all the tears held in check since my parents' death. I cried for them, for Marty, but mostly for myself and the waste of my youth. I ignored the bleat of seagulls and the taste of sand and briny morning air. I never wanted to move again.

And that was where he found me.

"NICE THROW. Hell of an arm you got there."

I looked up through my tears to see a man staring at the spot where I had pitched the ring. His mouth curved in a bemused smile, but when he turned and met my gaze sharp intelligence and concern lit his hazel-green eyes. An unbelievably handsome man, giving a new definition to the term sculpted. A long-sleeved gray T-shirt clung to his upper body. His shoulders looked like they could carry the weight of the world and the fit of the fabric showed off an awe-inspiring six-pack. His left hand had been shoved into one of a zillion pockets in his tan cargo pants that rode low on lean hips.

Dream or hallucination? It had been a brutal night, maybe my psyche had snapped like a dry twig. I started the perusal over. He wore his dark brown hair a little shaggy but oh so boyishly charming. Streamlined nose and high cheekbones were in perfect symmetry and deeply tanned skin covered lean muscle that he didn't exactly advertise but became evident nonetheless. The lightening sky over the crashing waves of the Atlantic contrasted his profile, casting him in sharp relief against a soft-focus backdrop, a living, breathing specimen of male perfection.

Great. Just what I freaking needed.

"Look." I narrowed my eyes on Mr. Gorgeous. "I'm kind of in the middle of a nervous breakdown and after that, I plan on having a very festive pity party, table for one, so unless you are here to put me out of my misery I suggest you scurry on your way."

He flashed me a whiter-than-Vanna White smile, which only succeeded in making me feel like dweeby Pat Sajak. I guess that meant God was Merv Griffin and He was laughing His ass off. The handsome stranger held his hand out to me and for some bizarre reason, I took it.

He pulled me to my feet and then turned to walk away. I stared at his backside, wondering if I had hit my head at some point, sure this couldn't be real because Merv Griffin only knows—actual people weren't so glorious. He looked back when he realized I hadn't followed him.

"It's best to keep moving, that way the demons can't catch you."

"That's easy for you to say, you were never the fat girl in gym class who couldn't outrun her own shadow," I snipped at him. Gesturing at the roaring surf, I continued, "Besides, I've hit the Atlantic. Running is no longer an option."

He strolled back over to me, locks of hair tussled in the early morning sea breeze. If possible he appeared even more magnificent in motion. Something in the way he moved choreographed lethal intent, a dangerous predator, lying low, waiting for the right moment to spring at his unsuspecting prey.

"Then you've got to swim for it," he informed me before he did just that. His easy gait morphed into a determined sprint and he crashed against the oncoming waves—one awesome force of nature against another.

I think a crab crawled into my mouth when my jaw hit the sand. Stupefied, I watched him swim in the cold water, a steady crawl full of power growing smaller as he neared the horizon. And then he vanished.

"Okay, Maggie, you're officially psychotic," I murmured to myself and sat down hard on the sand. My gaze trained on the spot where he had disappeared and I wondered what Freud would say about my vision. Probably something like I hated my mother and needed to get laid.

Maybe he was a merman, returning to his home beneath the sea where he could shag Ariel and tell tales about the chemically unbalanced woman he'd met on the beach.

"If she is an example of the people above, the land is ripe for the picking!" he would announce to his fellow merfolk as they dined on lobster before a roaring fire in the great hall. Although how the fire stayed lit underwater, or how they cooked the lobster for that matter...

"Hey!"

I looked up for the second time to see my dripping wet merman—sans fins—holding out his hand to me. He held my one-point-five carat solitaire, which looked none the worse for wear. I took it from him with a shaking hand.

"Oh my God." Water dripped from his hair, eyelashes, nose, and chin and I shivered in sympathy as the cool wind cut through my denim jacket. "Are you insane? You're going to get hypothermia!"

He *winked* at me. "Not likely. The water temperature is in the low fifties. I've been in much colder water for longer periods. It's not exactly comfortable, but I'll pull through."

Master of the understatement.

"Come on." This time he strode back up the beach without checking to see if I tagged along. Only an idiot would, but follow I did. He stopped short of the boardwalk where he retrieved a fraying blue towel and a small white card, which I instantly recognized as a hotel room key.

9

"You leave your hotel key sitting in the sand?" My tone sounded incredulous. "Where are you from, Mayberry?"

He didn't look at me as he dried his stylishly unkempt brown hair. "It's a magnetized card. If I'd lost it, I'd go to the front desk and they'd issue me a new one."

"Yeah, but someone could steal it, go through your stuff."

He shrugged. "Whatever, it's just stuff. Nothing irreplaceable."

I remained silent as he slipped on a pair of leather sandals and headed up the ramp to the boardwalk. He made no concession to the wind as it slapped his wet clothing, just strode along at a steady pace with me trailing behind him like a bitchy lost mongrel hoping for a good belly scratch.

The princess-cut diamond bit into my palm. I wanted to ask his name and how he had retrieved my ring, but even despite his assurance that he wouldn't freeze to death, I wanted him to get warm and dry as soon as possible. Answers could wait.

We were the focus of more than a few raised eyebrows as we entered the hotel lobby, not one of the pricier ones along Atlantic Avenue, but a nice little five-story place with quite a bit of charm. My haggard appearance might have drawn notice if I'd been alone, but my companion commanded all the attention. I figured the men were astonished by his sodden clothing while the women were checking out his magnificent bod. He dripped into the elevator and I paused, unsure if I wanted to go all the way. Into his room. Where he would get naked.

A low growl rumbled in his chest as he reached for my arm and propelled me into the elevator. I didn't resist, glad to follow a little while longer and study every detail of the merman. He pushed the button for the fifth floor. Coffee-colored hairs were visible on his forearms, along with thin white stripes, possibly old scars. He didn't shift or fidget, just gazed as the numbers on the elevator lit up with the car's progress. I tried to think of something to say, but my mind had gone out to lunch. He seemed content to absorb the Kenny Logins Muzak and drip on the floor. The door dinged open all too soon.

He ambled halfway down the hall as if he didn't have a care and inserted the key card. The light turned green and he gripped the handle, pushing the door open. My brain chose that moment to reappear and panic gripped my lungs in a vice.

"I'll just wait for you here." I toed at the carpet like a lost child.

He gave me a hard stare, allowing the silence to amplify my statement. A flash of something that might have been disappointment came and went. Or maybe it was just my severely battered heart, making me see things not really there. Wanting to be wanted. Hazel green eyes bore into me and it felt as if he sized me up like he could read my thoughts as easily as he had found a diamond in an underwater sand dune.

"You'll be all right." His deep voice sparked something in me, something totally unfamiliar that I craved with rabid desperation. I nodded even though he hadn't phrased it as a question.

Without a backward glance, he entered the room and shut the door. I stared at the brass numbers, 517, trying to jumpstart my brain. What the hell had just happened? Who *was* this guy?

I gazed at the ring in my hand through new eyes. When I had started driving last night, my only intention had been to exorcize The Jackass from my heart and get rid of this final reminder of him in one grand gesture. And I had. The ring had been cleansed in the ocean, a materialistic baptism that wiped the remaining vestiges of sentiment from my mind. I saw it now not as a reminder of The Jackass, but as the means to a fresh start. The gorgeous merman had known this and had given me a new chance.

"Thank you," I whispered at number 517. I touched the door, but jumped when I heard footsteps inside. I ran and only Merv Griffin knew how fast.

CHAPTER TWO

Run away, little girl. I leaned back against the door and closed my eyes as the soft whisk-whisk of her footsteps retreated. When I'd seen her on the beach, slumped in defeat as if the entire world had given her one hell of a beating, my first thought had been, *what a freaking drama queen.*

Something about her though told me her pain hadn't been choreographed. She wasn't Amber, didn't need to put on a show for the whole freaking world. And though it was selfish, I felt a moment's satisfaction knowing she was as beaten down. Just like me. *Misery loves company and all that happy horseshit.*

On the nightstand, my cell phone trilled and I groaned. For fuck's sake, what would it take to get a day of peace? Who needed saving now?

Deciding to roll the dice, I ignored the caller ID and flipped open the phone. Maybe it would be Amber. "Phillips." Even my voice sounded worn out.

"What's doing, Neil?" The pitch resounded several

octaves too low for the person I really needed to talk to. Sitting down on the bed I scrubbed a hand over my face. Was seven in the morning too early for a drink? "Do you need something, J.T?"

"I thought you were back on active duty."

"I am."

"So why aren't you here for PT?" In my mind's eye, I imagined the other SEAL nagging like an old fishwife, hands-on-hips. Bitch, moan, sigh.

When the hell did he turn into my mother? Wait, Mommy Dearest had never been this concerned with my habits. "Doctor's orders. A little down time before we go wheels up." I couldn't manage to hide the resentment behind the words.

A pause and then JT asked, "Did you see the boys yet?"

"No, Amber won't answer the goddamn phone." Maybe she wasn't there alone. I really didn't want to think about the possibility. She was still my wife and the thought of her with another man sent my mind reeling back into the darkness.

"That's harsh. You should go get laid." J.T.'s answer to all of life's little hurdles? *Get your dick wet.*

For no obvious reason, I thought of the frazzled brunette from the beach, with those luminous blue eyes and lush curves. So young, almost painfully so, but her eyes held the same weariness I'd seen in the mirror every morning. Too bad she hadn't come into the room. Even now I could be rolling around on the queen-size bed, finding out if she could possibly be as soft as she looked....

J.T droned on in my ear, something about meeting up later that night at one of the dive bars he and the other guys frequented while on liberty. "Now's really not a good time. I'll see you later."

I shut the phone with a snap and flopped back on the bed, uncaring about my soggy clothes or the effect the seawater would have on the hotel comforter.

How in the hell did I manage to find that ring? Disbelief thrummed through me that I'd gone in after it. Needle and a haystack had nothing on that challenge. But having a goal, a purpose again, felt awesome. I needed to get back into the field, to fight the wars I'd been trained to fight, outsmarting the bad guys. Idleness sucked rotten eggs.

Vividly, I recalled the look of amazement on her face. Total fucking hero-worship—like I'd hung the moon or some shit. If I'd pushed, she would have let me do whatever I'd wanted, taken her any way I'd wanted....

A groan escaped as I realized cargo shorts dipped in brine and an erection didn't mix worth shit. I stood and stripped off the wet clothes, imagining she had stayed here to watch, saw how hard I'd grown for her, blue eyes wide and inviting....

I lay back again, fisting my shaft, fantasizing about her pink little lips closing over the head when she took me in her mouth.

Fuck. This was so wrong, I didn't even know her name and she'd obviously been at the end of her frayed rope, but my hand wouldn't stop, the picture locked in my mind of her caressing my balls while laving me with her tongue.

"Come for me," she'd whisper, a soft lilt in her voice right before she took me deep.

Who was I to say no?

I RAN FROM THE HOTEL, only to stop short when it dawned on me I had nowhere to go. My esophagus seized up from pure panic. I doubled over and took a moment to catch my breath. The lack of direction and sleep made me punchy and I turned in a circle, considering my future. I'd had dreams. Most were of the pie-in-the-sky variety but until that moment, the here and now had always demanded more attention. The voice in my head—which sounded suspiciously like my mother's—reminded me that *God helps those who help themselves.* My eyes focused on the small ring in my hand. There *was* something I could do.

With a purposeful stride, I marched into the hotel next door from the merman's.

A quick scan of the lobby revealed that tourist season had indeed ended because the only voices came from the blaring television and the gray-haired woman behind the concierge desk appeared totally enthralled with Al Roker. I decided to wait for a commercial. It's a good idea never to come between a little old lady and her Al time.

"Do you have a phonebook?" I queried in my most respectful voice. The effect was somewhat ruined because I had to shout to be heard over the shattering decibels blaring from the television. The woman squinted at me through glasses thicker than windows on the space shuttle. Even the coke-bottle lenses couldn't mask the suspicion in her eyes. The polished brass plaque on the wall behind the desk flaunted my reflection and I winced. I looked like a strung-out junkie, with wild, windblown hair and a serious hint of desperation in my eyes.

"I had a rough night." Maggie Sampson, mistress of the understatement.

The commercials ended and the woman obviously had her priorities in order, whether I happened to be a crazed psycho or not.

"There's a pay phone with one down the hall by the elevators. It's attached, so don't be getting any ideas."

Because there's such a high demand for used phonebooks on the black market. I waited until turning the corner before indulging in an exaggerated eye roll. At least she hadn't called the cops. The book hung by one corner and I flipped the battered pages until seeing the pawn shop listings.

First, I called a tow truck to pick up my POS car that had crapped out at the I-264 interchange. Hopefully, it hadn't been impounded because I did not have the funds to spring it. Next a cab company to take me to my destination.

It seemed like a good idea to wait across the street from the hotel, and I half hoped to see the merman again. The idea *he* might not want to see *me* kept me from returning to room 517. So, I climbed into the cab with a final wistful glance at the Atlantic. I directed the cab driver to the address I had memorized from the book, a pawn shop up near the Navy base at Oceana. The driver agreed to wait and I went inside and haggled over the sale of the ring. I returned to the taxi three hundred dollars richer, sans the cab fare. I'd been had, but was too excited over the money to be bothered by it. After a lifetime of spinelessness, this didn't even rate as worth a second thought. Besides, the ring would make some Navy sweetheart very happy. Hooyah!

I requested the driver bring me back to the strip where I paid him and headed into the nearest McDonalds. I bought two bacon, egg, and cheese McMuffins and two large coffees I hate the noxious brew but I either needed toothpicks or some serious caffeine to keep my eyelids up. Any grease-filled port in a storm.

After purchasing a copy of the *Virginia Pilot* I took my cache to a bench on the boardwalk. The coffee burned the roof of my mouth and scalded my tongue, but I didn't care. Opening the paper to the classified ads, I searched for what I needed most—a job. With no intention of going back to Richmond hat in hand, I read ad after ad in the help wanted section. Slim pickings, considering I possessed a high school degree, one job where I slept with my boss, and no references. The food service column held a bit of potential, but I needed a place to live and doubted minimum wage would cut it. The only things going for me were my complete lack of pride and determination to survive.

I found the perfect listing under childcare help wanted. The listing advertised a live-in position for a nanny of two young boys, with no experience required. I blanched slightly, wondering who would leave his or her children with someone with no experience. This ad must be a sign from the almighty, telling me since I wasn't a pervert these kids needed me as their nanny.

I took the paper to a telephone booth and called the number on the listing. A recorded message picked up.

"You have reached the Phillips's residence. No one is available to take your call right now. If you are calling in regards to the nanny position, it has already been filled. Please leave a message after the beep."

My heart sank. Terrific, back to square one. The phone beeped and I was about to hang up when a breathless voice answered. "Hello?"

"I'm sorry to bother you," I apologized. "I read about the nanny position—"

"Oh thank God!" the woman exclaimed. "When can you start?"

My eyebrows drew down in confusion. "I thought the position had been filled."

"The Nanny I hired ran off with her sailor boyfriend who just got back from a six-month cruise. He's her new husband now. God, I hate this Navy town!"

So, why do you live here? I almost asked, but the thought cut off as a jet roared by overhead. Probably shouldn't question a possible future employer, even one who sounded like she might be a shovel shy of a toolshed. I didn't have to like her. Heck, I'd loved my last boss, and look how well *that* turned out. "What is it you do, Ma'am?"

"I'm an insurance agent at Geico and I've had to take off work every time I can't find someone to be with the boys. I'm desperate! When can you be here?"

Seriously? "Um...?"

"Would tomorrow be too soon? Or even better, tonight. I have a date and I really don't want to cancel. Could you be here by seven, Miss...?"

"Sampson. Maggie Sampson." I supplied. "Yeah, I guess I could come by tonight."

"Wonderful! My name is Amber Phillips." She rattled off her address, which I wrote down on my newspaper.

"The ad said something about live-in help. Where exactly will I be staying?"

"I have a guest bedroom all set. It's right next to the boys' room, so it'll be convenient to get up with the baby. He's been colicky."

Convenient for her, perhaps. Well, I didn't have many options and this job didn't require wearing a hairnet. How hard could it be?

"I'll be there at seven, Miss Phillips."

"It's Mrs. Phillips, but not for much longer. Call me Amber, hon," she simpered in that golly-gee-whiz-aren't-we-gonna-be-chums kind of way. Gack.

I never knew what to make of women who 'honned 'other women. Especially ones they didn't know. And I really didn't know how to react to the "but not for much longer" remark So I said goodbye instead and stared out at the water for a long time.

ONLY ONE OTHER time in my life had I felt so lost. With nowhere to rush off to, no brother to care for I sat and gazed at the ocean, inhaling the sharp tang of sea salt and just being. The crashing waves with the incoming tide lulled me into a weird trance and I couldn't help but think about that dark time.

I'd been out on a date—a really horrific date my mother had arranged for me. Sad, but at seventeen and with high school graduation looming near, I'd never gone on a date before. Of course, the rumors that I might be a lesbian hadn't helped an already dormant social life. I happened to be in love with my best friend's brother ever since the Camaro incident. If not for those rumors and the idiotic hope my beloved would hear about my new romance and be over-come with jealousy, I'd have been at home that night, butt planted on the couch next to my dad.

I'd recognized the police officer from a few of the assem-blies at school regarding drug awareness, but he appeared paler now and so tense he almost vibrated.

My body went numb. Some niggling premonition caused a knot to form in my stomach and the evening of horrors got bumped up to a whole new nightmarish level. I listened silently while the female officer told me about the accident, a gas leak which had engulfed our house in a fireball, taking my parents along with it. I remember not blinking as the hits just kept on coming. She informed me my father was already gone. *Whump.* My mother had been rushed to the hospital with third-degree burns. *Thwack.* Did I know where my brother might be?

Marty.

Supposedly he'd been sleeping over at Frankie Pullman's house, but Marty had a way of migrating, even at sixteen. Vivid flashbacks of the ride to the hospital, windows rolled up against the unseasonable heat, with the occasional siren disrupting the calm May night. I must have walked down the hospital corridors, but the next thing I knew, had been seated in an uncomfortable plastic chair, staring at a crack in the utilitarian linoleum flooring.

Why hadn't I been there? The question made no more sense to me now than it did all those years ago, but it wouldn't go away. I was *always* there! Fat Maggie Sampson never had anything to do on a Saturday night. She watched television with her parents, shows her father recorded during the week because he hated commercials and was too tired to watch after a long day at the hardware store. Mom sat next to him, her crocheting in her hands to keep herself from foraging in the fridge like a hungry bear, always fighting the craving for a late-night snack. I usually flipped through a magazine looking for beauty tips and daydreaming about a man far away who would help me discover life beyond primetime television.

I looked down at my flowered dress, the one my mom had picked out for me to wear to Easter service, reliving the fight we'd had about wearing it on my date. The polyester fabric itched, especially after hours of sweating. Tears filled my eyes. Why hadn't I agreed right away? I *always* caved in the end and the precious minutes spent arguing had only been for my pride.

"Maggie?"

I looked up to see a distorted vision of Marty—his too-lean frame a shadow of our father's domineering presence. I had no idea what time it might be, but Marty wore plaid pajama bottoms and a white T-shirt, one Mom had told him time and again to get rid of because of the hole in the seam of the left shoulder. He kept it to drive her bananas.

"Hey, Sprout." I wiped the tears from my eyes, striving for a real smile for my brother who had obviously been pulled out of bed and given the news before he could change his clothes.

I searched for something comforting to say to him, something that would overcome the terror in his pale blue eyes, but before I could get my mouth to work, a doctor came over to us and begun to use words, like "stabilized", "internal bleeding" and "critical condition".

"Will she get better?" Marty asked. The hope in his voice was almost painful to hear because it mirrored my own.

"There's no way to know." I had heard of clinical detachment before and this doctor had it down to a cold, unfeeling science. "We've done all we can to make her comfortable, and she might improve, given time." I picked up on his subtext. He didn't think Mom had time.

"Can we see her?" I asked, a quaver in my voice.

The doctor nodded and we followed him into the ICU. Mom lay wrapped up like a mummy, one leg in an elevated cast. Her face had been blistered and with her eyes closed, I couldn't believe it was really her. The steady beeping of machines and the smell of antiseptic permeated the air and made the situation even more surreal.

Marty shook his head, the typical bravado of a sixteen-year-old replaced by a frightened young boy. "It's not her. There has been a mistake, it's not her. Mom's fine."

"Marty—"

"No! Maggie, listen to me. This isn't Mom! It isn't her! Mom's at home, wringing her hands over the last tier of chocolates and waiting for you to come back from your date so she can grill you like a steak! You have to go home, Maggie! You have to, she's waiting for you! Go home and you'll see!"

His voice broke on the last word and he started trembling. I pulled him over to a chair, forced him to sit, and wrapped my arms around him, understanding exactly how he felt. For a moment, I had hoped it had all been a mistake, that the woman in the bed was a stranger. But I'd seen her ring. A small gold wedding band engraved with her and

Dad's initials. There had not been a mistake, no matter how badly I wished it otherwise.

"I'm here, Sprout. I won't leave you. I'll always be here."

My brother sobbed on my shoulder while I listened to the steady beeping of the machines and concentrated on breathing. Nothing else. Thinking was not an option.

CHAPTER THREE

H*e's dead, Jim.* The words echoed in my fatigued brain as I surveyed the rusty heap that had been my car. On some level, I had known all along, but the reality of it hit me hard. I didn't have the money to replace the alternator and the grease monkey who ashed his cigarette into a bin of oily rags informed me he could in fact rebuild it, but for a hefty fee and there was no guarantee it wouldn't crap out again. He made a disgusting snorting noise in the back of his throat and hocked a major loogie into the bin.

"They don't make cars like they used to."

Men either, apparently.

I retrieved my bags from the Jetta, donated the pee-pee mobile to charity, and checked into a sleazy motel that charged by the hour for forty winks. Feeling dirty after my nap, I scoured my body in a very hot shower until I was practically parboiled. At the first opportunity, I made a vow to wash everything I owned.

Since I had all of my worldly possessions to tote—meager though they might appear—I forced my thrifty self to hire another cab. My small nest egg, padded by the hocked ring had taken a severe beating, but there weren't many other options. Forking over a large chunk of my diamond money would only sit well with me if I could keep this job. I needed time to retrench.

I arrived at the address Mrs. Phillips had given me at ten to seven. My destination turned out to be a powder blue, two-story house with gleaming white shutters in a newer development off of Dam Neck road. The structure seemed to be in good condition, but the lawn desperately needed a trim. A blue Ford Explorer sat in front of a converted garage. The backyard had been fenced, but from the distance between the houses, I gathered it was minuscule. Overall, a nice place, not too stuffy, but in desperate need of some TLC. Didn't look like murderers bent on carving up innocent young women lurked within, but really, what could you tell from a paint job? Oh, hell, could I really go through with this?

Okay Maggie, put on your most confident veneer. You need this job, so keep the sarcasm to a minimum. The voice in my head sounded suspiciously like my mother.

I had too much riding on this interview to screw it up. A few nasty thoughts surfaced. Angry words directed at the rat bastard for putting me in this predicament and a few more at Margaret Delilah Sampson for allowing a man to ruin her life.

Never again.

Determination coursed through my veins and stiffened my spine as I reached for the doorbell. I could hear the pounding of running feet and a baby's mournful caterwauling. I picked a few pieces of motel crud from my red sweater dress and squared my shoulders. The door opened.

A small boy peered up at me. He had his finger in his mouth, which was rimmed with what I could only hope was chocolate. The hair on his head looked blond and in need of a trim, and he had a bug bite on his forearm which had scabbed over. His large green eyes were wary and belonged on a much older person. I felt a strange flip in my chest.

"Hi. I'm Maggie." I smiled at him.

His lips trembled. *"Moooomeeeeeeeee!"*

"Ssshhh, it'll be okay, buddy. You don't need to shout." His huge eyes welled up, so I quickly diverted my gaze and took the opportunity to check out the house behind him. The door opened directly into a living room. It looked like something out of a sitcom with kiddy clutter, blocks, and stuffed animals were strewn around on the tan carpet. The couch, one of those leather deals which look nice, but was hell to sit on during a sticky Virginia summer, came in blah beige. Beat-up miniblinds covered the large picture window, but couldn't conceal the sticky little fingerprints all over the glass. No curtains or color except for the kids' toys and the flickering picture on the television. An overhead ceiling fan and light combo illuminated the room.

"Joshua!" The harsh voice accompanied the tapping of high heels. A gorgeous woman in her late twenties carried the chubbiest infant I'd ever seen on her hip. Her ash-blond hair appeared neat and coiffed in fluffy ringlets that fell just so, her makeup a level of perfection I could never attain. She wore a jade green cocktail dress which ended several inches above her knees and revealed an ungodly amount of cleavage. It was such a ridiculous picture, elegant lady of the night holding this drooling tub-o-baby in his stained onesie. I had to bite the inside of my cheek to keep from laughing. The baby gurgled and pulled at a wisp of blond hair and the beauty scowled at him before returning her attention to the toddler with the soulful eyes. "I told you not to shriek. I just got your brother settled down for God's sake!"

Joshua ducked his head and hid behind the door. I

reached for his shoulder but he backed away from me. The woman's scowl melted as she noticed me and my suitcases.

"Are you Miss Simpson?"

I cleared my throat. "Sampson, but please call me Maggie."

The blonde offered a dazzling smile and gestured me inside. As soon as my luggage cleared the threshold, she foisted the infant at me.

"I'm Amber Phillips. This is Kenny. He needs to be fed and given a bath. Joshua ate already, but he can have a snack. I'll show you to your room, but then I need to be on my way."

So much for an interview. I looked down at the baby. Same incredible green eyes, almost hidden behind fleshy rolls of fat when he grinned and squealed. He smelled ripe and his shirt had been soaked with drool. Teething most likely. One dimpled fist found its way to his mouth and he sucked nosily.

"Um...Amber?" She was already gone. I looked back at Joshua, who stood plastered against the front door, as though he could melt through it. "Should I follow her?"

He didn't respond.

"Mary, are you coming?" Amber's voice sounded impatient.

"It's Maggie." Abandoning my bags, I followed the sound of her heels, only to stop short as I passed the kitchen.

Was that cheese stuck to the floor? It came in a different color than the copious piles of crumbs scattered across the linoleum. The walls had been spattered pink and red as if an abstract artist had enough of the tan paint job. The trash can had a flip-up lid, but it overflowed with diapers and the remains of several meals. A stool lay tipped on its side and a highchair sat in the corner, decorated with a disgusting rainbow of dried on baby food.

Do you smell what I smell?

I looked back at Joshua and had a sudden insight into why he stood sentry at the door. He probably hoped someone would let him out into the fresh air.

Beggars can't be choosers! My mother's voice reminded me. The irony was I had grown up in a home where I could eat off of the kitchen floor.

Technically, I could here too. The thought made me shudder.

I dragged my eyes away from the mess and navigated through the minefield of Legos and wooden puzzle pieces on the stairs. Amber tapped one foot as I climbed to the second level with difficulty, still carrying the squirming baby in my arms.

"This is the boys' room," she said with an impatient wave. I glanced in at the aftereffects of a kiddie tornado. Diapers had been strewn across the floor, though these looked clean at least. Toys and books spilled from shelves and a few piles of laundry created an obstacle course in the area between a toddler bed and a crib. Despite the clutter, it was a decent-sized room and someone had painted a solar system on the ceiling over Joshua's bed.

Plus, it didn't reek.

Amber scurried off again. "Here's the master bed and bathroom, but you will be sharing with the boys downstairs." She gestured at an alcove leading to a closed door. "That's your room. I haven't been in there since Becky left, so I have no idea what condition it's in."

She didn't appear concerned either, because she did a quick about-face and vanished into the master suite. Chubby baby secured on my left hip, I turned and opened the door.

The guest bedroom was the calm eye in the center of hurricane Phillips. Painted a soothing sage green, the space appeared small, yet functional. A full-sized bed took up two-thirds of the floor, and the only other furniture, a battered but functional antique dresser, stood vigil in the corner. The taupe carpet had a few bumps but had been recently vacuumed. A tiny window overlooked a postage-stamp-sized backyard and someone had gone to the trouble of hanging a shelf with a few coat hooks attached to the back of the door. Efficient use of space. I had a hard time picturing Amber assembling this restful room. She practically vibrated with frenetic energy.

"Looks good to me, Sport." I glanced down at Kenny, who drooled some more and then slapped me with a wet fist. "What do you say we get better acquainted. Just you, me, and your brother, hmmm?"

Already establishing a game plan, I headed back to the hallway. Since it was a warm night, I figured I'd throw open the kitchen windows and air the place out a bit. Take the garbage out and then hold a meeting of minds with my new charges. After they went to bed, I'd clean with a vengeance. Amber might be comfortable with the house as it was, but not me.

Several summers ago, I'd taught vacation bible school to first and second graders, so I knew I could handle these children. And I would push my dislike of Amber deep down into the cobwebby recesses of my mind to deal with her too. I tried not to be judgmental, but honestly, her lack of regard for her kids made my ass twitch.

Snagging a fresh diaper from the boys' room, I carried the sumo baby downstairs to check on Joshua. The television blasted out incomprehensible sounds, tuned to a cartoon I'd never seen before. The toddler had left his post by the door to sit cross-legged, his nose inches from the screen.

"Hey buddy, why don't you back up a bit? It's not a good idea to sit so close to the television." I set Gigantor-baby on the carpet, which looked relatively clean, and unbuttoned his onesie. The second he went horizontal, he started to howl.

"Why?" Joshua's gaze never left the flashing picture.

"Because it's bad for your eyes." I removed the wet diaper and grimaced at the splotchy irritation on the pale skin. I wondered if Amber had any of the smelly white gunk you're supposed to smear on rashy baby butts.

"Why?" Joshua queried again.

"You'll get eyestrain." Amber *still* hadn't come out of her room, and I didn't want to leave the half-clothed baby to search for the gunk. What do you call it? I opened the fresh diaper and tried to figure out exactly how it should go on. Tabs in front or back? My brain dug through the dusty memory archives looking for any helpful tidbits. *Come on Maggie, you got this one.*

"Why?" Joshua looked directly at me, but he hadn't moved back. I tried to think of an answer for him while stretching the tabby things across the baby. The first one caught, but the second one ripped off in my hand.

"Shit!" As the final syllable fell from my lips, I clapped my hand over my mouth. Joshua's enormous green eyes focused on me. "I meant, shoot."

"No, you didn't." Give the kid points for honest perception.

I looked at the piece of tape in my hand, at the useless diaper on the squalling baby, and then back to Joshua. "Now what?"

"Mom yells at me to get a new diaper. Dad uses duck tape."

I liked Dad's solution better, appealed to my thrifty nature. "Do you mean duct tape? Do you know where it is kept?"

Joshua finally moved away from the television and exited the room. I heard the phone ring and crooned a few bars of "Bye-Bye Blackbird" to Kenny, whose face had mottled with red like his poor little bum, but he only screamed louder. I stood him up, and he stopped. Almost as if I'd flipped a switch. Of course, the diaper fell off and he laughed while he peed on my dress.

"Did you find it, Joshua?" I tried to keep my tone even, but a note of hysteria slithered across the question, poised on the razor's edge of sanity.

No reply from my helper but I did hear the phone peal again.

Soaked through with urine, I carried the baby to the kitchen and debated for a moment if I should answer. I hadn't received a list of job requirements, so I stood there while the machine picked up.

"Hi, you've reached the Phillips's residence...." The same automated message I had heard that morning, so I decided not to monkey with it. Amber would get to it when she felt like it. I had bigger problems.

"Joshua?" I called again over the machine, wondering where the kid had gone.

I'd been in charge for five minutes and the house looked like hell, the baby remained diaper-less, the toddler was UA, and my dress had been soaked in pee. The fryer at McDonalds was looking better and better.

"Amber, it's me, pick up the phone." The male voice coming through the answering machine rang full of authority and had the slightest hint of a Bostonian accent. He sounded familiar, but I chalked that up to a lack of sleep.

A floorboard upstairs creaked and Amber's voice filtered through the machine. "What do you want, Neil?" Her hostile tone led me to believe Neil was not someone she wanted to talk to.

"I want to see my kids. I've played by your rules, Amber, but I'm probably going wheels up, most likely OUTCONUS, for the next few weeks and—"

"Speak English, damn it!" Her shrill voice made me wince

and I bee-lined for the living room where I had to stop short to avoid running over Joshua. The poor little guy's eyes filled with tears and I held him to my non-urine-saturated side while we listened to his mother bitch.

"I told you Neil, the next time you show up here on a day you don't have visitation privileges, I'm issuing a restraining order."

Neil's voice took on a hard edge. "These visitation days are bullshit and you know it. Two Saturdays a month and I'm not even guaranteed to be stateside—I never see my boys. I've tried to work with you, left you alone when you asked. I moved out because that's what you wanted, agreed to everything you requested through your damn attorney and all I want is to see my children! Is that too much to fucking ask for?"

I didn't think so, but no one requested Maggie's input, so I dragged the boys down the hall into the small bathroom and ran the water in the bathtub. Even through the closed bathroom door, I could hear my new employer verbally duking it out with her soon-to-be-ex, while a virtual stranger cared for her children. She'd advertised for "no experience needed," and trusted I wasn't some kind of pedophile walking into their little lives, which were already filled with chaos. I swallowed my anger at The Jackass, at the heartless beauty queen upstairs, and let it seethe in my stomach. Some might view me as incompetent but I vowed I would give these kids my all.

I hugged the boys to me. "I'll take care of you guys, no matter what. I promise."

WHEN THE PHONE clicked in my ear I heaved it across the room. It hit the wall with a vicious thwack. God damn it—no

God damn *her*. She knew I'd never hurt her or the kids, even in my wildest rages, yet she used every weapon in her arsenal to keep me away. Was I really such a monster that she wouldn't let me see my own children?

I paced until the confines of the room became too small then trudged out into the hallway. Open space was what I needed right now, I craved the freedom to run and just keep going like I'd told blue eyes earlier today. Yeah, it was hard to swallow my own sage advice. Unfortunately, I had responsibilities, pint-sized ones who needed their dad, not his whole rucksack full of shit. Forget walking, I hit the beach at a flat-out sprint, reveling in the room to run.

Blood pounded in my ears as I sprinted down the shore, grateful the summer had come to an end and the tourist population was busy doing whatever the hell it did when not clogging up the city of Virginia Beach.

Why, why, why? No matter how hard I tried to force my brain around her stated desires, nothing Amber said or did made sense. We'd been happy once, or at least content. Doing the job I loved, believed in down to the pit of my soul and having her at home with first Josh and then Kenny—it'd been a good life. What made her so determined to toss it all away?

Another man? Or had I been that fucked up before the incident that still threatened my career?

Everything changed when she'd gone back to work. Though I'd never voice the thought out loud, my inner caveman rebelled at the idea of her working outside the house, leaving our kids with strangers while they were so small. Maybe I'd feel different if I did one of those nine to five jobs, but I was gone for days, sometimes even weeks at a time with my SEAL team. *Face facts, Neil. Women just don't want to be at home with the children.* How many times had my mother said those words?

My lungs burned and my muscles ached. God only knows

how far I'd run but the demons were still there, nipping at my heels. Moving without a purpose didn't mean jack-shit. I slowed to a walk. I needed to see my boys, threats of a restraining order be damned.

I headed back to the hotel, where my truck sat, waiting. Having an end goal was crucial—a task that kept my mind sharp, focused. Wayward thoughts needed to be avoided at all costs.

There was nothing wrong with wanting to be around my boys. Christ, I had little enough time to spend with them due to the nature of my job. Amber knew that, knew I planned on a full career with the Navy when she agreed to marry me. I'd wanted forever, she'd wanted…

Well that was the problem, right? I still had no idea what she wanted, from me, from life in general. Other than my parents' money.

I picked up my speed to an easy lope, determined to find the answers tonight.

"Hey, Sprout. How's it going?" The open bottle of ammonia on the counter by the phone made me dizzy. Bleary eyes searched in vain for the cap, but I missed my brother's reply. "Come again?"

"I'm on my way out the door Maggs, can I call you back?"

"Yeah, but I have to give you the—"

Marty cut me off. "Great, I'll catch you later." A soft snick and then only silence from the other end of the line.

"—number," I finished as the dial tone blared through the receiver. After replacing the portable unit in the cradle, I turned to survey my handiwork.

The kitchen sparkled and smelled, well, if not good, then at least not putrid. Amber had waved off my subtle query about setting the house to rights on her way out the door, so I figured she wasn't concerned. A quick perfunctory kiss to the top of each child's head and she was gone, leaving a trail of Vanilla Musk in her wake.

I'd opened the windows first.

Several bottles of unopened cleanser were lined up in an unlatched cabinet beneath the sink. After I'd finished scouring the counters and floor, I moved them to a cabinet above the refrigerator. What I knew about children couldn't fill an index card, but after one night with a teething baby and curious toddler, I figured they wouldn't mix well with the harmful chemicals.

Midnight closed in fast and I was beyond tired. Kenny's eyelids had drooped as I stuffed him into his pajamas, and he'd passed out halfway through his bottle. A little coaxing and I'd encouraged Joshua to pick up the toys on the stairs before I read him three bedtime stories. He'd almost smiled twice while we read *Harold and the Purple Crayon*. I resolved I would make him smile soon.

Amber still hadn't made it home and I wondered if this was typical. I pulled a load of laundry from the dryer, but I was too beat to fold it, so I brought it all up to my room, shutting off lights behind me. The boys snored with a vengeance, but I fastened the gate at the top of the stairs in case Joshua woke up before I did.

Ignoring the overhead light, I stuck the laundry on top of the dresser and was about to sink onto the bed when I remembered I hadn't used the bathroom. The thought of hurtling the baby gate and tromping downstairs almost made me want to hold it all night, but I'd been mainlining coffee throughout my cleaning binge and figured that probably wasn't the best plan.

Amber had decreed her bedroom and bathroom off-limits, but she wasn't home. And I had to go. Screw it. I moseyed down the hall, aware the bedtime story I had turned on for the boys had switched off. Strange that Amber would provide these kids with all of this great educational stuff and then never use it. I'd had to unwrap the CD from the cellophane and plug in the boom box.

Someone cared about these kids and I had a sneaking suspicion that someone was Neil, their father. The one who had obviously lost the verbal war with Amber, since he hadn't called back. After my own less-than-stellar love life I was in no position to judge Amber, but I did want a little more information about how I was supposed to handle this guy if he made a cameo.

Amber's bedroom light was still on and I had to restrain myself from attacking the mess. Dirty laundry abounded, exactly like in the boys' room. Magazines littered the burgundy carpet and several half-filled wine glasses were perched on the dresser and the night table. A large stereo faced the bed and the entire west wall was one huge mirror. No wait, it was a walk-in closet with mirrored doors. Tract lighting illuminated the bed and I noticed a dimmer switch on the wall by the carpet. The bed was unmade, with a golden comforter rucked up at the foot of it.

Welcome to Tacky-Ville.

I traversed the cluttered obstacle course and headed into the open bathroom door. Makeup to rival the L'Oreal counter at Macy's covered the vanity, but at least the bathroom looked clean. The open and half depleted box of condoms on the back of the toilet tank caught my notice and I proceeded to line the seat with toilet paper. I had a hunch this bathroom saw as much action as a rest stop stall off of I-95.

Okay, so stay out of boss lady's room Maggie, if not because you fear for your job, then for fear for your health.

There are certain things you don't want to know about the person you work for.

I flushed, washed, and left everything the way I had found it. Marty's room had always been two short steps up from a biohazard, but he was my brother and I was used to his funk. It seemed so wrong for the mother of two innocent little boys to be recreating the Copa Cabana in her bedroom before her divorce had been finalized.

Don't judge, don't judge, don't judge.

With my mind so intent on my mantra, I almost didn't see him. The shadowy shape moved up the stairs soundlessly and hurtled the gate in one fluid movement. He was tall, at least six feet even with a solid athletic build. I couldn't make out features from my hiding spot in the corner of the alcove, but he moved with confident determination. This was no strung-out junkie looking for something to steal. This guy knew what he was about.

But how did he get in?

The kitchen window. It took all of my willpower not to groan aloud. Great caretaker, I was turning out to be. First night on the job and I left a window open on the first floor. I couldn't have made it easier for him if I'd tried. This guy had probably taken one look at it and thought, *what, no welcome mat and glass of lemonade?*

He looked first to Amber's room, then to mine before he headed into the boys' bedroom.

I was too angry to be frightened. Angry at myself for being an irresponsible nitwit and at this guy for taking advantage of my foolishness. At Amber for putting that asinine ad in the paper, at The Jackass for existing...

The anger was a good start, but I needed to *do* something. I thought back to the self-defense class I had taken when I'd first moved to Richmond. I needed something to give myself an advantage. No mace or pepper spray, no Taser or stun gun to be found. The warning to never pull a knife because most women who did wound up impaled by their own blades was fresh in my head and I doubted I could use a gun even if I had one.

What was left?

A blunt object, something to incapacitate this bozo so I had time to grab the kids and sprint to a neighbor's house where we could phone the cops.

The kitchen was downstairs and I had a feeling Amber wasn't the type to stock iron skillets in any case. No floor-to-ceiling lamps in the hallway. *Come on brain, think!*

There. My salvation lay right inside Josh and Kenny's bedroom door.

Never in a bazillion years could I have moved as silently as the trespasser, so I choose to move with insanity instead. I charged like a rhinoceros, shrieking at the top of my lungs, and scooped the diaper genie from the floor by the dressing table on my way. The surprise on the intruder's face as he gaped at me was almost comical as I swung the diaper genie at his head with all the rage in my body.

But he wasn't there.

My assailant moved like a cheetah, swift and graceful, not a flailed limb to be seen. Before I could regain balance from my off-kilter swing, he ducked and stuck his foot out. His effort was completely unnecessary. My well-thought-out attack hadn't included putting on the breaks and I crashed into him like a wave on a rocky coast. The bottom of the diaper genie chose that moment to unlatch and the bag holding the dirty diapers split as it hit the floor. We landed in a minefield of baby poop.

Now what, Genius? I'd masterminded quite the predicament. The intruder was sprawled flat on his back with an arm over his face and a winded Maggie Sampson draped across his hard frame, pinning him in the land of excrement.

He was bigger than I'd thought in the dark, and covering him like a blanket made me realize exactly how much bigger. He was at least six feet tall and had forty or more pounds on me, all of it unyielding muscle. I couldn't think, or breathe, my heart was lodged in my throat, choking off all oxygen. He could snap my neck like a toothpick, in fact, he probably would when the idea occurred to him, and the boys would be left totally unprotected.

"I have a gun," I told him with my best Dirty Harry bass. The quaver in my voice might be mistaken for anger rather than fear, especially by someone not thinking straight.

"Then why the hell did you attack me with the diaper bin?" His clipped accent called my bluff and I retrenched.

"The police are on their way. Get out and there won't be any trouble."

"Lady, you sport trouble like some women wear perfume. I should never have said anything to you on the beach. Now, why are you in my house?"

I blinked, not trusting what my ears told me. With heat burning my cheeks, I scrambled off of him while my heart moved into my throat. Even in the dim illumination provided by a superman nightlight, I recognized the features of my merman.

Wait a second... "Your house?"

He grunted and heaved himself to his feet. "Don't wake up the boys."

Somewhere buried beneath an avalanche of shock, my brain was making an effort to function. "These are your children?" I squeaked.

Sighing in his sleep, Joshua rolled over in his bed. I clapped a hand over my mouth to remind myself to stay quiet.

The merman sighed softly and chucked his thumb at the door. "I need some coffee. And an explanation."

I tiptoed after him out into the hall. After closing the door to the children's room I whirled to face him. "I'm the new live-in nanny."

He didn't say anything for a minute, then turned down the stairs, unlatching the baby-gate. "You got a criminal record?"

"No." I followed, not offended in the least. Someone needed to ask these questions, damn it.

He flicked on the overhead light in the kitchen. Bug corpses littered the cover of the fluorescent monstrosity. I made a mental note to scour that out tomorrow.

"Mind if I do a background check?" He gazed around as if searching for something.

Poor guy didn't know where the coffee pot was in his own home. I took pity on him and hauled the twelve-cup machine out of the pantry. So what if I'd cleaned it and put it away only twenty minutes ago. After the assault by a deadly Maggie, he definitely earned a caffeine break.

"Suit yourself," I told him as I plugged in the machine and handed him the glass carafe to fill. "My name is Margaret Sampson. I was born on October 17, 1974, at St. Luke's hospital outside of Richmond. Both of my parents are deceased. I have one sibling, my brother, Marty who may or may not have a criminal record."

At his scowl, I took the coffee pot from him and scooped fresh grounds from the Folgers can. "Don't worry—he's not a bad guy, just an idiot. I won't expose the boys to him anyhow."

I glanced over my shoulder. The scowl had softened but was still in place. "I'm going to assume you're Neil?"

Surprised flickered over his chiseled features. "Amber told you about me?"

My teeth sank into my lower lip. Though he'd tried to hide it, the note of hope in his tone was unmistakable. I had no trouble picturing this god-like creature with Amber the fashion plate. Unfortunately, after hearing World War III over the phone, I could accept that maybe they didn't belong together. Neil obviously hadn't reached the same conclusion yet.

"In a roundabout way," I answered. Enough coffee had dripped into the carafe, so I poured some into a chipped mug and handed it to him.

"Want to tell me what was going on at the beach?" he asked, taking a sip.

I shrugged, the drama of the morning fading in his glorious presence. "Caught my thieving fiancée in bed with another woman. He admitted to her that he'd embezzled the inheritance money he was supposedly investing for me and my brother so I took the next logical step and had a mini-breakdown. I'm better now."

Neil blinked at my candor. "Did you call the police?"

"What could they do? The Jackass conned me, but as far as I know, he hasn't broken any laws. If anyone's at fault, it's me, for being a gullible dupe."

"Believe me, I know exactly how you feel," Neil grumbled almost inaudibly. He sipped from his coffee again, those firm lips erotically meeting with the ceramic rim. I clenched my fist at my side to keep from fanning myself. *Bad Maggie—he's the boss. Haven't you learned anything yet?*

He shook whatever thought he'd had off like it was a fly buzzing around his head. "You clean this place up?"

I nodded, drinking in his face as subtly as could. Honest to God, I'd never seen a man so perfect. It was like someone had made a call down to central casting for the personification of masculinity.

"Looks good, keep it up. A vast improvement over the last time I was here. Amber isn't exactly the domestic type." He actually spoke the words with a straight face.

"No shit, Sherlock." Crap, did I say that aloud? From Neil's dark glare, I acknowledged I had. *Be careful*, my mother's voice whispered. *You don't have many options here and those boys need you.*

"I'd hazard a guess you're responsible for the mural on the boys' ceiling." My smile was wan as I broached the new subject. It was the right tact. Neil smiled and the effect almost knocked me on my rump. What in God's name was Amber thinking, letting go of this man? I had half a mind to chain him to the sink for myself.

"That was fun. It's a reproduction of the sky in the northern hemisphere during the harvest moon. I did it about a week before Josh was born. When I was a kid, I used to lie awake and stare at the ceiling sometimes. The paint glows in the dark. I thought the boys would enjoy it."

"It's incredible. I'm sure they'll appreciate it as they get older." I stomped on the urge to pat his hand, the gesture seeming too familiar for our odd second encounter.

"What's Amber paying you?" Neil took another sip of coffee.

"Um, we haven't gotten around to discussing it," I admitted, my gaze falling to the plaid pajama pants I'd slithered into while my pee-covered dress soaked in the sink.

"I'm in the Navy and unfortunately out of town too often. Those boys need a steady influence, someone to be here for them every day, somebody they can count on. While you may be kooky, I'm pretty sure you're harmless." Neil stood and extracted his wallet from his back pocket. He dug some bills out and handed them to me.

I blinked as I stared at the twenties in his grip. "What's this for?"

He shrugged and waved the money at me with an impatient jerk. "A bonus to make sure you stick around until I get back."

I stared at him for a beat and then waved the bills away. "Your wife hired me, and there was no mention of a bonus. You'll have to take my word that I'll stick around."

Neil dropped the money on the table. "Keep it for the boys then, in case they need anything." He fished in his cargo pants pocket once more removing a keychain. "I'm going overseas so I'll leave my truck here. Use it if you need it."

"When will you be back?" I asked, for purely professional reasons.

"Don't know for sure. And when I get back I can't talk about where I've been." His tone brooked no argument.

Huh, well okay. "You don't seem like much of a talker anyway," I told him.

His blinding smile showed up again, like rays of sunlight after an intense storm. He needed to smile more often. "I'm getting better about some things, but I guess I'm still a sucker for pretty blue eyes."

Before I could process his meaning, he'd gone.

I shook my head and turned off the coffee pot, loaded the mugs in the dishwasher, and stumbled up the stairs to bed.

Sleep didn't come though. The mattress felt lumpy as hell springs sticking out all over the place, the room was unfamiliar. Even though my body felt like an overcooked steak, my mind crunched over the events which led me to this point.

After the explosion, Marty's friend's family took us both in for the night. I didn't sleep, but I ran a bath and sat in the tub for hours, mulling over nothing. I returned to the hospital at dawn, catching a ride on the bus. Sporting the same clothes as I'd worn the day before—since they were all I had left. Somewhere in the back of my head, a thought kept trying to voice itself, something to the tune of, *it would all have to be replaced*. Everything we had was gone, no clothes or books, no photographs or trinkets. But I couldn't focus on that now. I knew if Mom got better, she would take care of everything, the way she always did. So I focused all my energy on sitting by her bedside, squeezing her limp hand, and telling her about all my grand plans. She didn't wake up.

Three days after that awful night, my father was laid out at the local funeral home. We had no other family, so the responsibility fell on me for picking a casket, ordering flowers, and retrieving my father's new suit from the dry cleaner. How ironic, since he'd been wearing the same dark blue suit for as long as I could remember. Wedding receptions, church functions, Thanksgiving dinner, the blue suit made a cameo. But the blue suit was gone, so I picked out a gray suit with a maroon tie.

I stood vigil over the wake and funeral. Marty kept sneaking out the back to smoke cigarettes, so I was alone with my father's corpse. Even the mourners didn't seem to notice my still-life imitation and talked freely in hushed voices. The mortician had done an excellent job, everyone said so. One could hardly see the wounds where he'd been burned. We were lucky to have an open-casket service.

Lucky?

My stomach flipped over at the thought of my father being knocked unconscious and dying from smoke inhalation. I didn't care what anyone else said, he didn't look right. I couldn't figure out what it was, but he didn't look like my father. The mouth was all wrong, just a closed press of frozen lips, instead of his friendly smile. He was clean-shaven too, no red-brown stubble worn as a badge proclaiming his Highland ancestry.

The people who read the eulogies messed up, too. They spoke about his honesty and his business ethics. Nobody mentioned that he loved fresh green beans, or that he had bowled a forty-seven last Tuesday night. No one said how he liked butter on his mashed potatoes instead of gravy and he slept in flannel pajamas, even in ninety-five-degree weather.

As I took in the scrubbed-up and frumped-down congregation, it hit me.

No one really knew him.

I drove my father's car to the hospital and relayed my insight to my mother. I told her how Daddy looked wrong and had been dressed differently and everyone was so calm. I talked about all the things I knew my father to be until my throat was raw from talking and crying. I kept expecting my mother to open her eyes and shriek in outrage.

It didn't happen.

My mother slipped away quietly during the night, probably while I lay awake in a sleeping bag on the floor of the Pullman's sewing room. And I had to do it again. The phone calls, the sickly sweet flowers, which were supposed to be a quiet reminder of life, but felt more like a cloying mask for death, the service where no one really knew her. They praised her cooking and generosity but neglected her fondness for all things Elvis Presley. I wondered if this was how I was going to go too, with no one really knowing me, who I really was under the smart-alec remarks and imperfect physique. Arms around my sobbing brother, I watched as the mourners dropped more flowers on my mother's casket, and prayed I would be seen.

CHAPTER FOUR

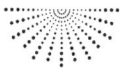

"**M**aggie," I spoke her name out loud as I took a cab back to the hotel, a smile on my lips. Here I'd believed I'd never see her again and then bam, she's working for me, hired by my wife? The coincidence was one thing, but this was uncanny. Maybe even....*fated?* A shiver gripped my spine as I paid the driver and exited into the humid seaside air. Something about her being there with Kenny and Josh just felt *right*.

At the same time, the idea of her in the same house as Amber was royally fucked up. One woman I slept with and the other I wanted to sleep with. J.T. would give me a high five and say something like "Yeah man, hit that threesome action."

Her eyes were just as blue as I'd remembered, but the fire in them was new. Something had shifted in her, no longer a lost babe in the woods, but a woman on a mission. There was fear there too, maybe because she thought I would fire her? I shook my head at the thought. *No fricking way, I have an inside man now.* One I had to stop thinking about undressing with my teeth.

I strode through the lobby and rode the elevator to my floor. It would be a good idea to head back to base, find something to do and be there for wheels-up in the morning. Bad enough I'd been forced to take this mini-vacation with the admonishment that I wasn't allowed back on base until recently. Everyone else thought I'd be home, recouping and getting myself back to mission readiness. Only J.T. knew where I'd really been staying, an unavoidable reality since he'd stood next to me when the messenger served me with divorce papers.

Packing was the work of minutes, and I strode the stairs down to the lobby. The bored, balding hotel clerk snapped to attention when I approached the desk. "Is everything all right, sir?"

"Yeah, I'm checking out." I handed over the key card and signed the receipt without looking at it. Probably a small fortune in on-demand porn, but I needed something to help ease the perpetual battle tension I'd come home with.

Maggie, the sick fuck in my head whispered. I ignored it and bee-lined for the street, hailing another cab. The drive to Little Creek took no time and it dropped me off at the base gates where I showed my I.D. then decided to walk in the hopes I'd wear myself out. I headed for the barracks where the majority of my team spent their nights when not on duty or in some woman's bed. Life in a Navy town.

J.T. and the rest of the guys were still out. I stowed my bag and lay down on a random bunk, staring at the ceiling, trying not to think about Maggie in the bed in my guest room. Or how much I wanted to be there with her. *I am so messed up.*

Wheels up at 0500—only six hours to kill. Maybe I'd actually be able to sleep.

The rock-hard erection I'd had since I'd been with her,

breathing in her fresh clean scent and feeling those lush curves beneath me said *hell no*.

THE SOUND of a baby crying didn't make any sense within the context of my dream. I rolled over, wedging the pillow over my ears, a desperate attempt to hold onto the dream of the gorgeous merman with his dazzling smile and his kingdom under the sea. Light from the open blinds brought reality seeping back. I was in the merman's house, only it wasn't underwater and Ariel had been stepping out on him while Maggie was in charge of the merspawn. One of whom happened to be in the throes of a major hissy-fit.

My feet hit the floor and I stumbled over my duffle before crashing into the doorway. The insistent wails from the boys' room grew louder as I lurched like Frankenstein's monster, brain screaming for my ritual caffeine fix. Good thing I'd taken the time to clean up the diaper bin last night after Neil's departure. I wasn't up to traversing a minefield of poop yet. No booze or feces detail before five AM.

"Hey there, buddy." I approached the crib, where the sumo-baby flailed like a pissed-off turtle on his back. "I bet you're hungry, huh?" Hefting him out of the bed, I took a moment to check on Josh, who'd somehow slept through Kenny's auditory assault. Poor kid must be used to it by now, sharing a room with his demanding younger brother.

Mentally adding earplugs to the list of stuff I'd buy with my first paycheck, I changed Kenny's diaper without needing the duct tape, happy to see some of the redness had faded. His caterwauling accompanied us out into the hall, while I struggled to unlatch the baby gate. We descended the stairs, where I confronted a dilemma. Should I try to hold him while I prepared his food, or stick him in the playpen and face his wrath later? Probably safer to put him down as I didn't remember where I'd stashed the baby paraphernalia and my clumsy morning self might drop him.

"Okay, big guy, time to go to baby jail. Worry not. Maggie will spring you in a jiffy." A blessed moment of silence followed his descent into the crib, but alas, merely the calm eye of the storm. With a humongous gulp of air, Kenny belted out a note which would put a pop diva to shame, and twice as ear-splitting.

"Baby food, baby food, baby frigging food," I chanted as I scurried around, opening cabinets, looking for something, *anything* that might be Kenny fare.

A can of formula had been half-hidden on top of the refrigerator and I made a few grabs for it before dragging the barstool over and clambering up. There, thank all that was holy. My blood pressure spiked and this prolonged screaming couldn't be doing the baby any good either, though he showed no signs of tiring.

Rereading the directions three times, I ran some tap water until it reached a decent temperature and filled the bottle up eight ounces, with a perfectly level scoop of formula added every two ounces. Might not be how Dr. Spock would do it, but screw him.

Big, fat crocodile tears streamed out of Kenny's scrunched-up eyes and he'd somehow managed to kick a foot out of his jumper. Gathering him up, I shoved the plastic nipple into his mouth and was immediately rewarded by blessed silence. His eyes popped open and I smiled as he began to feed with a vengeance. Amazing, as if someone had done a sleight of hand from demon child to Gerber baby.

Kenny studied me as he sucked back his bottle, his sea-green gaze roving my face. This was definitely Neil's child and for a moment I entertained myself with a mental image of how he would grow, shedding baby fat and morphing from a cute infant to an adorable toddler, then an impish little boy.

Not that I would necessarily be around to see all of it. Yes, last night I'd promised the boys I would take care of them no matter what, but eventually Amber and Neil would sort out their differences. Remarry, maybe each other, or brand new pretty people who would then become step-parents to these children. Maggie Sampson would not be needed here forever. If I was lucky, the happily ever after awaiting this crew would remain elusive until I got my sorry act together.

Kenny finished the bottle and, shifting his significant weight to my shoulder, he let out an enormous lip quivering burp, which reminded me of Barney the drunken barfly from *The Simpsons.*

"Oh, a man's man are you, little charmer? Can't remember the last guy who whispered a sweet nothing in my ear in quite the same way."

Kenny gurgled and slapped at me before stuffing a fist into his mouth.

"Let's go check on your brother, okay?" Sad though it may be, I needed my two-and-a-half-year-old charge to help clue me in on what to do next. Either Amber hadn't come home or she was sleeping off the excesses of last night. Whatever the reason, Josh was the key to further insight. My mother would have been horrified to witness how little her baby girl knew about small children.

Maggie Delilah Sampson, domestic goddess. In training.

Josh waited quietly at the top of the steps, his soulful eyes tearing another strip off my already flayed heart. Obviously, Kenny made noise and got rewarded for his demands with attention, but Josh was a different sort. He desired adult attention but seemed unwilling to seek it out.

"Hey, Scamp. Watcha want for breakfast?"

His face lit up. "Chocolate cake!"

I grimaced. Although cake might be *my* first choice for breakfast, no way was I gonna feed it to a toddler who I needed to supervise all day. "How about we check out the cereals first?

Josh scrunched up his nose. "No cereal."

"Eggs?" True, the last time I tried to make eggs I wound up throwing away the yolk-encrusted pan, but for my charges, I'd give it another whirl.

His lower lip trembled. Crap, what was I doing so wrong that he'd start off the day in tears?

When in doubt, show them something shiny. Hey, it still worked on Marty. "Let's go get dressed and then we'll tackle breakfast. What do you want to wear?"

Josh toddled into his room and returned dragging a huge red snowsuit. "This!"

"Um...."

And so it went. When given a choice, Josh would come up with the most inappropriate one possible. I'd make a few more realistic suggestions and then the lip would quaver and I'd feel like a career puppy-kicker.

By eleven-thirty, Josh and Kenny were fed, dressed, and sitting on my lap while I read a Scooby-Doo mystery to them. I always enjoyed Scooby's antics and the way the gang could crack any case. Granted, as an adult it seemed like every villain was scheming for real estate, so how hard could it be, but still superior to any of the stuff that passed for children's entertainment. When the hell did I get so old?

The front door opened. "Hello, hello!" Amber sang out. She drifted in and dropped a perfunctory kiss on each child's head.

"Hi." Shifting Kenny onto my hip, I rose to greet my employer. However, she was already halfway up the stairs.

"Um...Mrs. Phillips?"

"Told you the name's Amber, hon." A scarf was tossed on

the floor leading into her bedroom, followed by the distinctive sound of shoes plopping onto the carpet.

Hefting Kenny to my other side, I swayed back and forth in a gentle rocking motion. The baby's eyelids drifted closed and I figured naptime was fast approaching.

"I have, um, a few questions about the boys' schedule...." I trailed off as a pink *Victoria's Secret* bra was tossed in my general direction. Okay, really uncomfortable now. Having grown up as the fat girl, I never acclimated to the whole stripping in front of other women mentality, preferring to change in a stall, or in some cases, wear the sweaty grimy gym clothes for the rest of the day. Then there was the time Toothy Ruthie snagged my bra while my back was turned and used it like a sling shot, pelting the senior boys with day-old tapioca she'd pilfered from the cafeteria. I shuddered in remembrance.

Amber's blond head poked out of the doorway, startling me from my reverie. "Can we chat later, Marcy, I'm bushed and I've got a meeting with my lawyer at three o'clock."

"But the boys—"

"Just keep them quiet. Thanks, hon!" The door shut firmly in my face.

Apparently, getting information out of Amber was not going to be easy.

Kenny yawned and tugged on my hair.

"How about a little lunch, then?" Carrying him downstairs, I bit my lip, pretty sure I was on my own with these two, and prayed my best judgment would guide us.

"HIGHER, MISS MAGGS, HIGHER!" Josh's squeal of pure delight warmed my heart. I gave him another small push on the swing, basking in the warm Virginia sunshine. This park was a great find. From the Internet reading I'd done, I knew Mt. Trashmore was a treated garbage heap, covered over with dirt and grass and converted into a local and tourist hangout. A great place to fly kites or take a walk and complete with a huge wooden play area for kids to run and climb.

A quick glance showed Kenny was still snoring in his stroller, snuggled beneath the expensive baby quilt I'd found in the back of Neil's truck. Technically it was an SUV, a full-sized Suburban, black and fully-loaded. The car seats had been secured in the back and not a gum wrapper or old receipt littered the pristine interior. The Navy must be paying well these days.

I'd been doing well, taking life moment to moment, and pushing worries for the future away to be dealt with later. Both the boys were clean and contented, but I still had questions. What if one of them got sick or injured? What should I be feeding them? How long should each one nap and what about food allergies? Proper nutrition was important, but I'd never prepared a meal that didn't come out of the freezer before. Marty was the type to skip the warming and the bowl and eat straight from the packaging. Neil was out of town, and he'd left me no way to reach him. I might need to tie Amber to a chair for a full interrogation, but I had a sneaking suspicion she might not possess any helpful information.

I was not without resources, however. Later I planned to call my mother's friend, Mrs. Hamilton, and ask if she would send me a copy of the recipe book her church group had published. My mother had donated almost all of her recipes and several of her mother's as well. I could also dig up information on feeding young children, to see what exactly I should be doing with these boys. They deserved better than my bumbling about.

A secret part of me whispered my motives weren't entirely altruistic. So what if I thought proving myself to be

53

the nanny of the year would endear me to Neil? He was hung up on his ex-wife anyhow, what would it hurt if I crushed a little bit on the rebound from The Jackass? The kids would benefit and I had nothing left to lose.

Josh rubbed his eyes. I guess he needed a nap, too. If Kenny cooperated and stayed asleep, I might take one myself. Who would have thought caring for two small children would be so exhausting?

Alas, a nap was not in my future. Kenny woke as I transferred him from the stroller to his rear-facing baby seat and screamed his round little head off while I loaded his brother, wrestled with refolding the stroller, and put the enormous vehicle into gear. Josh, overtired and cranky started to sob and I flipped on the radio, hoping to find something to soothe the pint-sized beasties.

Never would have guessed Neil was an alternative rock fan. I'm not sure what I expected, he seemed so straight-laced and I couldn't picture him listening to *Nirvana*. Eying the controls, I decided fiddling with the radio was asking for trouble so we jammed to *Smells Like Teen Spirit*. The music didn't abate the histrionics from the back seat, but it did drown it out somewhat. Kurt Cobain did nothing for the toxic smell coming from Kenny's seat, so I rolled down the windows a smidge. Next time, I'd bring the diaper bag.

Both kids conked out as I turned into their subdivision. It was a nice little neighborhood, home to many military families no doubt. Lawns were small but well maintained, except for Amber's, which looked about a foot high. No way would I mow that mess. I may be a modern woman but still, yards and cars were man's work. I decided if the overgrown yard didn't bother her, I could ignore it as well.

I carried Josh in first, setting him down to nap on the couch, and went back for Kenny. He was in the middle of his demon baby impression, transforming to a horrible puce color in his rage, and I rushed him into the house, heading straight for the stairs and a much-needed fresh diaper.

Amber's door stood open and I guess she'd made her appointment. Unsnapping the onesie, I held my nose at the toxic stench. "Whoa mama, that's rank, little man."

Kenny's crocodile tears dried up and he gurgled at me as I removed the diaper and the biggest load of poop. It was still smeared over thirty percent of his body, taking on a gelatinous consistency of green funkiness. I fought with the vacuumed-sealed package of wipes, and my forearm landed in the poop as I ripped them open.

"Cripes," I muttered, scooping a moist wipe from the floor and cleaning him. Five wipes later, I decided a bath would be more efficient. "How about some tubby-time?"

Kenny lifted his legs up and farted at me. "Oh. I see how it is." Deciding to use Amber's bathroom, I picked the baby up and headed into her room. If anything, the mess had grown since last night, more clothes heaped on the floor, more shoes missing their mates to traverse on my way to the bathroom.

Adjusting the water temperature, I wondered if I should scrub the tub out before putting Kenny in. The logistics had me stumped though, as I had no idea how to hold sumo-baby and spray cleanser, bend down, wipe with a sponge and rinse the porcelain all at once. The open box of condoms worried me, as did Amber's flighty behavior. Who knew what sleazeballs Mommy brought home and fornicated with against the tile walls?

"Poor Daddy," I said to Kenny as I left the bathroom, choosing to risk waking Josh over infecting Kenny with God only knew what. How long had Amber been living like this, vibrating with chaotic energy, always dashing off, leaving the kids with strangers? The thought of all that activity made me yawn and my feet were lead as I trudged downstairs.

Had she always been like this? Or had motherhood snapped something in her brain, causing her to regress to high school level maturity? Whatever the cause, Josh and Kenny suffered for her self-indulgence. So did Neil. It occurred to me as Kenny splashed in my arms that I was painting Neil as the Dudley-Do-Right and Amber as the evil temptress. Life, at least *my* life, was never simple black and white. Perhaps Neil had cheated on her first, maybe while she was pregnant with one of his sons. Maybe Amber didn't sleep around. She might have one steady guy who she ran to for solace, too brokenhearted to get her family priorities straightened out.

Yeah and if I bought into that one someone would try to sell me a bridge in Brooklyn.

After finishing Kenny's bath, I wrapped him in a fluffy towel and carried him upstairs. I found sleepytime lotion and rubbed it into his chubby limbs, cooing nonsense as I dressed him in a clean outfit. Since the kid had been awake for almost an hour now, I knew he'd want to eat like five minutes ago.

"Who the hell picked this out for you?" The ensemble was like a little mini sailor suit, navy and white striped and pleated navy slacks. There was a hat too but I wasn't that frigging cruel. Kenny's bulbous little body gave the impression of the new recruit who had yet to suffer through boot camp. I adopted my best command voice. "Down and give me fifty, you big baby!"

Kenny laughed and farted.

"Yeah, that's what I would say too. You want tasties?"

"Numie-numie-numie-numie." I had no idea what his words meant but took it as an affirmative. We paraded downstairs and I vowed I'd do laundry as soon as he ate his fill. Which might in fact take till dinner but he was so damn cute I couldn't resist him.

I mixed the fruit and cereal and formula like an old hand. Safe in his baby torture device— also known as a high chair —Kenny pounded on the plastic tray with the ring of keys I'd given him. I spooned the first bit into his open mouth when a crash sounded from upstairs.

"Oh, God." I left Kenny and darted upstairs. Josh was still asleep, sucking on his thumb. Whatever the noise had been, it'd come from my room. I opened the door and immediately found the source of the problem. The double-paned window had lost a fight with a baseball.

"Son of a mother effin goatherd!" I crossed to the far side of the room and peered out through the broken glass. A small boy, probably ten or so booked across the cul-de-sac and disappeared into the house there. "You won't get away so easily, little menace."

I sighed and shut the door. Amber wouldn't be happy about this if she noticed at all. Not like the broken window was in her room. I was the one who had to sleep with the draft until the glass was replaced. Sure the money Neil had slipped me would cover this but why should I pay for it?

"Well, I'm not gonna, Kenny, so there!" I stomped over to where he'd struggled halfway out of the chair, straining for the dish I'd put down. "Guess I can't leave food in your sights, right handsome?"

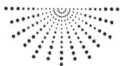

CHAPTER FIVE

"**H**ello?" I called through the open screen door into the shale blue Cape Cod style home across the way. "Is anyone here?"

I hoped so. Not only did I want to get the window situation remedied ASAP, but it was colder than witch's britches out here. The temperature had dropped as the wind picked up. For coastal Virginia in October, the mid-forties was an arctic blast. To me at least. Whoever lived here must be some whack-job northerner—they were all sorts of screwy when it came to temperature.

Kenny's porky little butt was in the stroller and Josh was bundled to the hilt and sucking his thumb. "Fingers out of your mouth, Scamp. It's a bad habit."

The thumb popped out. "What's a habit?"

"Something you do all the time but you don't really think about it." Like me getting shafted by the universe. Cheating fiancé, lusting after married man, baseball through a window, check—my life was a bad made for T.V. special.

"*Hey!*" I practically bellowed through the screen door. Nothing.

"When I get my hands on the little punk..." Having no decent way to finish that thought aloud I envisioned telling off the irresponsible parents who let him latchkey himself into being the neighborhood Dennis the Menace.

We were halfway across the cul-de-sac bulb when the voice called out. "Sorry, I was in the darkroom. Were you looking for me?" I turned and saw a stunningly good-looking man about ten years my senior and dressed all in black. Even from a distance, he reeked of Big City. His hair was well cut and his silver belt buckle and shoelaces confirmed my diagnosis of a northerner even without the New Yawk accent.

"Hi." My irritation vanished. I needed to tread carefully as my job was on the line and I could neither ream this guy out nor let him skate on the window issue. "Sorry to bother you, but your son—"

Mr. Metro didn't let me finish. "Aw, hell, what did he do now? *Peter!*" The last was directed inside the small house.

I smiled. This might not be as bad as I first imagined. "I'm pretty sure he broke a window with this." I pulled the baseball out of my pocket and extended it to him.

"What is this, the neighborhood where clichés go to die? Pies cooling on the sill, wives with their noses pressed to the glass watching our every move, and now the baseball thing!"

"I feel your pain." I smiled, liking his style.

"Please, come in while I find my nephew." He actually came outside and helped me heft the front end of the stroller through the doorframe. "I'm Leopold, by the by."

"Seriously?" I wanted to clap my hand over my mouth to capture the rudeness but I'd never met anyone named Leopold before.

He grinned at me. "I shit you not. Well, Mom always called me Leo for short, but I've been trying out the extended edition. What do you think?"

I glanced around the room. It was beyond immaculate, even with a child in the house. Windows gleamed in the late afternoon sunlight, the taupe curtains hung straight, pressed with military precision. The leather furniture gleamed as if it were part of a showroom display. Black and white architecture prints hung on the wall, shot from unique angles and perspectives. "Either fits, but I'd stick with Leo for the general population. That way when you make it big, everyone will be stunned. I had no idea Leo from the cul-de-sac was The Leopold!"

"The Leopold. Of the one named crew with Cher or Madonna. I like it! And you are?"

"Maggie Sampson."

"Like the cartoon baby on Fox?"

"Not Simpson, Sampson. You know, as in Sampson and Delilah."

"Oh and she's down with the bible thumping terminology. It fits with the cute little accent and sprinkles of freckles across the nose."

"Hey Leopold, in case you haven't checked, we're in the commonwealth of Virginia. I'm not the one with the accent here."

He shook his head. "You're a peach, you know that, right? Oh for the love of grief, *PETER!*"

His bellow woke Kenny who went from zero to fuss-budget in no time flat. I almost threw my back out picking him up and popped a binky in his face to quiet him.

Leo looked sheepish. "Sorry, Peter's staying with us while my sister is on deployment. We've had a few...issues of late. Regina was supposed to be sending us money, for an after-school program, but something got mixed up and of course, the bank won't deal with us without her there. Bunch of drones, with nary a scrap of compassion."

I rocked side to side, Josh wrapped around one leg, and

Kenny not in the mood to be pacified. "How much longer until she gets back?"

"Two months. I have a blissful reprieve every day from eighty thirty till three, then he's home, stirring up trouble."

I winced sympathetically. Leo obviously had his plate full over here. "You know what, don't worry about the window, I'll handle it."

Leo scowled. "Don't be stupid. He needs to take responsibility."

The boy I'd seen fleeing the scene of the crime peered around the corner, shooting me stink eye. Leo snapped in a most diva-worthy fashion. "Young man, get your sorry carcass in here, pronto."

"You're such a fruit," the kid said to Leo.

I sucked in a breath but Leo rolled his eyes. "Clever *and* original. Your rapier wit wounds me. How about you tell me something I don't know, smart guy? Like how you're gonna pay for the window you broke."

"Dunno." Peter shrugged.

Looking at Peter's impudent scowl and Leo's frustrated expression the words slipped out before I could ponder the full implications. "Chores."

Both of them stared at me with identical expressions of *say what now?*

"He can do chores to pay me back for the window. Cut the grass, wash the truck, help me entertain the boys. Every afternoon after school, if that's all right with you."

While Leo didn't exactly have tears in his eyes, his look of thanksgiving was unmistakable. "Sounds like a plan to me."

"Peter?" I queried.

He focused on his sneaker. "No way in hell will I change a diaper."

What was I doing? Taking on another child, apparently. I set Kenny back in the stroller, stalling for time to think. Did I have a plan here or was I hoping to anoint myself for Saint-hood? Maybe I could apply to the government as a charitable organization. "Don't worry, no poop patrol for you. I have something *much* worse in mind. Come over tomorrow after you do your schoolwork and I'll get you started."

"Whatever," he grumbled and skulked out of the room.

Leo gripped me in a chokehold/hug. "You're a goddess and don't let anyone tell you otherwise."

I patted his back. "You're very welcome."

ANOTHER GODDAMNED DELAY. I was losing my mind, but that was Uncle Sam's Navy for you—hurry up and wait. I'd been up since the ass crack of dawn ready to go but brass couldn't seem to decide if we were coming or going. Even a training exercise would be welcome at this point.

With nothing better to do, most of the guys decided to hit the gym, seabags standing at the ready. When the call came we would need to move out, lightning quick.

"Phillips," Lieutenant Commander Roberts barked from across the weight room.

This was not shaping up to be my day. As the team lead, Roberts was driven, ambitious, an exemplary officer. The problem was he didn't know how to be anything out of uniform other than a raging asshole.

"Sir." I saluted crisply, hoping he wasn't looking to pick a fight.

"Walk with me," he ordered. Damn it all.

I fell into step beside him and waited, knowing enough that he needed no lead-in to get to his point.

"Hollis told me about your wife."

I was gonna beat the shit out of J.T. "Yes sir."

He came to a stop at a random corridor and turned to

face me. "Give me one good reason why I shouldn't bench you."

Oh, fuck no. "Sir, the shrink cleared me for active duty."

Roberts narrowed his eyes at me. "Was she aware that your marriage was falling apart?"

I didn't say anything because no, I had not mentioned to the good doctor that Amber had served me with divorce papers.

"The field is not the place to work out your personal issues, Phillips. If your head is not in the game it could cost lives."

My molars ground together. "I am well aware of that, Sir, and I would never take an unnecessary risk that might jeopardize the mission or the lives of those involved."

He surveyed me for another minute then nodded. "Don't let me down, Phillips."

"I won't, sir." We saluted each other and as he strode off to crap on someone else's day I let out a breath I didn't even realize I'd been holding.

"AMBER?" I knocked on her bedroom door, trying yet again to garner my employer's attention. Man alive, I was so glad she wasn't my mother. I'd have serious abandonment and self-esteem issues. Oh wait, I did anyhow. "The boys are in bed for the night and I need to talk to you about the window."

The door opened and I was hit by a cloud of *CK One*. Gagging, I backed up and she breezed past me, her blond hair fell smooth and shiny down her back. She wore a strapless black dress that hugged her petite frame and fuck-me pumps which showed off her well-toned legs. It was hard to believe so slight a figure could have brought a baby the size of Kenny into this world.

"I'm running late, hon. I'll get back to you later. Might not be back 'til tomorrow night! Thanks, Mindy, you're a life-saver!" Heels and all, she took the stairs like a champ and went out the front door before I formed a reply.

"And you're a selfish ho-bag," I muttered. Jeeze, she didn't even check on the boys this time. Was it any wonder she couldn't remember my name when she cared so little about her own children?

In a temper, I stomped downstairs to the laundry room. The basket of colored clothes sat on top of the dryer and I carried it into the living room to fold. Clicking on the television, I hunted for a decent blood-n-guts action flick to enthrall me. Maybe there was popcorn in the house, I could nuke a bag and settle in down here for the night. Did I know how to have a rollicking good time or what?

The phone rang and I leaped to catch it before the noise disturbed the boys. Maybe it was Neil.

Stop that! I scolded my wayward self. The last thing my heart needed was to play the birdie in another round of romantic badminton. Although he was on the rebound and so was I, so maybe a fling would get us both over the hump, so to speak.

Sniggering at my own idiocy, I pressed the talk button. "Hello?"

"Who is this?" a woman demanded.

"Um, Maggie. May I ask who is calling?"

"I'm Laura Phillips." She waited for a beat and when abject adoration wasn't forthcoming added, "Neil's mother."

See, my own mother's voice whispered in my head. *You brought this on yourself by mentally lusting after a married man. Shame on you, Margaret!*

I worried my lower lip, trying to ignore the voices

residing in my own skull. "Hello, Mrs. Phillips, I'm the new nanny. I'm sorry, but your son isn't here right now—"

"What sort of way is that to answer the phone?"

Um, a commonly accepted one? I bit my sarcastic response back. "May I take a message for Neil?"

"No. I have Neil's contact information. If I wanted to speak to him, I'd call him directly."

So why the hell was she calling here at an hour sure to disturb her grandchildren. "Then…?"

She sighed, her disgust radiating over the phone line. "I need to talk to Amber about this nonsensical divorce."

Made perfect sense to me, but since she hadn't asked, all I said was "I see. Well, I'll be happy to leave her a message—"

"Where is she?" the harridan demanded.

"Excuse me?"

"Are you slow, girl? I asked where my daughter-in-law is at ten o'clock on a Saturday night."

Many possibilities came to mind—most had Amber on her back—but I kept my yap shut. "I don't know. She left about half an hour ago and said she might not be back until tomorrow."

There was a pause as if Neil's mother had trouble assimilating the information. She retrenched with amazing speed and homed in for the kill. "What are your credentials?"

"I live in a little gingerbread house and lure plump children into my home so I can feast on their tender flesh." Shit, did I say that out loud?

The sound of her indignant spluttering confirmed it. "You are exceptionally rude, young lady, and I will see to it my son and his wife hear about this disgrace."

Somehow I didn't think either party would be too outraged. "Okeydokey, no message then?"

Click. Huh, I wonder why she hung up.

I replaced the receiver and began hunting for popcorn.

Before I'd found any, the phone rang again. "Phillip's residence," I said into it this time.

"Maggie." The deep voice rumbled in my ear and the receiver slipped. Did Neil's mother call him and report me already?

"I can explain," I started.

"That doesn't sound promising. Are the boys all right?"

I realized how my words must have sounded and winced. "Oh yes, perfectly fine, I didn't mean to worry you. They're in bed right now."

"Good to know," he said. There was a pause and then "So, what did you feel the need to explain?"

"Oh, I um, was rude to your mother and she threatened to report me."

"You were rude to my mother?" he said in a tone of almost awe-like respect. "I didn't know that was possible. At least to her face. What did you say?" Scuffling sounds and wordless noises made hearing him a bit difficult. Neil wasn't a shouter by nature. I muted the television and clutched the phone tighter as I resumed my snack search.

"I'm not exactly sure but I think I mentioned there was a possibility I eat children." *Bingo.* Popcorn located. Hmm, only two bags left. I guess grocery shopping was on tomorrow's to-do list.

His laughter rumbled in my ear. "Good for you. My mother is…."

"Difficult, demanding, cold?" I supplied and stuffed the popcorn into the microwave. The funny thing about being at rock bottom, it emboldened me to say things I normally wouldn't have because I had nothing to lose. Well, my job, but I doubted Neil would fire me for being a smartass, he seemed a proficient one himself.

He chuckled. "All of the above. She's a corporate attorney."

The popcorn dinged. I pulled the bag out by the corner and set it on the island. "So I should expect to be sued by a large conglomerate? Skippy, something to look forward to next week. So Neil, what exactly is it you do for the Navy?"

There was a pause, as though he had to think about his answer. "I'm a SEAL." The way he said it made me feel like an idiot for not knowing what being a SEAL meant. Before I could dig further he asked, "How did you and the boys make out today?"

"Pretty well. I had a rough time getting Josh to eat anything and Kenny wants to eat *everything*, but otherwise, they're perfect angels."

I heard the smile in his voice. "They really are. I wish—"

The noise in the background picked up to a thunderous roar, like a jet engine warming up to full burn and he shouted something unintelligible, probably directed at someone on his end of the line. After a beat, "Maggie, I need to get off here. I'll call you soon. Kiss the boys for me."

For no good reason, tears sprang to my eyes. "Will do." I wanted to say something inane like be careful, as I had this ominous feeling about those noises. But something stopped me. "Talk to you soon," I said instead.

"Bye."

As the receiver clicked in my ear I abandoned my popcorn and movie plans. The computer took forever to boot up, but I waited as it whirred to life and then did a search for Navy SEALs. If I thought the knowledge would give me some kind of comfort I was totally wrong. These guys did *everything*. Well, everything everyone else couldn't. I skimmed the history, totally engrossed in the descriptions of demolitions experts who swam, flew, belly crawled through the muck, and made up the best of the best. My merman was more of a Superman, able to leap tall buildings sans the red cape. The job went beyond high risk and well into *you must*

67

be Looney Tunes territory. Shit, what would possess a guy to do this sort of thing for a living?

"Here I was worried about him thinking I'm crazy," I muttered and logged off the computer. I returned to my movie but my thoughts were elsewhere.

CHAPTER SIX

J
ust a sneak and peak. Relief coursed through me when our mission turned out to be one of the fact-finding variety. SEALs go forth and find out if the bad guys really do have the big bads or they're endeavoring to bluff our balls off.

No hostages to rescue, no innocents in the line of fire. We'd be in and out like...well I was trying not to think like a frat pledge, but after hearing the soft lilt of Maggie's voice in my ear sex was on my mind.

I couldn't believe she'd actually given my mother guff. Undoubtedly Laura Phillips was leaving a detailed message on my cell phone at this very moment. Too bad I'd stowed it in my locker.

As the military transport rumbled over the ground to our drop-off point, I sat with my back to the side, weapon at the ready. We'd insert about five miles shy of the border, crossing before moonrise to hunker down for the day in some of the caves that populated this region of the world. The secret to almost every operation was timing and the reason SEAL teams were so effective is that we functioned like the finest Swiss watch.

Hurry up and wait.

Roberts was on his sat phone, double and triple-checking our intel. J.T. had scowled when I'd climbed aboard the transport but didn't say a word. He didn't have to—I knew he was surprised Roberts had allowed me to come on the mission. Big fucking baby couldn't keep his yap shut. I wondered if I had picked up some random barfly and screwed her brains out if he'd have finked on me. We'd need to have it out.

Later.

But not now, I thought as the vehicle rolled to a stop. Weapon ready I waited to disembark. Time to get serious.

"YOU CAN'T BE SERIOUS." Peter gave me a black scowl as I handed him his assignment.

"I'll admit it doesn't happen often, but yeah, I'm serious. Now mow the lawn."

"I'm twelve!" He whined better than a girl half his age.

"Your point is…?" No way was the little punk getting out of this. I'd shelled out all of the money Neil had left me with, plus some of my hocked engagement ring cash to replace the window, even after the guy gave me a military discount. I'd dipped deeper into my own pocket to buy diapers, formula, rice cereal, pasta, coffee, and microwave popcorn. Crazy, naive, even moronic at times, but benevolent, I was not.

The sullen boy kicked a tire. "I don't know how to work it."

"It helps if you move it out of the shed and sit it on the grass."

With more grunting than the situation warranted, Peter backed the power mower out of the shed and onto the lawn.

Josh rode his tricycle in circles on the driveway and Kenny gurgled merrily from his baby prison/playpen. It was a beautiful autumn day, the birds tweeted merrily and I was looking forward to surprising Neil with the fruits of a young delinquent's labor as well as how contented his offspring were under my watchful care.

"Now what?" Peter grumped.

"You'd better be careful, your face might get stuck, and then you'll wear a scowl for the rest of your life."

"Whatever."

I crouched next to the power mower. It was a nice piece of equipment, shiny and relatively new. "This here's the dipstick. Before you begin check the oil and the gas levels, and refill either if necessary. Screw the cap on tight. Here's the choke. No, there, move it all the way to the right. Good. Now hold this lever and yank back on the cord as hard and fast as you can to start the engine."

Peter gave a half-assed tug. I cocked my head and put my hands on my hips. "Really, that's the best you can do?"

He made a face and yanked again. I glanced heavenward, wondering if Marty and I had annoyed our parents this much.

"Peter," I said as I bent to meet him at eye level. "I know this sucks, but it's a life skill, so maybe you wanna try a little harder. Your wife will thank me some day."

"What if I'm fag like Uncle Leo?"

I made my eyes wide. "Leo's gay? Shoot, there go my wedding plans!"

From the way Peter bit his cheeks, I could tell he was trying not to laugh. "You're so not funny."

"And you're such a master of the obvious. Tell you what,

you cut the grass without griping and I'll send you home with fresh chocolate chip cookies. Give you extra if you laugh at my jokes."

His eyes lit up and he tugged the mower hard enough so the engine turned over. Ah, the good old days of pre-pubescence when a body could be bribed with chocolate chip cookies. Wait, I could still be bribed with homemade cookies.

I traipsed over to the baby cage and put my back into picking up the little tike. "Come on Kenny, let's go make some numie-numies."

"Numie, numie, numie, numie."

"You got it, Sport." He'd been drooling like crazy this morning and I wondered if he was starting to cut a tooth.

"Josh, let's go in now."

Josh stared up at me but didn't get off the tricycle. "Why?"

"So we can make cookies."

If I thought my answer would be enough, I was wrong. "Why?"

"To give some to Peter."

"Why?"

"Why, indeed." I shook my head. The little guy was stubborn. I thought of what he might be like as a teenager and grimaced. Good grief. Well, I could always resort to bribery "Don't you like cookies?"

His thumb popped into his mouth and he nodded. I pulled it out and made a face at him.

We paraded into the house and I supervised Josh washing his hands and wiped Kenny's with a damp cloth. The wash-cloths smelled funky as if someone left them sitting in the washing machine too long. I'd add them all to the next round of wash along with a splash of white vinegar and be glad I wasn't paying the utility bills. Between the laundry and the vacuuming, I'd been cleaning almost nonstop since I walked through the door.

Kenny squealed as I plopped him in his high chair and handed him a zwieback cookie. "Nosh on that, little man." He complied with relish.

I peeked out the front window and winced as I saw Peter making donuts in the grass. Whatever, it was shorter. If I could live with it, so could Amber and Neil.

The words sounded so...wrong in my head. Amber and Neil. Even though I promised myself I wouldn't, I did the stupid name thing in my head. Maggie and Neil. Mrs. Maggie Phillips. Damned if I didn't like that!

"You idiot," I whispered as I scoured the cabinets for flour and sugar. Hell, they were still married and a few conversations with Mr. I'm-Too-Sexy did not equate to a relationship. I set the oven temp at three hundred and fifty degrees and measured out ingredients, most of which I'd bought that morning with my own money.

I guided Josh through the mixing stage and he did really well, perched on his little step stool, a dishtowel safety-pinned to his shirt instead of an apron. If there was an electric mixer in the house, I hadn't run across it yet, so I stirred by hand. "Shoot, no vanilla." I crossed my eyes and stuck my tongue out at Josh and he giggled. Ah, we'd make do.

"Now, for the chocolate chips," I announced and produced the bag with a flourish. "Would you care to do the honors, sir?"

He grabbed the bag and dumped it, scattering milk chocolate chips all over the island countertop. "Like dat?"

"I like your enthusiasm, but your aim needs work." I swept them into my hand and poured them on top of the creamy batter.

I lowered my voice and leaned in close. "Now, here's a super-duper big secret Josh. I can trust you to keep a secret, right?"

Those big solemn eyes regarded me. "You bet, Miss Maggs."

God, the child was his father's clone, with the green gaze and confide-in-me air. I shook my head to clear the weird feeling away and demonstrated how to work extra flour into each cookie to make them super soft. It was a messy, sticky job and Josh had dough in his hair when we finished.

We glanced over to Kenny and laughed as we saw he'd created a fine mushy paste with the zwieback and somehow smeared it into his eyebrows.

"No doubt you two are boys, the way you cover your-selves in crud." I grinned at them and decided to run a bath.

The lukewarm temperature felt right to me and I had stripped them down to their birthday suits and cookie mush when the doorbell rang.

"No way could Peter have done the entire yard by now. Don't pee on me, okay big guy?"

Kenny laughed, somewhat maniacally in my opinion as I scurried to open the door.

"Peter, you need to do the backyard, too."

As soon as I caught the drone of the lawn mower from off to the side I realized my mistake. A woman in her late fifties wearing pearls and *Donna Karen* scowled at me through the screen.

I swallowed. "Laura Phillips, I presume."

WASN'T THIS FLIPPING FUN? Neil's mother stared me down from across the room, a robin eyeing a worm, deciding which segment to nosh on first. Laura had planted her expensive behind on the couch and watched as I went about the rest of my day. Of course, she showed up as I was getting the boys into the bath, the kitchen was a wreck and Peter made a total mess out of the mulch around the deciduous trees and took the paint off the siding with the weed whacker. I fed the boys, built cardboard block towers with them, read half a dozen stories—stalling for time—and reluctantly put them to bed. Everything I did was overlorded by a condescending sneer or a pithy remark. Then there were the questions.

"Why is that local urchin cutting the grass? When do you expect Amber? How much are you giving him to eat? (Kenny.) Who cleaned this house?"

"I did," I responded to the last as she followed me into the laundry room and sneered at my folding technique. Not like she was volunteering to do it.

She raised one overly waxed eyebrow. "I thought you were the nanny."

"I am." I snapped out a pair of my pants, dropping a not so subtle hint she should leave me to my work, utilitarian as it may be.

"So, you tend the children and then clean the house during your off-hours? What are your rates?" The question sounded more like an accusation.

"Why don't you ask your son all of this? I'm just the hired help."

"Mouthy creature, aren't you?"

"You have no idea," I murmured in a voice too low for her to hear. What kind of world did she come from where she could employ a nanny *and* a housekeeper?

Neil comes from that world, too. An insidious voice reminded me. *This is his mother, so obviously he's accustomed to privileges you've never known.*

Never before had my inner voice been so harsh with the reality checks. I eyed Laura as she made a face at something in the kitchen. Why oh why didn't I have a number for Neil or Amber? This was not my own personal cesspool needing a thorough cleaning.

"So, young woman, tell me about yourself." Though her words were clipped, it was more than obvious she was from the north, the moneyed WASP north where they beat you with sticks to rid any trace of an accent, or so I'd heard.

Gah! I rolled my eyes heavenward. Was there any way to answer her that won't give her an aneurysm? No? Okay then, it's on your head big guy.

"Well, I'm a Virginia native, born and raised."

Laura didn't look impressed. She regarded me warily her gaze probably searching for telltale signs of inbreeding. Damn, and here I left my moonshine in the bathtub!

"What about your people?" She raised a questioning eyebrow.

As if we were herds of nomads who sheered our own sheep and lived in caravans. "One younger brother, who graduated last spring."

"Surely you have parents."

"They died," I said flatly.

My candor brought her up short. While she didn't offer condolences the way a human being might, at least she stopped grilling me like a steak.

Keys rattled in the door and Amber entered, somehow looking exactly the same as she had the night before when she'd departed. Same clothes, hair straight and smooth, skin unblemished. Laura's eyes narrowed as the new target set itself in her sights. Oh goody, this should be more fun than a barrel of wet monkeys.

"Where have you been?" Laura barked.

Amber's head whipped around in surprise. "Laura? What are you doing here?"

Laura stalked over to Amber. "After speaking with your newest nanny, I was so concerned about the situation I canceled my day and flew down here, only to find you unreachable! You leave some strange woman, whom you know next to nothing about with your children? I expected you earlier and now, I've missed my flight back to Boston. What exactly was so important that you ran off, leaving your children under the care of a stranger for over twenty-four hours?"

Rabid wolves couldn't have chased me away. My eyes must have been as big as dinner plates and I bit my lip, wishing I could settle back on the couch with my popcorn and watch Amber sweat. This was how I'd wanted to talk to her all along. Maybe Laura wasn't such a bitch after all.

"You," she whirled on me. "Bring my bag upstairs. I'll be staying the night."

I mentally retracted the last thought and looked at Amber. "Do you have more than one guestroom?" I already knew the answer as she shook her head no. Great, a night on the couch.

Laura's designer travel bag weighed next to nothing and while part of me shrieked and wanted to toss the thing at her head, I thought about Kenny and Josh, who neither woman downstairs seemed to be worried about in actuality.

Laura didn't hug or cuddle the children, hadn't gotten involved with their play. Josh had offered her a cookie and she'd actually scowled at him. In her own way, she was almost as bad as Amber.

What must Neil's childhood have been like? I couldn't begin to imagine this harridan looming over my everyday life. My teenage years had been rocky enough without a judgmental harpy on my back.

Since I was already upstairs, I stripped the bed and put my things back in my own duffle. I was sure Laura would find something to bitch about, but the cleanliness of the room wouldn't be part of it. The lamplights spilled pools of light onto the blacktop bulb of the cul-de-sac and I stared at the cheery light in Leo's window. He was probably in the throes of an argument with Peter, the light as deceptively artificial as the sense of community home and hearth.

Bag in hand, I skulked back to the top of the stairs and sat down to eavesdrop.

"You have no right to judge me!" Amber was saying, more riled than I'd ever imagined she could be. "He's gone all the time and I have needs!"

"So explain what you need to Neil. He's a reasonable person. A mistake now and then is no reason to end a marriage."

I shook my head. Poor Neil, with these two deciding what was best for him. Granted, I didn't know him well, but I had a hard time believing he could forgive and forget. Or maybe I only projected what I thought of the situation onto my image of him.

You need to stop worrying about Neil and start worrying about Maggie, my mother's voice whispered. She was right—I had a hard time shutting off the caretaker switch. These two were not my charges and their issues were none of my beeswax.

Decided, I clomped down the stairs. "I'll be back in the morning before the boys wake up. You two have a pleasant evening." I smiled as I shut the door on their shocked faces.

Shoot, I'd forgotten to snag the keys for Neil's truck. Probably just as well, Laura might report the vehicle as stolen to the police and the last thing I needed right now was legal entanglements. The first thing I needed was a place to stay.

I marched across the bulb and knocked on Leo's door. He opened it, dressed in a bright blue button-down smock and orange wind pants. Whoa, he sure knew how to make a statement.

"What's up, my favorite new neighbor?"

I chucked my thumb across the street. "This is going to sound screwy, but my employer is arguing with her soon-to-be ex-mother-in-law and I really need to get out of the line of fire. Mind if I crash on your couch for the night?"

He waved me in with a flourish. *"Entre vous, mon ami."*

CHAPTER SEVEN

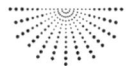

Leo set me up in a guest room across the hall from Peter's. "'Scuse the mess. George is eventually going to set up his office here, but we're still in the deciding stages. You know themes, layout, paint choices, and all that jazz."

The "mess" was a stack of boxes, hip-deep and piled neatly in a corner. To me, it appeared as though some movers dropped the boxes off and no one ever bothered to open them. "What does George do?"

Leo eyed me for a minute, his expression inscrutable. "I can trust you, right?"

I set my sorry-looking duffel bag on the floor. "I didn't murder your nephew, though I was tempted at times, so yeah, I think it's safe to say you can trust me."

Leo nodded and exhaled audibly. "George is career Navy."

"Okay...." I watched Leo, searching for a clue about what I was so obviously missing. Leo raised an eyebrow and gestured to "the mess" again.

It hit me like a two-ton elephant falling from on high. "Oh, the gay thing! Sorry, I'm an idiot."

Leo grinned. "You are too freaking cute. The freckles, the soft drawl, the absolute naiveté, like a little caricature of a southern housewife."

I rolled my eyes. "Haven't you heard? No house will have me. Too high maintenance."

"Come on into the kitchen. You can sample my cheese-cake and dish about the woes of your love life."

I followed him down the hall. Peter slumped in a beanbag chair a video game remote in his hand, the blue light flickering over his zombie-esque stare. Leo shook his head but didn't comment. So in typical Maggie fashion, I piped up. "For future reference, I'm gonna tell you a secret. I can easily be bought with cheesecake or any highly fattening food."

"Jeeze, did no one teach you how to play hard to get?"

I thought of my mother and all her lectures. *That is not a nice boy, Margaret.* She'd said about The Jackass. *A nice boy would be at home helping his poor mama. You find yourself a nice boy, one who goes to church and knows how to treat a lady.* "Not for lack of trying, I suppose."

He gestured toward the kitchen table, a sleek mahogany deal, polished within an inch of its life. I licked my lips as he swooped the cheesecake from the refrigerator, hip bumped the door closed, and presented it for my inspection.

"Holy crap," I breathed. "I can't eat that Leo—it's a work of art!" He'd made meticulous swirls of strawberry and chocolate creating a web work pattern that pulled me in like a fly to a spider's web. Despite my words, I would find the will to choke some—if not all—down.

He grinned. "Martha Stewart, eat your black heart out."

I licked my lips as Leo retrieved a plate and fork as well as a pie server. Without asking, he poured me a cup of coffee and set out the cream. I eyed it with longing. "I can't have caffeine after five or you'll have to pull me from the ceiling."

He made a face. "Decaf, darling, ever hear of it?"

"My father always said decaf was for communists."

"Try it," he coaxed. "Promise I won't report you to the tribunal."

I took a sip. "Doesn't suck."

"Thanks ever so much." Leo's tone was dry as he cut a piece of cheesecake. "So, tell me about your life." He spritzed little dollops of Reddi Wip onto the plate at strategic places to enhance the visual impact before he slid it to me.

"The long or abbreviated version?"

He folded his hands over his middle and watched me "I have nowhere else to be."

I took a forkful and moaned in bliss. "This is truly excellent Leo. Aren't you having any?"

He shook his head "Diabetic. I have to live vicariously through others."

Another bite and I set it aside. "In that case, I'll give you all the dirty details, for a fair exchange. Where do you want me to start?"

"Well, how did you wind up across the street?"

"A long time ago in a commonwealth far far away...I, Maggie Sampson, was engaged to a jackass."

He laughed. "Do tell."

I smushed a stray bit of the crust onto the plate. "I guess I should start with my first real date."

While telling Leo, I relived every detail of that night. His name was Mitch Greeley and he was a sophomore at a Christian college. I don't remember much about his appearance, but he smelled like bologna. Still can't eat Oscar Myer products. I am ashamed to admit my mother arranged the date—she was always a sucker for lunch meat.

"He's a nice boy who helps his mother run the church rummage sale every Saturday. Just be nice, Margaret. He'll love you."

Notice she didn't tell me to be myself.

It turned out the "nice boy" was actually pilfering from the church rummage sale, a fact he made known when he picked me up in his rolling pawn shop.

"Can I interest you in a lawn ornament?" Bologna Boy asked as he opened the trunk of his 1976 Oldsmobile. I stared at the collection of ceramic lawn gnomes, farm animals, and even a small birdbath which appeared to be hand-carved. There were knitted blankets, crochet rugs, small still-life paintings of fruit and flowers, and several sachets of potpourri which smelled infinitely better than my date. All he needed was a plastic cover on the backseat and a little old lady watching *Matlock* and he'd have his very own rolling retirement village.

"I tell you what since your mom is a friend of my mom's, I'll cut you a deal. Anything you want, half off."

I respectfully declined and Bologna Boy got into the car. I turned around and could see my mother's and father's silhouettes as they settled in for a riveting night of *MacGyver*.

I swear the smell was stronger in the car and I remember trying to subtly scope the interior for Oscar Mayer packaging. There wasn't any to be found and I rolled down the window.

"Where do you want to go?"

Home was my first thought. But I had promised my mother I would be nice. Since the only surefire way for me to be so required my mouth to remain closed, I shrugged instead.

He stared at me for a minute. "We could go to the diner. You look like you have a healthy appetite."

Exactly what every teenage girl wants to hear.

Bologna Boy—A.K.A Mr. Smooth—took me to the diner where I ordered a burger, fries, and a chocolate milkshake. My mother had slipped me a twenty on my way out the door, whispering that it was the nineties and all women should offer to go Dutch. "The good ones won't take you up on it," she had informed me.

I glanced over at the guy who had tried to sell me pilfered lawn gnomes and figured he'd have no problem splitting the check.

"Stop, I can't take anymore." Tears of laughter streamed down Leo's face. "That has got to be the most awful first date in the history of the world."

"I'm glad you are enjoying my pain," I teased as the front door opened. I couldn't see who came in, but the smile on Leo's face spoke volumes.

"Hey you, come meet our new neighbor."

The man who came in could have stepped off a Navy recruitment poster. His uniform, the casual blue dungarees pressed to crisp precision, boots gleaming. He had a dark brown mustache groomed to perfection on his upper lip, the hair the same color as his eyes. He removed the navy ball cap and extended his hand to me. "George Landowski. You must be Maggie. Thanks so much for helping out with Peter."

"Nice to meet you, George." I smiled and shook his hand. Witnessing the adoration in Leo's eyes, I liked him instantly. They made such a cute couple, I thought as he kissed the top of Leo's head. I'd never known gay guys before, well, I was sure I had met a few, but not ones I could observe in their natural habitat. Actually, the Jackass and I didn't hang out with any couples, gay, straight, or otherwise. Hadn't that been a big, fat clue? I'd had no one but my brother to tell about our engagement. "I'm such a moron."

"Uh oh," George whispered. "It's that reflective time of night when all single girls start taking stock of their ill-spent lives. I've seen this on the ship but have no idea how to treat such a disease."

"Well, I've already applied cheesecake therapy. The next step, make her watch pointless television until her brain won't function anymore. And look, *Sex in the City* will be on in a few. Kim Cattrall to the rescue!"

"Really guys, I'm tired and need to get back across the street before the little guys are up and prowling. I think I'll turn in."

"Wait, you have to tell me about how you ended up working next door. What happened next?"

"My parents died, I slept with my boss and then tossed my engagement ring into the ocean, met a married man, and moved in with his family. Night."

I shuffled down the hall past Peter's coma room and to my own. I brushed my teeth and changed into my cow pajamas before flopping on the bed. What the heck had possessed me to come here? Not so much to Leo's house, but to Virginia Beach? Why hadn't I had a direct confrontation with the Jackass? The SOB owed me and my brother some serious money. That was our inheritance, all we had left from our parents and I'd turned my back on it because of some bruised feelings?

What could I do now though? Call the police? Hire a lawyer? Even if Marty and I pooled all of our resources I doubt we could swing the cost of a consult with a lawyer, never mind a full-out court battle. Not like I could disappear regularly, or drag Kenny and Josh into court in the hopes that at least some of my money could be recovered.

God, I was *such* an idiot. Look at the mess I'd made of my own life, and of Marty's. I'd sat around judging Amber when I couldn't get my own act together. What hope was there for Kenny and Josh under my watch? A tear slid down my face and dropped onto the high thread count Egyptian cotton pillowcase.

"Knock, knock," Leo called out softly. A brow went up when he saw my pajamas but all he said was, "I wanted to see if maybe you changed your mind about T.V. time."

"Yeah, I think I have." I stood up and dried my eyes. "You are the best friend I've ever had, just so you know."

Leo grinned. "A guy does what he can for his neighbors. How about telling me the rest of it?"

So I did, between commercials. My father's friends held a small memorial service in their home and the cloying smell of flowers got to me. Marty had disappeared again, and my head throbbed. I slipped off my new chunky heels, sneaked into the kitchen and out the laundry room door, and sprinted across their backyard. It was late by my parents' standards, but I didn't care as I made my way to the ruins of our house. I hadn't been back there since I went on my date with Bologna Boy. Who knows what I'd expected to see but it wasn't the bare foundation covered by blackened debris and ash.

I'd picked my way around the rubble, my stocking feet accumulating soot and grime with every step. I couldn't get my bearings, couldn't tell what had been our homey kitchen, or my father's study. I tried to cry, but the tears wouldn't come, I was too frightened.

"I thought I'd find you here."

It was The Jackass, suavely clad in what even in my naiveté I could tell was an expensive suit. Heedless of the ruined structure, he picked his way over to me, tearing the leg of his trousers when they snagged on a broken two by four.

"You shouldn't be here, dressed like that, you could get hurt."

"Tetanus is the least of my problems right now," I told him with more venom than necessary.

"It sure as hell won't help anything." He grabbed me around my waist and flung me over his shoulder in a fireman's hold. I squeaked, but couldn't form any other kind of protest. He was right, I was being stupid.

Some things never changed.

He set me down on the driveway, a dozen yards from the worst of the ruin. "I wanted to talk to you."

That was a first. "About what?"

"Well, I wanted to know what your plans are."

"I don't have any." It was true. Planning took too much effort.

His silver eyes narrowed in on me and I could easily imagine him as he had been, a thoughtless and callow teenager, only out for number one. But then he smiled; a small, knowing, man of the world smile, and my heart fluttered.

"Do you know how much insurance your parents had?"

I shook my head. "I got a call from their lawyer earlier. I'm supposed to go to his office tomorrow to discuss the details."

"I'll go with you."

And he did. He picked me up at eight-thirty and drove me into Richmond. He sat next to me during the meeting when the stuffy British solicitor informed me that even after the funeral expenses; I had inherited a quarter of a million dollars and guardianship of my brother.

"The house is a different matter," the lawyer told me in what I assumed was his kindest tone, one used for comforting women on the verge of a nervous breakdown. "It was mortgaged to the hilt and all of your father's assets were tied up in the purchase of the hardware store."

"Purchase of the..." I hadn't known anything about this.

"Hardware store. Your father had made the owner an offer and it had been accepted, so as the executor of his estate, you are now the owner."

"What am I supposed to do with a hardware store?"

"Well, you have a few options. You could run it yourself

like your father did, or hire someone to run it for you. Or you could sell it."

"I'll have to think about this."

"Think quickly, the business is not doing so well right now, and the longer it's closed, the more clientele will go elsewhere."

I shook the man's pasty white hand, which I imagine was similar to grasping a stunned trout, clammy and limp.

My companion placed a hand on the small of my back and guided me toward his BMW, which was the same silver shade as his eyes. He pulled out into the mild midday traffic and headed for the highway.

"What do you think you'll do?" His tone was gentle, but I could feel his eyes on me.

"I really don't know. I should discuss this with Marty; after all, it's his inheritance too—"

"Marty is a teenage boy. We both know how badly teenage boys sometimes behave...." He trailed off and there was an awkward pause as we both remembered the Camaro incident. It was the closest he would ever come to an apology, but at that point, it was more than enough for me.

I smiled over at him. "What do you think I should do?"

His response was immediate. "Sell the store and your property, and let me invest the money for you. I'll set both you and your brother up for life by the time he graduates."

I envied his confidence. He was so sure, while I was so lost and needed someone to lean on.

"Where will we live?"

"With my mother and Justine until your finals are done. Then I'll hire you as my personal assistant until the investments pay off."

"Why would you do this for us?"

"Does it matter? I like you Maggie, and you and Marty have gotten a raw deal."

It was a half-assed answer, but I was too busy basking in the revelation that this man liked me to worry about his motives.

He drove me to his family's house, where Justine greeted me with a hug and her tipsy mother assured me it would be fine if Marty and I stayed with them. My benefactor wrote me a check to supplement my and Marty's wardrobes and gave me his business card with the instructions to call if I needed anything. I slipped it into my purse and gave him an impulsive hug accompanied by sincere thanks.

"Ah, I get it now." George had turned in a few hours before, he needed to be up for PT at five AM, but Leo had stayed up to hear the whole sob story. "You needed a hero, then poof, there he was, the one you'd wanted all along."

I sighed and snuggled under the afghan he'd covered me with. "Like I said, I was a moron."

"No, sweets, not for loving someone. We all make stupid mistakes."

I swallowed and confided in him, this relative stranger who'd taken my sorry ass in for the night. "I'm scared, Leo. What am I supposed to do now?"

"What you've done all along. Survive." He patted my knee. "How about some more cheesecake?"

I grinned at him. "Why the hell not?"

CHAPTER EIGHT

"**D**id you sleep under a bridge last night?" Laura Phillips snapped when she answered my soft knock. Dressed in a black pinstripe suit with shiny black pumps, even at six in the morning she was pulled together. Okay, so my hair was a little Wild Man of Borneo, but sheesh. She didn't move aside and I was afraid to brush past her. She might decide to physically take me down and I might puke, thanks to my cheesecake hangover.

"Good morning to you too, Mrs. Phillips," I replied cheerily. "Will you be leaving us soon?"

"In a few minutes. Now, Maggie, I need something from you."

I glanced pointedly from her to the house. "Usually when people require favors, it's customary to ask politely."

She stared at me until I swallowed hard. Hell, I was going to volunteer for whatever she had in mind even if she scared the ever-loving crap outta me. The woman was a force of nature I didn't want to cross. "What do you need?" I asked, careful not to commit to anything.

"Evidence. Neil insists on using military lawyers for

representation during the divorce proceedings, while Amber has hired one of the best divorce attorneys on the East Coast. I need you to catalog when and for how long Amber leaves the house so he doesn't get wiped out in the settlement."

My eyebrows hit my hairline. "Wait a frigging second. You want me to *spy* on my employer?"

"Do you really think the children would be better off in Amber's custody than my son's?"

No, I didn't. "Children deserve to have both parents."

"Well, they can't, not in this situation. I tried talking to Amber last night, but she is beyond reason. They don't have a prenuptial agreement and with his job taking him out of the country at regular intervals, he doesn't stand a chance in hell. He needs you, Maggie, the kids need you."

Shit. I could have easily said no to her, but for Neil and the boys…? How much integrity did I have? Or perhaps the better question, what exactly did I owe Amber—the woman who couldn't remember my name?

"Think it over. I've hired a P.I to keep track of her movements but seeing as how they are already legally separated she's free to do as she pleases. I will make sure you are adequately compensated for your efforts."

God have mercy, I couldn't make a deal with this devil woman, could I? I knew it was bad because I really wanted to say yes, like when I eyeballed the second piece of cheesecake last night. Anything I desired so badly couldn't be good for me. "I'll consider it," I told her.

She nodded and picked up her bag as a taxi pulled up. How she managed the perfectly timed exit was beyond me, but I watched her climb into the cab and disappear, the scent of brimstone vanishing with her.

I checked on the boys first thing but they were both still asleep. After dropping my bag off in my room, I headed downstairs to get breakfast prepped. *It is not your place, my* mother's voice whispered. *The Lord says "judge not, lest ye be judged." Trust in him.*

I thought about how Neil had saved me on the beach, maybe not physically, but he had shown me there was a world outside my own miserable bubble, possibilities I hadn't considered. No one asked him to intervene, but he'd done it for the greater good. Shouldn't I try and do the same thing?

I made coffee and mixed up Kenny's cereal as well as some pancake batter. Maybe Josh would actually eat this morning. The day stretched out before me like a great big question mark. What should we do? Where should we go?

"The beach," I said to myself as I took the first sip of coffee. Ahh, strong enough to curl your chest hair.

"What did you say?" Amber stood behind me, Kenny in her arms.

I jumped and flushed before holding out my hands to take him from her. "I was thinking out loud that I might take the boys to the beach today if it's all right with you."

"Oh, sure thing." I noticed she didn't say anything about where the brand new container of flavored coffee creamer came from, but she definitely helped herself to it. "I'll be gone overnight again. If the phone rings, let the machine screen, all right?"

Hmm, worried I'd give away more info to Laura the Harridan maybe? Well, I couldn't blame her. "How did everything go with your husband's mother?"

"I hate her. What a vicious bitch. It's no wonder Neil has no human feelings, with half her genes."

"Yowch," I said. "You know—"

"I have to go. I'll see y'all later." An awkward pat on the top of Kenny's head and she was off. Though Amber hadn't seen Josh for forty-eight hours, she didn't bother waking him up to say goodbye.

"I'm nobody's snitch," I informed Kenny while I shoveled rice cereal and pureed pears into his gaping maw. He blew raspberries at me, spewing cereal gook everywhere.

"Behold, the reason why I didn't wash my hair and look like a bridge dweller." I picked a clump out with a paper towel. I couldn't remember the last time I'd had it cut. Maybe part of the reason Laura's offer seemed so appealing was my current financial state.

"We need to get out of the house, look for shells, crap like that," I told Kenny. So help me, if his first word was crap, I could kiss my job goodbye.

Excited about the prospect of the beach, I woke Josh and got him right into wind pants and a T-shirt. In late fall, the Atlantic was too cold to swim in—even for the merspawn—but they would have fun digging in the sand. We'd all enjoy a relaxing day at the beach.

Or so I thought.

It was like a little mini Easter egg hunt to find their sand toys. A shovel under the bed, a bucket in the living room filled with cars. A funnel and waterwheel in the bathtub and sunglasses nowhere to be found, at least by me.

"Fine, you can wear a hat instead."

"No." Josh folded his arms over his chest and the lip came out half a mile.

Kenny's bowels decided to chime in. It was an uber nasty poop that exploded out of his diaper and stopped halfway up his back. "Josh, bring me the diaper bag."

"No."

I gazed heavenward. "Lord, if you are trying to tell me something, you need to be more specific."

"It's always a terrific sign to find the nanny praying for divine intervention while changing my kid's diaper."

"Daddy!" Finally a word other than no out of Josh.

93

I'd been so focused on the chaos I hadn't heard the door. "Neil! Hi! I didn't think you'd be back so soon."

He dug through the diaper bag. "You want me to take over here?"

A man who actually volunteered to change a child's diaper? "I'm already covered in it, so you might as well assist."

He handed me a wet wipe and I self-consciously cleaned his son's ass. "So dear, how was work?"

He laughed. "Well I didn't blow myself or any of my teammates up, so that's always a good day."

Oh, shit, I couldn't tell if he was joking. "Um, wow, okay, well glad everyone still has a pulse. Oh, and here's another piece of good news, you just missed your mother."

This caused him to make a face. "What did she want?"

Hell, I hadn't thought this through. "To talk with Amber. You know what, this isn't working. How about a bath Kenny?"

"No," Josh said.

I hefted a half nude Kenny up off the changing pad and carried him downstairs.

"Why don't you use the one in the master bedroom?" Neil called out and I winced as I heard his footsteps heading in that direction. Maybe Amber had cleaned up in there last night.

"Son of a bitch! Motherfucker!" The stream of profanity drifted down the stairs.

I guess not.

"How are you holding up?" I squinted at Neil, who had camped out next to me on the oversized beach towel. Kenny —in between meals for a change—was sound asleep in his stroller. After eating half a peanut butter sandwich, heavy on the sand since he kept putting it down to dig, Josh ran back and forth filling his bucket with water for his moat.

He watched his son play, his expression blank, and my heart went out to him. "I'm not sure. I mean, I had a feeling there was someone else, but seeing the evidence, it hits you like a mortar blast, tears shit up inside."

Trust me I know exactly what you mean. I didn't say a word though because I had the feeling he wasn't after empathy or commiseration. Sometimes you just needed to wallow in your own particular brand of putrescence until you were ready to move on. Not that I was anywhere near ready to move on, but life didn't look so grim with Neil by my side, even if he was hurting.

"I'm an idiot."

I glanced over at him and scowled. "Are not."

"Am too." He smiled a little.

"Are not and here's why." This was the moment I was supposed to say something insightful, some special phrase that would cement us together forever because I helped him through his personal crisis as he'd been helping me through mine. Unfortunately, my brain must have been on its fifteen-minute coffee break. Neil looked at me expectantly and I sighed and deflated like a balloon. "Ah hell, I've got nothing."

He chuckled and shook his head. "Thanks for trying, kid. By the way, what happened to the window in the guestroom?"

"One of the neighborhood kids sent a baseball through it."

"And Amber had it replaced already? She's usually so slow and scattered about household stuff. You must have nagged her into it."

"Hey, I don't nag!" Well, maybe if the occasion called for it I might.

"So when can I expect the bill?"

The sun had started its descent and I stood up, dusting the sand off my capris. "We should get the kids back to the house. Josh looks ready for a nap." Josh was busy digging like the Tasmania Devil on speed.

As I reached for the picnic basket Neil grabbed my arm. "Knock it off."

Heat tingled up my arm and the warm glow had nothing to do with the bright sunshine. "What?"

He cocked his head to the side and studied me and my girl parts woke up with a tingle under his scrutiny. God, those eyes!

"When you don't want to tell me something, you segue by doing something else, moving, fussing with the kids. Don't think I haven't noticed."

I shrugged. "So I guess I shouldn't play Thursday night poker with you then?"

He laughed and pointed. "And there's the second line of defense. Make a joke. Distract the target with your wits. Yet another stall tactic. Won't work though, I see what you're about."

My next retort died on my lips. "You...do?" I stammered.

Knock it off! He's married, for the love of Pete!

"Maggie," he whispered.

I couldn't say anything, wanting so much to leap at him and tell him everything, spill all my crazy secrets in his lap, even though it wasn't fair to Neil, he hadn't signed on to be my object of lust/therapist. God alone knew which I needed more desperately.

"Blink if you're all right."

Snap out of it before you start to drool, moron! My eyes hurt, probably because I'd been partially blinded by the sun. "Sorry, my mind wandered off for a second."

"So, about the window?"

"Don't worry about it. It's been taken care of." I sounded like a mob boss.

"Like sleeping with the fishes taken care of?" He flashed his killer grin and I tripped on the towel. Perfect timing for a spaz attack.

"Yeah, I have an arrangement with the kid who broke it. He's working off the cost by doing chores."

"Oh, so that's who mowed the grass." Neil nodded. "What else do you have slated for him to do?"

"Well, I'm fresh out of potatoes to peel so I'm open for suggestions."

"Clean the gutters? Organize the tools in the garage? Whitewash the fence?"

"You don't have a fence." I pointed out.

"Hell, I'll put one up just to see him out there doing the Tom Sawyer thing. So, did you ask Amber for the money?"

Cripes, Neil was like a dog with a rawhide. I wasn't going to lie to him. "You left me with some."

"Not enough for a double-hung window!"

I picked at a wrinkle in my pants. "I may have...dipped into my savings."

"You don't have any savings." I sputtered with indignation but he continued in the same even tone. "You told me I could run a background check, so I did, including financial information. You're broke, babe, have been for years so I'm asking again—where did you get the money?"

Though his voice never rose above conversational tones, there was a distinct hint of warning. Furious and desperate, I looked away. He'd backed me into a corner and I had to tell him or risk my job. "I took it out of my engagement ring money, all right? Are you happy now?" I wiped away an escaped tear. Traitor.

"Yes," he said and nodded. "Just don't lie to me, Maggie. No matter what, be honest with me. This situation is beyond fucked up and I don't know what to do. I need to trust you, I want to trust you. Don't try and spare my feelings, okay?"

I sniffled and narrowed my eyes at him. "Rip away the veil of polite society and bludgeon you with the cold harsh truth. Got it, boss, anything else?"

"Yeah, when we get home I want to see the bill for that window so I can pay you back."

"Don't you need to save up for your divorce?" Might be a little too honest.

He didn't even flinch. "I'm surprised my mother didn't tell you, she usually brags about how I'm a trust fund brat."

"We didn't exactly have girl talk. She ranted, I ran. So tell me, how did a spoiled trust fund brat end up enlisted in Uncle Sam's Navy?"

Neil had taken off his shoes and socks and buried his toes in the warm sand. He had really nice feet.

Stop that!

"Wish there was a better story there. Basically, it's the same old teenage rebellion crap. Daddy and Mommy are lawyers in Boston and I wanted nothing of their world. I miss the northeast though, especially in winter."

I shuddered. "Snow, black ice, freezing rain. Yeah, plenty to miss."

Neil stood in a one fluid motion and held out a hand to me, grin in place. "I've created a monster."

CHAPTER NINE

God, I want her. Understatement of the year. The more I knew about Maggie, the more I craved her. Unfortunately, my randy dick did not seem to get the message that Daddy boffing the baby-sitter was not a good idea.

No, it's a great one.

The way she was on the beach, concerned about me, but not like everyone else, waiting for me to lose my shit, she just...empathized.

Because she'd been through the same thing. No, actually I still had my job and my home, as evident by the muck I was clearing from the gutters while she put Josh down for a nap.

She was more like a mother though, so easy going with Kenny and Josh. That uber crude acronym from the America Pie movies kept running through my brain. M.I.L.F, for Mom I'd like to F—

"Who the hell are you?" I turned and stared at the boy scowling at me from the ground.

"Peter, right?" He glowered at me as I climbed off the ladder.

"Yeah, what of it?" His chin jutted up defiantly. Not the easiest kind of guy to deal with, what with the giant chip on his shoulder. Yanking off my glove, I extended it to him. He eyeballed it warily but reached out his own mitt for a real man-to-man handshake.

"I'm Neil Phillips, you can call me Neil."

Peter scanned me head to toe. "Are you Maggie's boyfriend or something?"

My lips twitched. "Sounds good to me. Come on, let's get you working."

"THIS IS UNBELIEVABLY FRIGGING WEIRD," I muttered as I stood at the kitchen window and watched Neil show Peter how to use the hedge trimmer. I figured he'd drop me and the kids then am-scray to whatever exciting adventure was waiting for him. Yet here it was late afternoon, the leaves turning belly up in the strong wind and Mr. I'm-Too-Sexy was in the backyard giving the neighborhood hooligan a crash course on power tools. Peter actually had a smile on his face, probably envisioning the havoc he could wreak.

"Anuhnuhnuhnuh!" Kenny bellowed from his baby prison.

I turned away from the window to scowl at him. "Knock it off, you don't mean it. You're just pissed because I put you down. Can't go through life being carried by others, big guy."

The boy had an incredible sixth sense for when my hands were free, therefore able to hold him. Other than when he napped, the kid had been in my arms or fed by my hands since I walked through the door. Wasn't there some rule about little kids being held too much? I looked at the contact list Neil had given me. I could always call the pediatrician to find out. Neil said he'd be by to take them to their next well checkup appointment but I didn't see how he could plan so far ahead when his job required him to drop everything at a moment's notice.

But when he was here... I glanced back outside. These hedges weren't gonna be winning any neighborhood awards but the look of joy on Peter's face was almost worth it. Neil saw me staring and waved. I blushed, returned the gesture, and skulked away from my observation station.

"The heck with it." I picked Kenny up and carried him over to the open space in front of the couch where I laid him on his back. The baby was definitely cutting a tooth— he drooled and jammed his fist in his mouth for a nosh, large sea-green eyes boring holes into me. The basket of toys had been upended so I reached for the squishy monster with a reflective spot on his belly. Holding the pseudo mirror up to Kenny I showed him his visage. "Who's handsome?" No way would this kid end up with an inferiority complex if I could help it.

The baby gurgled in delight. "Ahhhh diggy diggy doo," he squealed.

"There's a handsome guy in there. Who is that?"

Arms and legs failing going like a champion kickboxer, Kenny ripped the monster out of my hand and stuffed one of its tentacles in his mouth.

"No, not to eat. I'll get you a teething ring. No wild parties while I'm gone, okay?"

I stood up and stretched my back before turning towards the kitchen. Neil stood there, a weird expression on his face.

"God! Do I need to put a bell on you? You scared the heck out of me!"

He blocked the doorway—a trick he must have learned from mommy dearest— still lost in whatever thought had captivated him.

So, the dilemma. Should I try and squeeze past him, or

wait till he was done with his reverie? I know what I *wanted* to do and almost giggled like a moron at the thought. "Neil?"

"You're so good with him," he stated, eyes still focused on something I didn't see.

The compliment warmed me, but I shrugged. "Kenny and I have an understanding. He's the boss and I'm here to serve him. It's not the best deal I've ever made, but it keeps him happy."

Neil shook his head, like a dog emerging from a swim in a cold lake. I smiled at him, willing to cut him about all the slack I could find. Who the hell was I to get in the way of his mental lapses?

"You gonna hang around for dinner?" I scooted past him, breathing in the smell of salt and surf which clung to him like an aura. The sinful thrill tingled up and down my spinal column was so worth my mother's mental chastising. Funny, in the *Playboy* stories the daddies always seduced the baby-sitters, not the other way around.

Stop that! My mother hissed.

Make me! I answered, hopefully silently.

Does your upbringing mean so little to you that you would throw it away for a fling with a married man? It's a sin, *Margaret!*

Nothing is going to happen! I'm building a comforting little fantasy world. Any woman in my place would do the same. Why I felt the need to explain my motivations to my own personal Jiminy Cricket who resided in my skull was beyond me.

I washed my hands before extracting Kenny's teething ring from the fridge. Neil hadn't answered me, nor had he moved. I half wondered if he'd fallen asleep standing up with his eyes open. According to the Navy website, SEALs were trained to take combat naps whenever it was convenient. In the middle of our conversation was a little odd, but I could roll with it.

Ah, who was I kidding? "Neil, are you all right?" I touched

his hand, the briefest contact possible without being a total slut bag.

"You're a good mother," he said, eyes still focused on something I couldn't see.

"Whoa there, big guy. I'm nobody's mo—"

"Get down!" Before I could absorb what was going on, he took me to the floor in a full-body tackle.

He sprawled atop me like a human shield, his eyes still watching something I couldn't see. "Fuckers came out of nowhere," he hissed. "Jack, someone's shooting up the market! We're pinned down!"

Kenny started to cry. All fantasies aside, he was heavier than he looked. "Neil, can you hear me? It's Maggie. I need to get to Kenny, he's upset."

His gaze swung to me, but I would swear he still didn't see me, caught up as he was in the past. His hand roved over my head and he pulled it back quickly to examine the palm. "Oh fuck no, Anise, wake up! Chief, I need a medic, the contact has been shot!"

Whatever Neil was experiencing, it was very real to him. His face lost all color, his hands shook like a crack addict going through withdrawal. I tried to shove him off, tugged on his hair, repeated his name but nothing got through. He was as solid as a mountain and just as immovable by my hands.

"The baby, oh God, the baby!" He looked in Kenny's direction but not really at him. "I'm sorry, I'm so sorry," he apologized at the wailing infant.

Panic made my voice shrill. "Neil, you're here in your house, in Virginia. I'm Maggie and no one's been shot, goddamn it!" What hell was he reliving?

"Daddy?"

Shit, Josh was up from his nap. This was not the kind of memory he needed. Taking a deep breath I apologized and kneed him in the groin as hard as I could from the awkward position.

He grunted but didn't roll off as I'd hoped. Shit, I'd run out of defensive maneuvers. Kenny was wailing now, and Josh stood wide-eyed in the corner. My panic level wasn't helping anything. What else could I do? How had everything gotten so far out of control? Could anything else go wrong?

"What the hell is going on here?" Amber stood in the doorway, looking down at us, eyebrows meeting at the bridge of her nose. She strode in and picked Kenny up off the floor, though he continued to wail.

Neil shook his head, blinked a few dozen times in a row before focusing on me. "Maggie?"

I closed my own eyes. Yep, things could always get worse.

NOT AGAIN. Everything was too sharp and bright around the edges, the main picture hazy, Amber's voice piercing as she screeched at me, Kenny and Josh bawling as they picked up on the charged atmosphere between the adults. Maggie's large blue eyes were full of panic. What the hell did I do this time?

With a muttered oath I rolled off of her, hating myself for this weakness. These episodes were supposed to be over. Roberts would take me out of field duty if he knew I was still suffering flashbacks. And that concern was secondary to the devastation in my own home.

"Do I have to take a restraining order out on you?" Amber shrieked, doing nothing to help settle the boys down. Maggie composed herself quickly and took Kenny out of her arms. He settled immediately, more comfortable with the nanny than his mother. The kid was sharper than his old man, knew which side his bread was buttered on. Seeing

Amber next to Maggie this way was like experiencing a gale-force wind pushing against a gentle ocean breeze. Amber buzzed with frenetic energy which made the hair on the back of my neck stand up. Maggie eased something deep inside me.

And I'd attacked her.

Amber pointed to the door. "Get out, Neil. I swear, I'll report you if you come back."

I watched Maggie cuddle Josh into her side, as Amber ignored both of our children. Yeah, I needed to leave, but not because of my wife's shrill demands.

Maggie's gaze was locked on mine, her concern evident, though whether it was for me or because of me, I couldn't tell.

"I'm sorry." Though the apology was offered to the room, I meant it for Maggie. Turning, I left without a backward glance, feeling as though I'd shattered something precious.

WELL, at least I didn't get fired, I thought as I put Kenny to bed for the night. After recovering from the shock, Neil had left in a hurry with his wife screaming at his back. She'd actually grabbed one of the neighbor's lawn gnomes and thrown it at his truck as he drove away. Poor guy.

The "poor guy" physically assaulted you! My mother scolded.

No, he was trying to protect me. Or at least whoever I represented in his flashback. Shit, things had become pretty real in a hurry.

From the moment I'd seen Neil on the beach, he'd appeared... otherworldly. I'd built him up in my head as this fantastic hero figure, someone able to rescue me from my lonely—and possibly destitute, life. This afternoon the smoothly polished veneer had melted away to reveal a glimpse of a shattered soul and somehow that made him even more dangerous to me. It made him accessible.

I trudged back downstairs to where Josh sat two inches from the television screen, enthralled with *Aladdin*. Amber was gone again, having stopped in only for a quick wardrobe change. To my surprise, she'd blamed the entire event on Neil, insisting he was "three shades of crazy". She'd made me swear I wouldn't allow him back through the door.

"Our divorce hearing is next Monday and I'm filing for full custody," she'd said.

"So, when is Neil going to get to see the boys?" I had asked.

She'd tossed her hair and the indifferent motion made me want to rip it out. "Only under supervision. He's too dangerous to be around them."

I stared at Josh while he watched Robin Williams as Genie sing about how we'd never had a friend like him. He'd been so happy on the beach today, building a sand fortress with his dad. It might be wrong of me, but I couldn't help thinking the kids were better off with their father's possible freak-outs than their mother's constant negligence.

She's not negligent, she has you! Old Maggie-the-doormat rides to the rescue.

"Why don't you back up, buddy?" I said aloud.

He didn't turn a hair. I sighed and got up to drag him away from the television, exactly as my father did to Marty and me. He'd either go blind or grow out of the habit.

I turned back to the couch and almost screamed when I saw Neil looking in at us. Since I was forbidden from opening the door to him I slid the window up. "Did anyone ever tell you lurking in the bushes is not a very attractive trait?"

"I'm sorry," he said but didn't move any closer.

The stupid screen was tricky and it took all my concentration to push both latches in and slide the bugger up. "You coming in? Or should I climb out?"

He didn't move as he asked, "Aren't you scared of me now?"

I sighed, not wanting to shout. "Do I realize you're dangerous? Yes. I received that memo but I'm not afraid of you. She's a nitwit if she believes you'd ever hurt her or the boys. Now, do you want to help me put Josh to bed, or are we gonna fart around like idiots all night?"

Still, he paused and I rolled my eyes heavenward. "Hey ma, if you aren't too busy could you ask the man upstairs to light a fire under some guy's backside for me?"

"Move over, wiseass."

He leaped through the window with amazing speed and stealth. Josh didn't hear or see him, he was so quick. If I attempted the same maneuver, I would have gotten stuck like Winnie the Pooh in the tree stump.

Once he replaced the screen he stood, gazing around like he'd never seen the place before. "Will you tell me what happened?"

I nodded to his son. "As soon as he's squared away."

His mouth kicked up on the side. "That's a Navy term, you know."

"I figured. George used it the other night when I was over there and it stuck in my brain. Hey Josh, look who's here to read you a story!"

Seeing the kid's face light up was all the reward I needed. He flung himself at Neil. "Daddy!"

I fussed in the kitchen while the two of them read a stack of Dr. Seuss. Once *Green Eggs and Ham* was finished, I supervised the teeth brushing and pajama donning. Josh went to bed a happier child than he'd been when he woke up.

Neil kissed Kenny—who snored like a wild boar crank starting a model T— and I set one of the CDs of sleepy time tunes spinning. We backed out of the room like we were traversing a minefield, wary of creaky boards which might wake the youngsters.

"Want some coffee?"

"So long as it's not decaf."

My kinda guy. I led the way downstairs to where I'd already brewed a pot and poured him a steaming mug full.

He took a sip and I cocked my head to one side, studying him. "Did you eat anything?"

His green gaze surveyed me for a second, those dark brows drawing together. "No."

Without asking I whisked out the baked spaghetti and prepped a plate. He looked like he was going to protest, but I gave him my best stink eye and the smart man knew when to bite his tongue.

I pushed the microwave buttons and let the modern-day wonder work its magic. "How much do you remember?"

He refused to make eye contact. "Nothing. Being out in the yard with Peter and then coming inside. Next thing I knew, Amber's screaming, and you looked like I'd scared ten years off your life."

"Well, you did." The microwave dinged and I retrieved his plate. "Parmesan cheese?"

"I really shouldn't be eating here. Amber won't be happy about this."

"Tough shit," I said and slid the steaming plate in front of him. "I paid for it, cooked it and I'll feed who I darn well please."

"Tell me about what happened," he said and tucked into the food.

So I did, point-blank, leaving out my nonessential flights of fancy. Did he really need to know I'd rubbed up against him like an alley cat? My pride chorused a resounding hell no!

"And then you just ...woke up." I finished lamely. He didn't say anything as he cleaned the plate and got up to rinse the dish. Was it wrong of me to check out his ass while he did so? *Only if he catches me in the act!*

"So do you want to hear the whole story or the short version?" Neil asked with his back still to me.

I sobered out of my lusty stupor. "Whatever you feel like telling, but not because you owe me anything. No harm, no foul."

"I've been diagnosed with PTSD; it stands for Post-Traumatic Stress Disorder. Mine was brought on by a particularly nasty SNAFU I was involved in six months ago. People... died. What happened earlier, the blackout/flashback episode used to happen several times a day. It's why Amber threw me out."

I didn't say a word. He sighed, arms spread to either side of the sink to support the weight of the world he carried. His shoulders were big but I could tell the pressure was bowing him. "It took months before I was allowed back on active duty and I still need to go to therapy once a month. It's helped, though not enough. I'm broken, Maggie."

"I don't think so." I whispered, then cleared my throat and projected more forcefully. "Neil, you aren't a car that either runs or doesn't. Sure, you've got a serious headfuck going on, but who doesn't? Get over yourself pal, you aren't so special."

He turned and shook his head at me. "You're something else."

"Aw, I'll bet you say that to all the women you tackle."

A spark passed between us then, something electric as our gazes locked, and my heart kicked into high gear.

"What is this?" I whispered, mesmerized by the fire in his gaze. I hadn't meant to speak aloud and under any other circumstance would have blushed, but I had to know if he felt it, too.

He broke eye contact first. "I don't know, but it's a bad idea. The boys have had too much upheaval in their lives and we're both..." He made an obscure motion with his hand as if searching for the right phrasing.

"Wacky as all get-out?"

He grinned and nodded. "Sums it up nicely."

The little seed of hope which sprouted in my heart withered and died. So what if Neil felt the pull too? He was right—we couldn't do anything about it, not with so much at stake.

"I'd better take off. Thank you for dinner, it was excellent."

I smiled and followed him so I could lock up behind him. At the open door, he turned and enfolded me in his arms, resting his cheek on my hair. "Thanks," he whispered and slipped into the night.

Stunned at the pure rush of pleasure I'd felt with the contact, I stared out into the darkness. Tenderness gave way to frustration. "Well, this bites."

I shut and locked the door, turned off the lights, and slogged up the stairs. Wasn't my luck the pits? First I get bowled over by a smooth-talking rat bastard and then I find a decent—albeit married—man who desires me back and yet I still wasn't getting anywhere. Same shit, different pile.

I changed into my sleep shirt and was folding my jeans when I felt a bump in the back pocket. There was another wad of money stuffed in there. Here I'd hoped he'd been coping a feel. Nope, just paying me back for looking out for his kids when he couldn't.

Irate, I opened the new window. "You're a real son of a bitch, you know that!" I called into the night.

"You're welcome. And next time, close the blinds before you change!"

Damn it, I hate when someone else gets the last word.

CHAPTER TEN

What does one wear to a divorce hearing? Of course, *I* wasn't getting divorced. No, some crazy man would have to marry my sorry ass first but still, I'd been requested by Amber to bring the children and we were to sit in the hallway outside the Judge's chambers.

The timing of this fun-filled afternoon couldn't have been worse. Kenny was asleep and would be crabby and Josh was fading fast, denied his normal afternoon naptime. And then there was me.

Picking up the phone, I speed-dialed Leo. "I have a fashion disaster," I told him.

"Honey, you are a fashion disaster," Leo responded cheerily.

"No time for jokes, Leo. I have two duffel bags and not a clothing choice in sight suitable for sitting in a courtroom hallway!"

"Maggie, are you kidding? Are you really going to drag the poor children down there to wait and see what cards the hand of fate deals the three of you?"

"Amber's lawyer wants us there, for the sympathy factor. I think she only wants to throw Neil off his game, which is why we're going to show up late." I held up a low-cut black wraparound top with red flowers. Too slutty.

"Did you consider taking his mother up on her offer?"

"My soul feels dirty even considering it." I had been keeping track of Amber's comings and goings, so to speak. I'd written everything down in a little notebook. The average time she spent with Kenny and Josh in the past five days? Eight minutes. So if someone asked me, well I had to tell the truth, didn't I?

"Damn it, Leo, I have nothing to wear!"

He sighed. "Black is classic, slimming, and professional. Can't go wrong with a black top."

"All of mine are in the laundry!" I shrieked.

"Borrow something from Amber's closet," Leo suggested.

I held the phone away from my ear and stared at it. Was he serious? No way I could fit my mega boobs into anything little miss size double zero wore. And even if Amber was lackadaisical about her offspring, I was pretty sure she'd notice me raiding her closet like some sorority house gal pal.

"Next option," I said and poked my head out into the hallway where Josh stacked cardboard blocks.

He heaved a great big put-upon sigh. "I need to see what we have to work with. I'll be there in two minutes." The receiver clicked in my ear.

I stared at the mess of my few worldly possessions. My mother would be so ashamed. No church duds in the bunch.

You're darn tootin' I'm ashamed. I raised you better than this, young lady! What would Pastor Maxwell think?

Probably that I'm Satan's whore and I should be drawn, quartered, burned at the stake, and have my ashes doused in saltwater so the Dark Lord doesn't resurrect my wicked self. Pastor

Maxwell had been our church religious leader of the fire and brimstone variety.

I ran down to greet Leo at the door. He stopped before he crossed the thresholds, hands-on-hips. "Just because I'm gay doesn't mean I know shit about women's fashion, Maggie."

I rolled my eyes at him. "I didn't call you about this because you're gay. I called you because you are the only friend I have in a sixty-mile radius."

Mollified, Leo nodded and gestured me back inside. "Well, okay then, lead on."

Ten minutes later, I was dressed in jeans, a white sweater, and sneakers. "This is the best you could come up with?"

"I'm going for the fresh-faced innocence you exude so well. You look responsible, respectable, and dignified. An excellent childcare giver."

"Should I put my hair in pigtails too?"

"Ungrateful wench." But he smiled. "You really sure you should do this?"

"I'm sure." I wanted to be there for Neil—even if he didn't know it until after the hearing ended. A friendly face in the crowd. Plus, I needed to know when I would see him again, damn it.

"Kay, I'm off. Peter has a field trip this afternoon and I'm chaperoning. Trade ya?"

"Two kids for twenty? Not even if I was drunk as a skunk and half-dead would I make that deal."

"You'll do fine in court." With a jaunty salute, he left.

Packing up two small children, even for a five-mile trip down the road, classified as an ordeal. The stroller folded down and strapped into the back of Neil's truck. Diapers, change of clothes for both children, juice, snacks, bottle for Kenny, teething ring, board books, mini Etch-A-Sketch, paper, crayons, and the primary source of entertainment, me.

I was loaded down like a pack mule ready to navigate the Grand Canyon.

"Let's do this thing, boys! Come on, troops, move 'em on out!" I called and Josh scurried out the door so fast he almost tripped on the sidewalk. Kenny was deadweight, still mostly asleep. With any luck, the short car ride would knock him into a deep sleep.

I'd printed directions off Map Quest and the midafternoon traffic flowing from Dam Neck Road to Princess Anne was relatively light. We cruised past Naval Air Station Oceana and were serenaded by the sound of jet noise. Unlike some of the residents of the area, I found the roar of the monster engines reassuring. Kenny and Josh didn't even flinch, old hands at the game.

"Do you like planes, Josh?" I glanced at my charge in the rearview mirror.

"Nope," he replied and gazed out the window.

That sounded definite. "Why not?"

He didn't answer. And I was about to miss my turn onto Nimmo Parkway so I let it slide for now.

Apparently, it was a good day to get a divorce because the Virginia Beach Circuit Court parking lot was hopping. I cruised around for a bit and then pulled into a parking space where I was sure the truck would fit in without damaging the doors. How I missed my maneuverable little Jetta, even if it was the color of stagnant urine. Of course, the truck smelled like leather and Neil. I took a hearty breath before unloading my cargo.

"Judicial Court, building ten," I muttered to myself. Fortunately, the man getting out of the car next to me overheard and pointed the way. I thanked him and pushed the stroller while Josh hung onto my belt loop.

By the face of my watch, we were thirty-seven minutes

late. Perfect. Amber would be riled, Neil wouldn't know and everything was going to be just—

As if summoned from my thoughts, Neil, sporting military dress uniform—be still my heart—stormed out of a nearby door. His face was as dark as the sky before a violent thunderstorm erupted.

"Hey," I called out, my voice trembling a little. Maybe I shouldn't have come at all, for he didn't look delighted to see the cheering section. His stride didn't slow as he maintained course past us and out into the parking lot.

"Daddy." Josh started to cry. I bent down and hugged him. *This does not look good.*

"NEIL, MY MAN?" I stared out of the truck windshield at J.T. Huh. I was back on base, must have driven there because I was in the driver's seat and the engine was still running.

The fact that I couldn't recall the drive made me realize I really shouldn't be driving. I shut the engine off and climbed from the truck.

"Everything all right?" J.T. had been avoiding me since he'd squealed like a stuck pig about the divorce. Suddenly having it out with him was what I wanted to do most.

Except as I looked down I realized I was in full dress uniform, supposed to conduct myself as a gentleman while standing as a symbol for the Navy. Not the wounded rabid animal stirring deep inside.

Got to change first. I strode off to the barracks, JT. falling into step beside me.

"What's up, Chameleon?"

I laughed the sound hollow and devoid of any real humor. "Don't think you can call me that any more J.T., I've forgotten how to blend."

"You've hit a rough patch Neil, it'll come back, you just need to—"

Fuck the uniform. I lunged at him, pinning him against the wall with my forearm under his Adam's apple. "Stop telling me to go get laid! If I wanted a fuck buddy I could have…."

"Who?" J.T. challenged me. Uncaring that I was minutes away from choking the life out of him.

I backed down. "No one you know. But she's beautiful and witty and deserves someone who isn't fresh from a fucking divorce hearing."

J.T. blanched visibly. "Aw hell, that was today? Shit, Neil, you should have said something."

"Yeah, well, I didn't and now it's over."

J.T. nodded once, then his face brightened. "Hey, come out with us tonight, we're heading over to the bar down the way. We'll turn it into a freedom party for you. I'll make a sign and everything, congrats Neil, way to ditch the bitch. You can get hammered and I promise by morning you won't even remember your own name, never mind hers."

I was about to refuse, not wanting to be around people, but J.T was determined to help. Maybe if I acted normal, like in the pre-Amber days, my teammates would quit treating me like a walking raw wound.

"A drink sounds good," I lied.

"Hey, what are friends for?"

"AND YOU HAVEN'T HEARD from him since?" Leo asked as we sat on the glider swing together and watched Peter chase Josh around the backyard. Peter made monster noises and lumbered after my eldest charge, who squealed in delight. I crinkled my nose at Kenny and snorted like a pig while he laughed and jumped in his bouncy seat. The weather was gorgeous, about seventy-five with a breeze blowing off the ocean and everyone in the neighborhood was out, planting bulbs, riding bikes, walking dogs.

Except for Neil and Amber. "I haven't heard from either of them. They could be holed up in the hotel room he stayed in, having post-divorce sex."

"And how would you feel about that?" Leo kicked the glider into motion.

"You know, for a six-foot-tall, slim gay man, you do a great impression of Dr. Ruth."

"If you'll observe how craftily she dodges the question. Well, sister, you can't fool me. Every third word out of your mouth is "Neil" and then you go on to explain what fantastical thing he's done lately. Admit it, Maggie, you're interested in him."

No, I was half in love with him but I'd bite my own tongue off before I said so out loud. Neil was right. Nothing good would come from our mutual attraction. "His ex-wife—who I think he still has feelings for—happens to be my employer. I've already learned my lesson about mixing business with pleasure, thank you very much. Besides, I'm not ready for a man yet."

Leo took a sip from the herbal iced tea I'd made. "Whatever you say, chief."

Peter roared and suddenly the game changed from fun to scary. Josh screamed and started to bawl. It seemed like the kid spent more than half of his young life in tears.

"The end of tranquility hour. Peter, apologize to him!" Leo called. I was already on my feet.

"You're such a baby, it's just a game," Peter taunted as I picked Josh up.

"Peter, he's little and he's tired."

"No." Josh managed to stop snuffling enough to deny my claim.

"You wanna help me make dinner, pal?"

"No."

"We'd better go. Peter has homework he needs to do."

"Whatever." Peter shrugged Leo's hand off his shoulder and headed for the house.

"Remember, whatever doesn't kill us, makes us stronger." Leo rolled his eyes and followed his nephew.

"Or suicidal!" I called out and turned back to the house. I plunked Josh on the couch.

"You forgot the baby," he accused.

"Jeeze, I didn't forget him, Josh. See? I'm going out to get him right now." No way could I carry both of them at the same time.

Kenny scowled at me as if he too was accusing me of negligence. My mouth felt dry and I swallowed as I wondered if Josh had gotten into the habit of reminding his mother about Kenny because she truly would forget him.

I busied myself getting them cleaned up and fed, though I couldn't manage to swallow anything for myself. Baths, racecar time, story time, still no sign of the parents. I dallied as long as I could, but by nine o'clock, both kids fell asleep watching *101 Dalmatians*. No use denying the inevitable. I carried them one by one to their room.

Where in the hell are you, Neil? I had the emergency number, but this wasn't an emergency, just me being nosy. I called Marty, seeking reassurance. I should have known better.

"So you're a nanny goat, whose brilliant idea was this?" I could tell Marty was eating chips by the crunching between the insults.

"I raised your sorry ass, didn't I? Didn't let you stick your tongue in a light socket and die, though the world might have been better off."

"Nice one, Maggs. So when are you coming back?"

I gnawed on my lower lip. "I don't know if I ever will."

"What about our money?" For once, Marty sounded serious.

"Do you need some? I could wire you—"

"That's not what I mean, and you know it. Are you gonna let him get away with stealing our inheritance? Money could give us a few options."

"I don't know if there's any way we can get it back," I told him.

"Of course you don't, you're hiding in Virginia Beach." More crunching. Had he always been so rude and spoiled?

"You know what, Marty? You want to find out what happened to the money? Then get off your dead ass and find out! I provided for you, now maybe you could give a little something back, you ungrateful waste of flesh." I slammed the phone down. Was I livid because Marty was lazy or because he was right?

Before I could chew on that juicy morsel the phone rang again. "Look, Marty I—"

"Hiya, gorgeous," Neil greeted me. "Whatcha doing?"

"Watching the fruit of your loins, what else? Neil, what the hell happened today?"

"It was a bad, bad day." His tone relayed absolute sorrow.

I narrowed my eyes as reality sunk in. "Holy crap, are you drunk?"

"Dunno, let me ask. Hey guys, am I drunk?" A room full of male voices verified.

My brain was whirling, plotting what needed to be done. "Where are you?"

"Don't think I should tell you," he slurred. Jeeze, he really was shit-faced. But I couldn't leave him there to maybe get hit on by some young, hot babe. No, that would be irresponsible of me.

"How about you let me talk to one of your pals, okay?"

He didn't answer and there was a great deal of fumbling. Finally, another man picked up. "Is this Maggie?" he asked in a soft southern drawl.

Wow, I guess Neil had mentioned me. "Yes. Could you tell me where you are?"

"This is J.T Hollis, ma'am. I understand you know our boy here?"

"Yes. Do you know what happened today?"

"No, ma'am. Neil hasn't spoken about it directly. The boys and I decided to take him out for a night of bucking up."

"Sounds like he's about to buck himself into a coma."

"Yes, ma'am. He needs to go somewhere he can dry out for the night." Other than the potential for this guy to ma'am me to death, he sounded all right.

"Tell me where. I'll pick him up." Shit, what was I going to do if Amber had gotten her way and he wasn't allowed back in the house? One problem at a time.

"Do you have something to write with?" J.T gave me an address and directions, which I scribbled on a paper towel. "I apologize for this, ma'am—"

"Please, call me Maggie, and no apologies necessary." I hung up and called Leo.

"I need a favor."

"You're a needy bitch today. First, I have to dress you up like a life-sized doll—"

I interrupted him with the tidbit I knew would get his attention. "Neil called. He's drunk as a skunk and I need to go pick him up. Could you come over and sit with the boys until I get back?"

"Did he tell you what happened?"

"No, and I need to find out. Please, Leo?"

"I want details for this. Excruciatingly vivid details. Plus some more spaghetti pie."

"Done." I had my jacket on and paced like an enraged water buffalo while I waited. Okay, the boys would be looked after, and I knew Neil's general vicinity. I'd yank him off of his barstool and find out what the hell had happened at the courthouse. Everything would all be all right. I had a plan.

"So here I am, in all of my glory!" Leo sang out as he entered the house. "Where is he?"

I relayed the address and somewhere deep in the recesses of my brain, I registered his appalled expression, but I was anxious to get moving. "Thanks so much for doing this! I'll be back as soon as I possibly can!"

"Wait, Maggie, that's a—"

I shut the door and sprinted for the truck.

CHAPTER ELEVEN

"**A** freaking go-go bar?" I said as I stared at the shanty-like little building with a neon sign advertising live girls. It reminded me of the place my father had always stopped for live bait on his way to our fishing hole—unfortunately in more ways than one. "Drunken sailor at a go-go bar, you've totally lost originality points with this one, Neil."

Get in, grab the big, strong dumbass and get out. I was waiting to hear from my mother's ghost, which had been noticeably absent all afternoon. Funny how the little delusion brought me worlds of comfort and I didn't realize it 'til it went away.

I slid out of the truck and onto the ground. The parking lot was mostly dirt with the occasional stray piece of gravel. The cars ranged from station wagons older than me to two-seater brand new deals. It really must take all types.

A cloud of musty air almost stopped me from going in, the scents of booze, grease, sweat, and sawdust were thick in the small space. The room was dimly lit and had an odd reddish glow, but it was packed full of sailors like sardines in a can. I was given the once-over by about fifty pairs of eyes. The only other woman in the room was on the stage, twice my age and covered in glitter down to her white bikini. Her gyrations did nothing for me but held her audience captive. *Men.*

I glanced around but didn't see Neil. Hell, I could barely see myself in this light. Maybe I should ask the bartender.

Since the entertainment was up front and I wasn't grinding as if my life depended on it, my progression to the bar on the right gradually lost its audience. The bathrooms flanked the battle-scared bar and the leather-clad bartender looked like he might have rolled out of bed and onto a Harley to get here. His hair was wild, his cheeks flushed as he filled orders. No wait staff I noticed. Hard times when a patron had to get off his ass and refill his own drink, interrupting the sparkly show—he might miss a crucial plot point.

"Excuse me," I said, "I'm looking for a sailor?"

The bartender didn't look up. "Take your pick, lady. Sheila has 'em all raring to go."

I rolled my eyes. Well of course he thought I was looking for a bed partner. What else would I be doing here? "No, I mean, my...friend. He's had a little too much to drink and I'm here to drive him...somewhere."

The man chucked a thumb over behind the stage. "Probably part of the private party. Behind the curtain."

Shit, I really didn't want to witness Neil enjoying the private party. "Can't you go ask them to send him out?" I smiled my best.

"I have to tend the bar unless you want to take over for me?"

Visions of men with alcohol poisoning filled my mind. "Never mind, thanks." Taking a deep breath, I strode to the curtain and scooted in behind it.

The private show was not much better than the public

one, though the main event was younger and wore a gold bikini. The biggest difference was in the back she was pretty much ignored while the men drank and laughed. There was a waitress bustling between tables, refilling glasses.

One small, dark-haired man spotted me immediately and staggered over. "Here to join the party, sweet cheeks?"

I glared at him. "Do I look like I'm here to join the freaking party?"

He looked me up and down. "Well, yeah. Aren't you another dancer?"

My head hurt from the pulsing bass in the music and I made a mental note to inform Leo his wardrobe choice made me look like a stripper. "I'm looking for Neil Phillips."

"Maggie!" Neil grinned like a kid on Christmas morning. If I thought the other guy had staggered, Neil looked like a loose-limbed cripple. His catlike grace was nowhere in sight as a behemoth of a man helped him limp my way.

"Maggie," he said again, the liquor heavy on his breath.

"That's my name, slick." I looked way up to meet the big guy's gaze. "J.T?"

"Yes, ma'am. Again, I apologize for making you come down here, but we can't take him back to base like this or he'll be in hot water."

"Don't worry, one more thing I can cross off the old bucket list. Go-go bar, check."

J.T grinned. "Neil's right, you're a class act."

I eyeballed the stage. "It all depends on who you're standing next to. Help me get him to the truck, all right?"

"We can go out the back." J.T dragged Neil out the exit door and I breathed in the fresh air, leaving the noise and smoke behind us. Circumnavigating the building was definitely a better choice than winding through the entire club.

"Look Maggs, it's a compensation car," Neil said, pointing out a Camaro.

"What's a compensation car?"

"You know, if you drive this, you must be compensating for a shortage in another department?" He wiggled his eyebrows so I'd get the message.

I sighed. "Where were you twelve years ago when I needed you?"

We made it to the truck and J.T. actually boosted Neil up, while I reached around him to buckle him in.

"Sleep it off, Neil. We have P.T at oh five hundred."

Neil made a noise which might have been an agreement as his head lolled to the side. "What'll happen if he doesn't show up?" I asked as we closed him in the truck.

J.T. shrugged. "Neil's the golden boy of the squad—never even had a parking ticket. So probably nothing more than a slap on the wrist, but I'd hate to see him spiral down because of her."

"You know Amber then?"

He nodded grimly. "She was a SEAL groupie, liked to collect trident pins like some women do pro athlete jersey numbers. Our boy there made the mistake of marrying her. He was new to the Teams, still wet behind the ears. She cheated on him constantly, though lost her taste for the military men at least. But she was out screwing around every time he was deployed."

"Why did he stay married to her all this time?"

"You'll have to ask him, but my guess is for the kids."

"Son of a bitch." I glanced up at Neil. "Thanks for letting me know."

"Be good to him, Maggie. He really likes you."

I blushed to the roots of my hair. "I really like him, too." Understatement of my life.

I circled the front of the truck and climbed into the driver's seat. "So now I have you but what the hell am I supposed to do with you?"

"Do I get to make a suggestion?" Neil asked, his eyes still closed.

"No." But I smiled into the darkness. "Feel like telling me what happened today?"

"Not especially."

I started the truck. "Kay. So where do you want me to chauffer you?"

"Let's go to the beach. I like going to the beach with you."

Not exactly what I had in mind, but okay. The little thrill of pleasure skittered around my body and I chastised my thoughts. He was drunk, practically incoherent, and here I was taking pleasure in his admissions. The fact that he'd talked me up to his friends, and we were alone— headed toward the beach and the moon was out, the go-go bar far behind us. It was a night made for romance.

Neil groaned. "Pull over. I'm gonna be sick."

Or not.

"FEELING BETTER?" I smiled as Neil climbed back in the cab of the truck. The good news was he hadn't barfed inside the vehicle, so by my calculations, we were still ahead of the game.

"Not really." He closed his eyes, the picture of misery.

"We're almost there. Maybe a walk will help."

He gave me a speaking look and I swear I heard him mutter yeah right. Traffic was light, all the sane people at home. The pleasant breeze from earlier had whipped up into a lusty gale, but he hadn't changed his mind about the beach.

I parked in a public lot, glad they wouldn't charge until tourist season started up next spring. Since I'd never been to the beach off-season, never given a thought about the people who had this quick drive then bam, they were there to enjoy everything the sea might offer year-round.

Neil spilled out of the car before I could come around and help him. He didn't look green or drunk anymore, just depressed. We crossed Atlantic Avenue next to the very hotel he'd been staying in when we'd first met—what felt like eons ago. I mused aloud as to why he'd been staying there and not on base.

"I'd come back the day before. Amber tossed me out like a mongrel dog that'd pissed on her favorite blouse," he replied.

I winced. "Sorry, I didn't mean to pry."

He glanced at me but didn't say anything. "You know, I wasn't quite as drunk as I was pretending to be."

Like I was going to argue with him? "Whatever you say, slick."

"No really, the guys wanted to help, and I didn't have it in me to say no. But I wanted to leave almost as soon as we got there. Don't feel like dealing with people, you know?"

No, I didn't. "Do you want me to go?"

He didn't say anything as we crossed the boardwalk but he shot me another of those indecipherable looks. I took my sneakers and socks off when we reached the sand. It was cold as it swallowed my feet. Much colder on an October night than under August's sun. He waited for me but didn't remove his own shoes.

"Doesn't that bother you?" I asked as sand spilled into his shoes.

"SEALs are trained to run in full gear on the sand. Swim, too. There are times when stripping to normal beach wear isn't the best idea."

"What made you want to become a SEAL?" I asked as the wind lifted my hair off of my neck.

He smiled as he stared down at our footprints. "My

parents are both lawyers and had my future all mapped out. College, law school, marry the debutant, make partner by thirty. What a yawn fest. I enlisted in the Navy to scrap their plan."

An image of his mother's disapproving scowl popped into my mind. "I really understand the why behind your choice."

"Yeah well, after I'd been in for about six months, the novelty of the idea wore off. Then one night, I was walking the beach, except it was colder, February, and I'd started out farther to the south. There's a line with a fence between the regular beach and the base at Dam Neck. Being a smart-assed punk I decided to hop the fence. After all, I had a military ID so why the hell not? No big deal. It was weird, I had this feeling as I wandered down the beach like someone was watching, but no one was there. I remember looking at the fence and debating if I should climb back over. I'd done what I'd set out to do, right?"

Engrossed in his tale, I nodded.

"Well, as I turned back around these dark shapes rose from the dunes—where I would have sworn there was nothing a half a minute before—pointing rifles at me. I'd stumbled into the middle of a SEAL training exercise. Almost pissed my pants on the spot."

"Wow. Did you get in trouble?"

"You bet. The team leader reamed me a new one, then the captain of the carrier company I was attached to took a turn. I spent three days in the brig and then was assigned kitchen detail for a month. But as soon as I was eligible, I applied to the BUD/s program."

"You wanted to run with that crowd, I guess. Skulk through the night and scare the hell out of other young dumbasses."

"At first. By the time I made it to BUD/s, I'd read everything out there about the SEAL teams and knew I'd found where I was supposed to be."

We walked along, past the lights from the hotels and restaurants, past several piers, and listened to the waves as they crashed against the shore.

"I envy you, Neil. You know where you belong."

He bent over, picked up a rock, and bounced it in his palm. "The judge granted us joint custody of the boys as long as I remain in counseling."

I let out a huge breath, utterly relieved. "That's great, fantastic really—"

"They made me apologize to her."

"What?"

"To Amber. For being a SEAL and being gone all of the time. I had to sit there in front of the judge and her lawyer and look her in the eye and tell her I was sorry for running off to save the world."

I watched as he tossed the rock into the ocean, mulling over his words. "They made you apologize to your wife—the ho-bag—for being a patriot while she gets off scot-free for being faithless skank?"

He nodded. "Her lawyer argued that I didn't need to accept every mission. I'd volunteered for quite a few of them and he claimed it was to dodge my family responsibility."

It still wasn't computing. "So by doing your job, providing for your family, and protecting your country, you somehow abandoned your familial obligations?"

He picked up another rock. "That about sums it up."

I thought about Amber and her flightiness. What J.T. had told me about Neil's marriage and her affairs. Envisioned him sitting across an uber shiny table, and being told he owed her something. I clearly pictured him shifting in his seat and clearing his throat, thinking of his sons as he looked at the woman who'd abandoned and betrayed him and said *I'm sorry, I made you do it.* No wonder he'd been so pissed!

"Oh, fuck this!" I snarled and grabbed his hand. "Let's go."

"Where?"

"To settle the score."

CHAPTER TWELVE

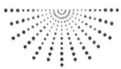

The lawyer was up first. I picked his address out of the phone book a kindly hotel clerk lent me and then hustled for the truck, Neil in tow. His absolute lack of objection was enough to spur me onward. Somebody needed to fight this battle and if the SEAL refused, the nanny sure as hell would.

Amber's attorney lived in a prestigious neighborhood in Sandbridge. Neil remained quiet as I circled the block, probably wondering what in the hell I was thinking. I'd be sure to let him in on it as soon as I figured it out.

The radio played some mediocre love song sung by one of those boy bands whose combined weight totaled my left thigh. I scowled and clicked it off and when I looked up salvation presented itself. "Bingo."

With a half-assed plan, I drove to the nearest 7-11 and bought a stack of paper lunch baggies and a lighter, plus two Slurpees. Back in the truck I handed Neil the drinks and left the bag on my lap before heading back to our destination.

"Why are we stopping at a dog park?" Neil asked.

I parked the truck and glanced over at my companion.

Smile in place, I reached over his lap to open the glove box. "You'll see."

Man, we were too close for comfort in this position and I removed what I needed in a hurry. I grinned as I heard him suck in a breath, glad I wasn't the only one affected. "Why are there rubber gloves in my truck?"

"I've been giving roadside prostate exams out of it in my spare time. Want one?"

His lips twitched. "Maybe later."

I snapped them on. "My father told me there are certain things you should keep in every vehicle. An emergency kit, a hammer—in case you need to break a window—a flashlight, a tire pressure indicator, and a patch kit as well as a full-sized spare, Windex, rubber gloves, and paper towels. Oh, and a copy of the Eagles Greatest Hits."

Neil shook his head. "In some universe, that might make sense."

"My dad was a smart guy. Wait here, I'll be back." I slithered out of the car and darted like a sneak into the park. Three steps in and I found the little poop collector bin where noble patrons discarded their little darlings' leavings. Lucky me, it hadn't been emptied in a while. I yanked the bag out and proceed to dump its contents into one of the lunch sacks and then headed back to Neil.

"Come on slick, we're walking from here."

We hustled along the road, me trying not to breathe too deeply. "Do you know if this guy is married?" I asked.

"I don't know, he wasn't wearing a wedding ring, but that might not mean anything." His tone was bitter and helped to firm my resolve. This man needed closure.

"Maggie," he whispered. You're not gonna do what I think you are planning to do, are you?"

I held up my prize. "One flaming shitbag deserves another."

Neil groaned and grabbed the arm which wasn't holding the bag of poop. "What are we, twelve? Can you imagine what kind of trouble we'll be in if we get caught?"

I glanced over my shoulder. The house was right in front of us, security lights on.

"He's a parasite, Neil. He makes his living by profiting off of other people's pain."

"So what are you, Robin Hood, redistributing the crap to the deserving?"

"Look, your protests are duly noted and if pressed, I'll take the heat. But I'm tired of playing the cards I'm dealt within the narrow scope of morality, aren't you? Look where it's gotten us. I need to do *something*, Neil, can't you see that?"

He hesitated so I took advantage of his waffling and elbowed him in the stomach. "Sorry!" I called over my shoulder as I sprinted for the house. The adrenaline kicked in as I scooted around the back deck out of view of the security light and circled to the front stoop. Nothing could stop me now.

Skulking through the dormant Azalea bushes, I took a chance to peek through the window. Didn't want Mrs. or Junior to take the heat. My target was in his office, talking on the phone. I gauged the distance to the door and unless someone else was sitting right behind it, he would definitely be the one to answer the summons.

Giggling like a mentally unhinged lunatic, I deposited my package and lit it up before ding-dong ditching back to my hiding spot. Through the window, I saw him frown, put down the phone, and rise. He called out to someone and proceeded out of my line of sight.

I shifted to get a better view of the flames. Cripes, the smell was awful, even from yards away. Some doggie was in dire need of canine Pepto-Bismol. The front door opened and the man poked his head out into the night, looked down, and gasped at the sight of the micro inferno. I sat up as his slippered foot lifted over the bag, practically vibrating from excitement.

Splat. I was knocked face-first into the ground, my breath escaped in a huge rush. A hand clamped over my mouth. What the hell? Did the lawyer have security ninjas? I flailed impotently and almost screamed when my assailant rolled me over. Neil's voice whispered in my ear, "Shut up unless you want to get caught."

I ceased my struggles, quit moving altogether, and listened. His body was warm on mine, his scent luring me in until I forgot where we were and why we were there in the first place. His rock-hard body conformed to every inch of mine, like two halves of a mold. Our noses were inches apart, and while his gaze focused on the front door, mine remained fixed on him.

"God damned idiot kids!" The lawyer cussed from the front door. "I'm gonna catch you, you worthless punks! Wait and see if I don't!" The sound of a door slamming and Neil smirked down at me.

"Mission accomplished?" I asked, winded from his assault and his nearness.

"If he'd look over here, he would have seen you! You're wearing white, like a freaking *here I am* glow-in-the-dark beacon! First rule of sneak and peek, camouflage is your friend."

I couldn't think when he looked at me all stern and scolding and close. And hard. "Any other tips?" I whispered.

"Yeah," he exhaled and his hands cradled my face. "This."

His lips met mine, the pressure hesitant at first, gentle and almost reverent and there was that damnable spark which flared up between the two of us, the intensity binding us together, feeding the need. He kept my arms pinned, but I wrapped my legs around his waist so I could hold him to me.

The kiss changed, intensified as I opened my mouth to welcome him, greeting his advance with the reserve of need he'd built up in me.

Were we about to do it in some guy's bushes on the night of his divorce? The idea seemed icky and wrong on every level, but if he asked, I would have said *game on*.

He didn't ask though, just broke the kiss and rolled off me. I shivered as the breeze washed over my flushed skin, bereft at the loss of his comforting weight.

Neil wouldn't meet my gaze. "Let's go before they get here."

"Who?" I asked as the sound of distant sirens pieced the night's tranquility. "Aw hell, he called the cops."

"Told you this was a bad idea," he reminded me and scurried into the night. I sighed and followed, wondering to which part he'd been referring.

God, I want to fuck her. Of course, this wasn't a newsflash to the Almighty and I expected some serious compensation for not sliding inside her wet heat there in the bushes. She tasted like every good memory I'd ever possessed, sweet and soft, welcoming in every way. She would have let me too, which made dropping her off at my house and not going inside, not being inside her damn near impossible. Her need was like an untapped reservoir, and I wanted in more than anything else in my life.

But it wasn't fair to her. My hands shook slightly as I drove back to base. Still early despite our exploits that evening. I headed straight for the shower and ran the water, glad no one else was around, but knowing I would have done it anyway.

Her ass would be the death of me. The way she swung her

hips was far from practiced, and I imagined gripping those curves as I eased her down on my shaft. The hot water pounded, my mind alternating between imagining her on her back while I tongued her wetness, tasting just how sweet she really was, and imagining the feel of plunging inside her again and again until she cried out my name in the throes of her release.

Locking my gaze with her in my mind's eye, those baby blues molten with desire for me sent my control over the edge, my body crashing into yet another hollow orgasm.

This shit needs to stop. I rinsed the shower and grabbed my towel, redressing. The difference between ejaculating via old righty and with another human being? Well, instead of being sated and content, I was keyed up and still restless as hell. All I'd done was take the edge off, but reality smacked me upside the head.

I was no longer married, free to do whatever I wished with whomever I wanted. And I wanted Maggie, but did I want her more as a mother to my boys or in my bed?

Not just in bed, everywhere. I craved her company. Wasn't that why I'd called her from the bar after overindulging in liquid courage? Christ, I had more fun with her fully dressed and skulking through the bushes, committing misdemeanors, than with any other women I'd had naked and spread. My mind made a neat segue to her naked and spread.

And he's up. My cock twitched and I forced myself to think about what was best for Maggie. I looked down to where the hard-on was tenting my pants. *And you are not it.*

"THAT'S IT? He didn't say anything else?" Leo sat on the bench and bounced Kenny on his knee. "I said I wanted details, you were out until well after midnight for heaven's sake."

"Sorry, Mom." I pushed Josh on the swing and made a face at my friend. "Leo, I'm not holding out on you or anything." How I wished I was though.

"So when are you going to see him again?"

I shrugged. "Not a clue."

"She gives me nothing to work with. You see this, right Kenny?"

"Down," Josh demanded.

I stopped the swing. "What's the magic word?"

"Down, pweese," he said. I lifted him off and let him down onto the woodchips. He darted off to the pirate ship. I moved to a better vantage point. "All I care about is the kids." The lie fell easily from my lips.

Leo lowered his aviator-style sunglasses and looked at me over the rims. "*Riiiiight.*"

"Knock it off, you look like a cop, the one from *The Village People.*"

"The Indian chief was hotter," Leo pronounced as a woman nearby turned and issued us a disapproving glare and hustled her son away.

"Don't worry, it's not contagious," Leo called at her retreating form.

"How do you deal with this every time you go outside? Wouldn't it be easier to...I don't know..." I shrugged, not sure where the thought might be heading.

"Not be me? Been there, done that, got the crappy T-shirt. I'd rather have most of the world hate me than to hate myself the way you do."

"I don't hate myself. I only wish I could take a break from me every now and again. Have you noticed how irritating I can be?"

"That's not why he said it, Maggie. Stop looking for crap that doesn't exist."

Sighing, I scooped Kenny up. "What was I thinking, telling you about the moment? You've harped like an old fishwife all morning."

"Listen to you." Leo stood and made little air quotes with his fingers. "*The moment,* as in the pivotal moment of your life, the one that changed everything. And people call me melodramatic."

"I call you a pain in the—"

"Watch me, Miss Maggs!" Josh called from one of the connector tunnels.

"I'm watching, Scamp!" I shifted Kenny to the other side so my arm didn't go completely numb from holding him.

"Well, I'd love to stand here and be insulted all day, but I promised George I would pick up his dress blues from the cleaners. Big command function tonight." Leo didn't bother to hide his dismay. As the gay partner of a career military man, Leo wasn't going to the shindig.

Impulsively, I leaned in and gave him a hug. "I'll call you with an update later."

"Ta ta," he called and headed back to the parking area.

"I guess the course of true love never did run smooth," I said to Kenny, who gurgled at me. I sat and bounced him on my knee, doing my damndest to think of nothing in particular.

"Hey." Like a freaking phantom, Neil had snuck up on yet me again.

"You like scaring me, don't you." The grin on his face was all the confirmation I needed. "How'd you know where we were?"

"GPS in the truck. My swim buddy dropped me off." He eyeballed the remainder of the bench.

"Have a seat." I slid over so we wouldn't have direct

contact but not as far as I could have. "Is a swim buddy like you would have at summer camp?"

"Pretty much. When we're trained to become SEALs, we're paired with another candidate who becomes our partner in crime. For the rest of BUD/s training, we do everything as a unit because it's a bad idea to swim alone."

"You swam alone when you went after my ring," I pointed out

"Yeah, but you were there," he replied.

I threw my head back and laughed. "If your plan was for me to help you, you're totally off your nut, pal. I'm nobody's hero."

"Don't sell yourself short, Maggie."

"It's what I do best. The secret is in the practice. Besides, nobody else will let me treat them this shabbily. Gotta get the crazy out somehow."

He surveyed me in a most unnerving way, opened his mouth but Josh caught sight of him. "Daddy!"

Kenny had fallen asleep and while I planned on heading home before his nap, Josh was having too much fun with Neil, climbing, and sliding, being pushed on the swing. Miss Maggs would do in a pinch but there was nothing like daddy time.

This was what I'd always wanted, I thought as I pushed the stroller with the sleeping sumo baby back and forth on the walkway, and Josh and Neil climbed up the giant grass-covered mountain that used to be a landfill. I'd never been bogged down with ambition as much as a need to belong, especially since the only family I had left was off sewing his wild oats. How I envied Marty his freedom from responsibility. The luxury I'd provided after my parents died. *And it isn't even mine to enjoy.*

"Earth to Maggie." Neil waved his hand in front of my face.

"Damn it, don't do that!" I was irate at him for acting as though nothing happened between us last night and annoyed at my own foolish heart for hoping something had changed.

He sighed. "Are you mad about last night?"

Men could be so dense that light should bend around them. "Why would I be mad? You know you wanted me to do that. With the lawyer, I mean."

"I distinctly remember saying no, it was a bad idea…"

I snorted in derision. "Yeah, the way a milquetoast heroine in a romance novel does." Adapting a higher pitch and breathiness to my voice I said, "No, Maggie, I can't, it's not right."

He scowled at me and I pushed my luck. "You know you wanted to do it as much as I did. Like my little elbow to the solar plexus could have hindered you? Like I really out ran you? I'm the girl who memorized the T.V. guide listings so I had a tactical advantage when playing T.V. tag because everyone could catch me! You're a trained warrior, for the love of grief!"

He grinned, shook his head. "I can't fool you, can I?"

"Nope. The question is why would you want to when I'm on your side?"

He picked my hand off the stroller and bent low to kiss my knuckles. I shivered, despite the warm Virginia sun beating on my back. He really knew how to pull out all the stops.

"Thank you for last night, Maggie. I'm not sure what I would have done if you hadn't shown up."

"Probably something really stupid you would regret."

He laughed, the first real one I'd heard in a while. "I doubt I'll ever forget the look on the guy's face. Priceless doesn't begin to describe it."

I wouldn't know since I was too busy looking at yours. "Glad you had fun. You deserve it, Neil."

"Maggie." His mouth opened like he wanted to say something but no words came out. I bit my lip, wondering if I had what it took to initiate another round of face-sucking. I'd never been the aggressor before, too afraid of rejection which had been all too common throughout my life.

We stared at one another, this weird sense of *what if,* hovering between us.

"Daddy, I'm hungry." Josh to the rescue.

"Now there's a good sign," I said. "How about we head home for lunch?"

"Sounds like a plan." Neil scooped Josh up and we made our way back to the truck. Silence reined as neither one of us willing to push beyond the pseudo-neutral zone we'd managed to establish. Neil folded the stroller like a pro while I secured the kids and tossed him the keys.

"You get to be our chauffer today."

"Did I miss anything this morning?" He reversed out of the spot.

Josh coughed and I rolled up the window in case the air was too much in his face. "I think Kenny's going to start crawling any day now. He keeps turning over to his hands and knees."

We turned onto Rosemont and sat at a light. Josh coughed again, a pitiful sound that started deep in his chest. Neil glanced at him in the rearview mirror. "You okay, pal?"

"Yup," Josh said before projectile vomiting all over his little brother.

CHAPTER THIRTEEN

"I guess your dad was spot-on about the rubber gloves," Neil, who sported them with a surprising manly elegance said while he wiped out the truck's back seat. "Came in handy twice in twenty-four hours. How's Josh?"

I carried a now clean, though still somewhat irate Kenny, down to watch his daddy. "No fever, so it might have been something he ate. Are you sure he doesn't have any food allergies?"

Neil sighed. "I haven't been to a doctor's appointment with him since he was younger than Kenny. The timing is always off. Once, we were actually sitting in the waiting room when my pager went off and I had to go. Amber was livid."

I shifted my weight back and forth, trying to soothe Kenny. "You don't need to beat yourself up about it, Neil, it's your job."

He shot me a rueful grin over his shoulder. "I'm not, not really. I can't be in two places at once, though I hear the SEALs are trying to master that special technique. Best I can do is make the most of what time I've got, right?"

I nodded. "Yup. So how's this custody thing going to work out? Do you come and pick up the kids or what?"

He chucked the sponge into the bucket of water and it landed with a soft plop. "Well, the visits have to be here, since I'm staying in the barracks on base and can't exactly bring the boys there. Amber was not happy about that part, I guess my hanging around will put a crimp in her social life." His face remained stoic but I could tell the idea still scraped over his raw wound.

Though I doubted his presence would slow her up too much. I hadn't seen or heard from Amber at all since the day before. How she managed to have so much energy was beyond me. I kept all of this to myself since I doubted Neil would appreciate my observations about his ex's rip-roaring social life. "Any certain days assigned to you?"

"No, it's not conducive to my work schedule. I pretty much have carte blanche to be here whenever I'm stateside."

Be still my heart. "Sounds like you had an awesome lawyer."

Neil scowled. "I hate lawyers, turning shit that's supposed to be personal into a freaking business arrangement. It's so…cold."

I shrugged the shoulder that was free of Kenny duty. "It's the world we live in. Look at the bright side—at least she didn't manage to get the restraining order in place."

He tugged the rubber gloves off. "Not for lack of effort on either her or her lawyer's part. The counselor I've been seeing had written a letter explaining my…issues and he made a point of stating he doesn't believe I would hurt anyone while under the influence of one of my flashbacks."

Something in his tone told me Neil didn't quite agree with this assessment. "You wouldn't, I'm sure of it."

He smiled at me, and then looked down at his son. "Let

me go clean up so I can take him for you. You're probably dying for some time off, huh?"

I blinked. The thought never actually occurred to me, but other than the night at Leo's, I'd been with the Phillips boys in one way or another for a week straight. Was it weird I didn't want any time to myself?

"Don't hustle on my part!" I called at Neil's retreating backside, enjoying the view. Shoot, five minutes ago, I'd been ecstatic because Neil would be popping by whenever he was able. But now, I was supposed to go elsewhere and pretend to have a life? Well, if that didn't draw a thick line between employer and employee. I looked at Kenny.

"I can't catch a frigging break here, big boy."

"Diggy diggy doo," he replied.

I turned back to go in the house when an engine revved not far off. Probably some idiot teenager showing off for his girlfriend. Screeching tires, reminiscent of the *Dukes of Hazard* pierced the afternoon's tranquility and a black Plymouth Reliant left skid marks as it turned the corner too fast.

"Cripes," I muttered, recognizing the rust spot which resembled Alfred Hitchcock in profile. AC/DC's *Highway to Hell* blared from the amp-ed up stereo I'd paid for.

The car skidded to a stop. I bent down to glare at the driver through the open window. My brother grinned back at me. "S'up?"

"Marty, what the hell are you doing here?" Why didn't I see this coming? I'd hung up on him yesterday and instead of hiking up his big boy skivvies, Marty decided to hop in the car and harangue me in person. "This is where I work! You can't show up whenever the mood strikes!" What was I going to tell Neil?

"We have an appointment and I'm here to retrieve your sorry ass."

Kenny squirmed in my arms. "What do you mean by appointment?"

"Is English your first language, *chica*? Exactly what it sounds like. We need to get you ready so we can drive together and be someplace to see someone at a specific time. Jeeze, and here everyone thinks you're the responsible one."

"I can't up and leave! Joshua is sick and Neil needs me—"

"No, I don't." The man himself had crept up on me again and those three little words cut me to the quick. I handed Kenny over, missing his weight in my arms already, and full of ire made the necessary introductions.

"Neil Phillips, meet my brother, Martin Sampson."

Like a total douche bag, my brother lowered his sunglasses to examine Neil. I groaned and almost ran to hide in the house. Every so often, Marty got a wild hair up his ass and thought he was tougher than nature made him. Apparently, he'd decided to size up a Navy SEAL. Marty was living proof that Darwin wasn't totally right about natural selection.

Neil though was an excellent sport and didn't seem at all concerned with Marty's scrutiny. "Nice to meet you. Maggie's mentioned you."

"Did she tell you how she sold our father's business out from under me without so much as by your leave then ditched my stuff in a fleabag motel room so she could hotfoot it to the beach in search of the next eligible bachelor?"

I hip-checked Neil so I could open the door and get my ass in the car. "Okay, we'd better get a move on or we're going to be late! Wouldn't want to miss our appointment, now would we," I sang out cheerfully.

Neil blinked and glanced at me. "Boys and I will be fine. We'll see ya later."

"Ciao." Marty—who was apparently working on his

international road show repertoire—gave a two-fingered salute and lead-footed the gas. We whizzed around the cul-de-sac. I scrunched down in absolute mortification.

Maggie to reality, I've been plunked back down at the home base.

"Oh, you gotta be shitting me," I said and sat down with a thump. The lawyer blinked, probably appalled by my unconventional greeting, and smiled faintly, a buzzard scenting fresh meat. He was in his mid-forties with a protruding potbelly and thinning brown hair. It wasn't his fault I was sick to death of lawyers and their zany antics.

With a glare at my brother, I said, "I'm sorry, Mr. ...?"

"Yates, Norman Yates." He tapped the tarnished name-plate on his desk with a pen.

"Norman Yates, really?" I raised my eyebrows, but as Maggie Sampson, couldn't say jack about the coincidence. The rhyme explained why Marty had picked his name out of the yellow pages though, probably though this guy was some big shot he'd heard of in passing.

"As I explained to your brother on the phone, I think you'll have a very good case for a lawsuit against your former fiancé." He rose from behind his battle-scarred desk and retrieved a law book from the rickety shelves behind it. "What would have to happen first is we take you to the D.A. in Richmond and tell them your story. The prosecutor would then arrest him and hold a trial to determine if he was indeed guilty of larceny according to Virginia State Law. If convicted, we could then proceed with a cause of action in civil courts to try and recoup some of your loss."

My head swam at all the legal jargon. "Can we back up

here for a second? What exactly was his crime, other than being a jackass?"

Norm looked at me like I was impossibly slow. "Chapter six of the Virginia State Code section 18.2-178. He obtained money by false pretense. If found guilty, he would be incarcerated for two to ten years and pay a fine of no more than $100,000."

"To the *state*," I clarified. "So what the hell would he have left to repay us?"

Marty and Norm stared at me blankly. Sighing I shook my head. "Sorry to waste your time Norm, but I'm not willing to give up God alone knows how much more of my time proving he's a jackass. I might be a woman scorned, but I'm not willing to waste another day on him." I stood and left the room, furious that Marty would even think this existed in the same universe as a good idea.

"Wait, Maggie, just hear him out!" Marty scurried along behind me. 'There are ways we could get the money—"

"When, huh? Years, Marty, it'll take *years* before we see a freaking dime, and then we have to hand most of it over to Norman Yates? Did you even think about me for a second, how I'd feel sitting in a courtroom and admitting I was victimized by that opportunistic rat bastard? Don't you want to get on with your life? I sure as hell do!"

I slammed the car door with excessive force before he could shout back at me. We'd already caused enough of a scene for one day. Marty glared at me through the windshield and I refused to look away. He may have grown into a man's body, but my brother was still a child, waiting for someone to give him the golden ticket.

His attitude was my fault. I'd born the entire burden of our lives and let him skate. Did I make awful decisions at times, yes, but they were mine and I owned my own crap.

Marty had never been required to do more than whine like a constipated mule and I ran to do his bidding.

Well not this time, damn it. It might be selfish of me, but I'd given him enough. He didn't want to use the college scholarship I'd found for him? Fine, but no way would I relive my naiveté before a jury of the jackass's peers so Marty could settle on easy street.

He climbed into the car and turned the engine over without looking at me.

"Sprout, listen to me—"

He cut me off as he pulled out into eastbound traffic. "So what's your big plan, other than screwing your new boss instead of your old one?"

I blinked, sure I'd misheard him. "Neil and I aren't—"

"What, doing the nasty yet? Tell me, Maggie, why is it so wrong for me to want some of my inheritance you pissed away, but the old moral compass of yours doesn't twitch at you sponging off of the men you work for."

He braked at a red light and I didn't hesitate as I flung open the car door. Good thing we were in the far right lane. I climbed out and shut the door on his stunned face. "You know nothing about the shape of your own spoiled ass, let alone what I've been doing, you selfish prick, so have a nice life."

"Maggie, get back in the car!" Marty called and honked the horn like I was a bus blocking his way. I flipped him off and marched along the side of the road, with no particular plan except to get away from my last family tie, as soon as possible.

What was it about the men in my life that made me storm along the highway like a militant power walker? Rage, hot and slick, roiled in my guts as I darted across the highway having nothing but the most general idea of where I needed to go.

Three miles in, I'd crossed Rosemont Avenue and my ire had worn to a throbbing nub of irritation. Damn it, why hadn't I thought to steal my cell phone from The Jackass's office? Piss poor planning on my part, not thinking about all of the times I'd be stuck in the city of Virginia Beach sans transportation. Hell, I didn't even have my bag, thanks to Marty's impromptu arrival and my desire to get him away from Neil post haste.

I sat down on a bench outside a gas station and stared up at the puffy white clouds. This was my life, no home, no family, and nothing but an uphill battle to earn a buck. Walt Disney was full of mouse droppings, seeding the idea we would all live happily ever after. No one did, not me or beautiful Amber or handsome Neil or selfish Marty, or clever Leo. We were all pretty darn miserable, in our own right. What the hell was the point of it all?

"Having fun yet?" My brother stood over me blocking the sun and casting a shadow over my ruminating bench.

"Not especially," I told him.

He stuffed his hands in his pockets and looked at me, waiting. I stared back, thinking I'd rather decompose on this bench than apologize to him. "How did you find me?"

"I didn't, I needed gas." He pointed to where his POS was parked beside pump number two.

At least I wasn't suffering under the illusion he'd been searching for me. "Why all of a sudden, Marty? What made you so angsty about the money now? I broke up with the Jackass over a week ago and you didn't seem concerned about it then."

"Gloria kicked me out yesterday," he muttered, his voice so hushed I almost missed the confession. "All of my stuff is in the car, and I don't have much cash or the hope of getting any more."

"Marty." I sighed, not knowing what else to say. He

shrugged and I saw the sixteen-year-old boy who'd stood lost and afraid outside our mother's hospital room.

I closed my eyes, hating myself a little bit. "All right, I'll do it, for you."

He grinned. "You won't be sorry Maggie. This will fix everything, set us up for life—"

I held up a finger. "There are conditions to this, Marty. A lawsuit isn't a quick fix. You need to get a job, find a place to stay. And apologize for what you said earlier."

"I'm sorry." His tone was almost sincere.

"Do not embarrass me in front of my employer, or I swear to God, I'll beat the ever-loving snot out of you."

"Sure thing," Marty agreed as we headed back to the car. "Maggie and Neil, sitting in a tree…"

I glared at him.

"Well, I have to get it out before we see him again, right?"

I sighed as he continued singing "K-I-S-S-I-N-G."

"What have I done to deserve this?" I asked the sky. I swear I heard my mother's laughter in my head.

CHAPTER FOURTEEN

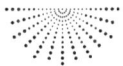

"Hey," I called out as I swung through the door. "How's Josh feeling?"

"Better, I think." Neil had Kenny tucked in the crook of his arm and the baby squealed in delight when he recognized the sound of my voice. "Did you have a good time?"

"Depends on your definition of good." I clapped my hands before taking baby butterball. "I think I might have made a decision."

Neil offered me his lopsided grin and it took everything in me to keep from sighing. "Sounds ominous. What about?"

"Marty convinced me to sue my former fiancé and see if we can retrieve some of the money he swindled."

"Agoo gee-gee," Kenny said with a giant grin.

"You betcha. Has he eaten lately? I normally give him a teething cookie to nosh on while I make dinner."

I was so wrapped up in talking to Kenny, who was obviously glad to see me, I missed Neil's dumbstruck look at first. "What?" I asked him, hoping he wasn't about to have another one of his flashes.

"You're going to sue your former fiancé?" he asked as if I hadn't already told him the answer.

Instead of replying, I took Kenny into the kitchen. He followed and I wondered if there was any way to get out of this conversation.

"Like for breach of promise or something?" Neil queried, his posture deceptively relaxed, ankles crossed as he leaned on the doorjamb.

I rolled my eyes as I tied a bib around Kenny's neck. "What is this, the Middle Ages? My father didn't exactly promise him the best ewes in the flock, Neil. No, the lawsuit is for the money he was supposedly investing for us."

"What brought this on?" His tone was too casual and even though his face remained neutral, I could tell he didn't like this plan.

"Well, it might be nice to not have to live off of the mercy of strangers," I said as I unwrapped Kenny's treat. The boy's gaze was trained on every twitch of my fingers. No sooner had I put it down on Kenny's tray than Neil whirled me to face him. I sucked in a deep breath and regretted it the instant I smelled his warm, spicy scent. So not fair that he both looked *and* smelled scrumptious all the freaking time.

"Knock it off," he said, his eyes blazing as he studied my face.

I shivered, whether, from his touch or my zinging hormones, I didn't know. "What?"

"Acting like I'm doing you this huge favor or something. You're taking care of my kids, under less than typical working conditions. If anyone has drawn the short straw, it's you. So let's try this again. Why are you bothering with a lawsuit? I know you don't care about the money."

"Who doesn't care about money? We live in a capitalist society."

He didn't respond to my segue argument, just stared at me.

I sighed. "It's for Marty. His girlfriend woke up and realized he's a lazy mooch and tossed him out."

"So, because your brother doesn't want to make his own way in the world, you are going to waste more of your life on that loser? Sounds fair to me."

"It's not like that," I huffed, even while I thought *Um, it's exactly like that.* "If I don't step up, he might snare some other naive young thing and wreck her life too. It's a public service, really."

Neil folded his arms over his chest, a smug smile in place. I glared at him. "Don't make me hurt you, slick."

"Why do you call me slick?" he asked.

"Because you're slicker than cat spit and though you aren't arrogant about it, you're more confident than the average shmoe."

He tilted his head to the side and studied me. "Are you really that afraid of me?"

"Yes." The word was out before I'd even thought about it. Crap, I'd handed him a big old weapon to use against me.

"Well good, because I'd hate to think I was the only one scared out of my mind."

He might be pulling my leg, but as I scanned the green depths of his eyes, I somehow didn't think this was the case. "Why would you be afraid of me?"

"I think you know the answer. We can't keep dancing around each other like this. I give you a day off and you go file a lawsuit."

"I didn't want a day off." Some inner streak of boldness made me step forward.

"Why not?"

I swallowed around the hard lump in my throat. Bravery

was so not my forte. "Because I want to be with you, whenever you're here, okay?"

He opened his mouth to respond, but a slamming door interrupted us. Neil closed his eyes and I groaned, thinking with the two of us here, it was easy to guess who'd stomped in.

"Do me a favor and keep Kenny in here, in case there are any fireworks." Neil stalked past me to meet his ex-wife. I wet a dishtowel and wiped the gook off of the baby's face, and shamelessly eavesdropped. I looked at Kenny and wondered if this would be how he felt if he understood what was going on, listening to the grown-ups decide his fate. If he thought about something other than stuffing his face.

His tone was low and steady, the words too soft for me to hear, like a gentle breeze overpowered by hurricane Amber.

"I'm going, Neil, you can't stop me."

"Think this through, Amber. You can't take the kids to California! I'm stationed here—I'd never see them."

I peeked around the corner. Neil's back was to me and Amber was too busy waving her finger in his face.

"So what, I'm supposed to put my life on hold because of your career yet again? I don't think so, pal. You want the kids, you can have 'em."

I sucked in a breath and Neil took a step back. His spine was so stiff it looked as though it had been starched. I could see in my mind's eye the expression on his face, jaw clenched, eyebrows forming a V. "You don't mean that."

Oh, I really hoped she did mean it. Well, not so much for anyone other than myself. Neil could move in here, we'd get busy, fall in love and the drama would die off like good taste at a *Bloodhound Gang* concert—happily ever after in my book.

Amber looked up and spotted me.

"Sorry, Michelle, you're fired."

"You just walked out of there?" Leo, bless him, served me a slice of German chocolate cake with Richmond chocolate frosting. How he could torture himself with these culinary masterpieces was beyond me, but I sure was grateful for the therapy.

"What was I supposed to do, Leo? She fired me!" I forked up some cake and crammed it in my mouth, trying to forget the ugly little scene.

Without being asked, he poured me a glass of milk. "So? Did Neil tell her where she could stick her pink slip?"

I took another bite to stall, then drank half the glass in one swallow. Leo made a face at my horrific table etiquette but was smart enough not to comment.

"He was already on the phone with his lawyer. Didn't even look at me." I eyeballed my empty plate. "Is there any more?"

"Not 'til after dinner." Leo took the dishes to the sink. "Did you tell him where you were going?"

My nose crinkled at the thought. "Because it's ever so romantic when you *force* the prince to chase after you. No, if Neil wants me, he can put a little effort into finding me."

Leo rolled his eyes to the ceiling. "Like walking across the street? Some big chase scene. I doubt either of you will win an Oscar anytime soon."

"What was I supposed to do, stand there and watch them bicker? It's not my family, Leo!"

"Do you want it to be?" he asked, his voice quiet.

I looked out the window toward the little house. "That isn't up to me. I'm still not over what the Jackass did, not even to the point of rebound fling yet. Though I doubt I'd know one of those if it bit me on the ass. Neil's even worse, the ink's still fresh on his divorce papers and Amber's dropped this huge bomb on him. And then there's Marty…"

"Oh yeah, about him." Leo's gaze shifted away and I narrowed my eyes at him.

"When did you meet my brother?"

"A few hours ago. I was raking the leaves out back and he popped his head over the fence, asked if he could sleep in the garage."

I winced, clearly able to picture the scene. "I'm sorry, I must have mentioned we were friends and to Marty, any friend of mine is good enough to sponge off. I hope he didn't cause a scene when you told him no."

He didn't answer and the truth hit me. "He's here? Oh hell, Leo, you're now putting up both the Sampson kids, aren't you."

He fussed with his perfectly straight table runner. "You'll be back across the street in no time and George is going on deployment. It's no big deal."

"Martin Chester Sampson, get your worthless hide out here, now!"

A door opened down the hall and Peter stuck his head out, caught sight of my expression, and disappeared. Marty sauntered down the hall, wearing an old T-shirt and paint-speckled jeans and boots.

"I know what you're going to say, Maggie—"

I stared him down, hands-on-hips. "Then why the hell do I have to say it, you little creep? Huh? Do I really have to ask why you thought it would be okay to mooch off of my friend?"

"It's cool, Maggie, I'm earning my keep." He waved his hands down the front of his pants and I blinked, sure I'd misinterpreted his intention.

Marty waited expectantly and I raised my eyebrows at him. He scowled and I chucked my thumb from him to Leo.

"Painting, jeez sis, get your mind out of the gutter. I'm painting Leo's project room."

"That's what I thought," I lied. I had no problem with my brother hooking up with men, but the thought of him trading sexual favors made me want to hurl. Relieved, I faced Leo. "Does George know about this?"

His smile was wan. "I haven't talked to him yet."

"That would be a no."

The doorbell rang and Leo scurried out of the kitchen like his ass was on fire, exactly the same way I'd left the Phillips house. I heard the scraping of the door and a few muffled words before he called, "Maggie, it's for you."

"We'll talk about this later," I hissed at my brother, as I finger-combed my hair.

"Can't wait," came his snide reply and he sauntered down the hall.

"Ungrateful, miserable pain in my...Amber!" I blinked, sure the cosmos was messing with me. I'd wanted a Phillips to chase after me, but in typical, screw with Maggie style, I'd gotten the wrong damn one. "What are you doing here?"

"Are you fucking him?" she asked me point-blank.

Somehow, I didn't think she meant Leo. "No."

"Good, then you can still walk away. He's a lunatic and you're better off without him."

"If he's such a lunatic, how can you justify leaving your children with him?" The hell with it, she'd fired me, I didn't have to pretend to tolerate her anymore.

She waved off my accusation as if swatting a fly. "Please, it's not like Neil is actually going to take care of them. His family will hire a whole bunch of tutors and au pairs to raise them. Neil might see them once a year."

Leo had made himself scarce and I stepped out onto the front porch and shut the door behind me. "How can you be so indifferent about your own children?" I asked her.

For the first time, I saw a spark of temper from the former Mrs. Neil Phillips. "Don't judge me, honey. You have no idea what I've been through—"

I held up a hand. "Save it for someone who gives a rat's ass."

She actually stamped her foot. "I didn't have to come over, but I wanted to warn you. Neil's a selfish bastard and it looks like he's already got you on his side." She paused and waited, but I didn't say anything.

"He'll do anything to get his way, and I mean anything. I bet my ten favorite handbags he'll be over here in an hour, begging you to come back, to take on the kids."

One could hope. "What if I refused?"

Amber glared at me. "You won't, you're already totally gone over him. I was the same way, in the beginning. He was great, the perfect hero. Actually pulled me out of a car I'd flipped on the highway. It was magical at first, like a fairytale, I was so in love with him." Her gaze went unfocused, lost in her memories. I swallowed, wondering if wore the same dreamy expression when I thought about Neil. It evaporated like morning fog under the noonday sun.

"He's pathological, needs to rescue people. It's why he became a SEAL, so he could do it all the time. But he doesn't actually care about any of them, only the thrill he gets from riding to the rescue."

I closed my eyes, thought of our first morning on the beach. How many people would have gone into the ocean after my ring? Why would anyone get involved with a stranger like that?

"You're wrong," I croaked. "He's not like that."

She smiled without humor. "I may not be the best mother in the world, but I'm a decent person. He'll seduce you, convince you to stick around one way or the other, and then go do whatever the hell he wants while you sit by the phone and wait. He'll take and take until you've got nothing left to give and then he'll move on. The only person Neil Phillips cares about is Neil Phillips."

"I don't believe you."

She scrounged in her giant shoulder bag and took out a receipt and a pen. "His SEAL buddies nicknamed him the chameleon because he can blend into any situation, pretend to be whatever he needs to be to get the job done. Call his pal JT and ask. He'll tell you the truth. This way you can't say you weren't warned, hon."

I didn't say anything as she handed me the number and strode back to her waiting car.

CHAPTER FIFTEEN

I *can't stay away.*

My mind worked up several scenarios where Neil was called out on some dangerous mission and left without anyone to watch the kids. Plus, Josh was sick, and what if Neil needed to bring him to the hospital? Who would watch Kenny?

While all of these suppositions were possible, I saw them as rationalizations for a woman desperate for an excuse to do what she wanted. Neil needed me, the boys needed me. My conversation with Amber didn't alter a damn thing, because there was nothing to change. Neil was my boss—well, my former boss who I was going to beg to rehire me. Besides, it was idiotic to think Neil would come across the street for me now because he was alone with the boys and didn't have time to track me down. I wasn't even a little upset.

Right. My inner voice gave me the old wink-wink-nudge-nudge routine. *You aren't at all concerned he'd write you off like he did at the hotel room.*

"Stuff it, self."

One last deep breath and I rang the doorbell. Shoot, not a

good idea as Josh was probably still asleep. I tried the knob but it didn't turn.

I hopped off the step and peered through the window, cupping my hands around my face to see inside. Eyes glared out at me.

"Shit!" I fell back into the forsythia.

Neil opened the door. "What are you doing?"

"Practicing my dismount, what did you think?"

"The Russian judge is taking off points for the cursing." He extended his hand and helped me up.

"Why didn't you let me in?" I dusted off the seat of my jeans.

He folded his arms across his chest. "You bailed on me."

Shocked he thought so, I sputtered. "Did not."

"Did too." He didn't even twitch, a man standing his ground.

"Amber fired me "

He raised an eyebrow. "Was she the one paying you?"

"She's the one who hired me."

"Nice dodge. And you call me slick."

We glared at each other, two pissed-off people engaged in a battle of wills. As no one was paying attention to him and we dared to put him in the baby prison, Kenny shrieked like a pterodactyl. We broke our staring contest to look at him, flailing like a kickboxing champion ready to be set loose.

"So," I said, peeking at Neil's profile. "Am I still fired?"

He sighed. "You never were, you know I need you—"

"To watch the boys," I finished the sentence, not allowing myself to get caught up in the fantasy again. "Well good, so long as we're on the same page."

He watched me for a beat. "Maggie, sometimes I don't think we're even reading the same book."

"Mine starts out 'A long time ago in a commonwealth far far away, I was engaged to a jackass.'"

161

Neil laughed and stepped aside. "I'd better go check on Josh."

I rolled up my sleeves and freed Kenny. "Lots of stuff going on today, huh?"

"Abwee bwee bwee." He drooled on my shirt but I didn't care, glad to have him back in my arms.

At a loss for anything better to do, I strapped Kenny into the highchair and gave him a teething ring to nosh on while I made dinner. The breaded chicken was sizzling in the pan and I had egg noodles boiling on the back burner by the time Neil returned.

"Still no fever but he's zonked out." He slid onto a barstool next to Kenny.

I flipped the chicken, stirred the noodles, and said, "I'm sorry."

Neil sat back as Kenny grabbed a hold of one of his fingers and tried to eat it. "About?"

I thought that was obvious. "Amber and the whole scene earlier. You've had a rough couple of days and I'm sorry I didn't do anything to make it easier."

He didn't say anything else and I finished the dinner prep with my entire mind focusing on the chore.

I served Neil at the counter and cut up little bits of chicken for Kenny, planning to wolf down my dinner while his cooled. The feeling of alternate universe settled over me again, like maybe if my parents hadn't died, if I hadn't been duped by the Jackass, I might have met Neil first. Then, this domestic bliss would be mine to keep, instead of borrow like a book from the library.

"Penny for your thoughts," Neil spoke up.

"You'd get change back." Kenny's dinner had cooled and I pursed my lips, annoyed since I'm missed my chance at the hot meal.

"I'll feed him. Sit and eat." Neil took the plate from me

and vacated the barstool.

"What about your..." My gaze locked onto his empty plate. "Wow, how long was I zoned out there?"

"I think you probably reached the end of the universe. Anything interesting out there?" He popped one piece of chicken and two egg noodles on Kenny's plate. The man had obviously fed this child before and my lips twitched as Kenny grabbed all the food up and stuffed it in his mouth. Neil grinned and watched his son chew.

"I'm sorry to report there is no sign of intelligent life anywhere, especially not on Earth."

The phone rang and before I thought better of it, I answered. "Phillips residence."

"At least you learned how to answer the phone properly."

"Good evening, Laura. How are you?" I made a face at Neil and mouthed the words *she hates me.*

Join the club, he said and took the phone from me. "Mom."

I looked at Kenny. "How about a bath, little man?"

His answer was to slap the tray and send his now empty dish to the floor. "That would be a yes. You're lucky, in a few years I'll make you clean up after yourself."

Neil had taken the portable phone out into the backyard. His stiff posture told me Laura was on a tear and he was her primary target. And now he'd have to tell her about Amber's disappearing act? Jeeze.

Kenny was naked and splashing like a hearty sea god by the time Neil returned. We didn't speak at first, just watched Kenny's innocent play crammed together in the too-small bathroom.

"Peter's here," he said.

"Did you find something for him to do?"

"Weed the flowerbeds."

I looked at him. "Since when are there flowerbeds?"

He grinned. "Since never. I told him to pull up weeds

around the perimeter of the house, in case you want to put in a flowerbed."

"Oh, so we're torturing the flora now. Sorry to disappoint you but the Southern Belle gardening gene totally bypassed me."

"Don't you like to get dirty?" His tone gave me a delicious chill.

I cut my gaze to him. "Are you coming onto me?"

Neil winced. "Obvious am I?"

"You're out of practice." *But I don't care!* Luckily sense kept the last part to an internal shout.

"What is it about you, Maggie? Rationally I know we're a bad idea."

"But?" The word escaped before I could zip my lips.

He opened his mouth and his pager went off. "Shit, I need to return this call."

By the time Kenny was dry and dressed, Neil hung up the phone and started to pull on his boots.

"Go time?" I asked and he nodded once.

"I'll have someone return the truck in the morning so you aren't stranded here, okay?"

"Don't worry, we'll be fine." I hoped.

He stared at me for a few seconds like he needed to say something more. It dawned on me I was solely responsible for his children, he'd entrusted me, a virtual stranger, with their well-being.

"I'll be here when you get back. No matter what."

He nodded once and left.

HELLUVA PARTY ANIMAL. Here it was my birthday and I had nothing better to do than sitting on my ass and watch *Say Anything* for the thirty-seventh time. Well, John Cusack is hot and the whole radio over the head scene makes me wanna bitch slap some sense into Diane. "Damn boom box must weigh a ton! Look what you're missing out on, silly girl!"

Ranting at the television was better than dwelling on the fact that Neil had been gone for a full week and I hadn't heard from him once. The truck had been returned the next morning but whoever had done the deed skulked off before I could grill him.

Kenny snored and drooled on my chest. Josh was already in bed but I couldn't bear to put Kenny down for the night. If he was safely tucked into his crib, then I'd have to face the music and the tune was twenty-something with no friends, no great love, no prospects. Birthdays after twenty-one are the pits and anyone who says otherwise is peddling some late-night infomercial piece of shit.

The phone trilled and I picked it up. "Hello?"

"The fat man walks alone," Leo whispered.

I laughed. "Are you sure? Maybe he's blocking someone else out of the picture."

"It's code dearest, try and keep up. So, what are your totally fabulous plans for the evening?"

What was that saying my mother liked to use all the time? Man makes plans and God laughs. "Same shit, older pile."

"Ah yes, the cliché junkie is moving up in years. Speaking of which, I have something for you. Mind if I drop by?"

I sat up, cradling Kenny to my chest. "You got me a birthday present?" My own brother, who I'd sheltered and provided for the past several years couldn't trouble himself to call me but the homosexual across the cul-de-sac gets me a gift. Sometimes my life is just too weird. "Come on by."

He hung up and I built enough momentum to heave us off the couch and carried Kenny upstairs. A quick diaper check, but nope, he was dry so I kissed his head and laid him in the crib. Josh was out cold and I wondered what he dreamed about.

Leo knocked softly so as not to wake the boys and I let him in, grinning like a fool. He wore a black silk shirt tucked into pressed jeans and a rhinestone belt I was sure he'd thought twice about. "Thanks for coming by."

"Were you lonely, my sweet?"

"Maybe a smidge." I wiped at the baby spit-up on my sleeve.

"I have just the thing to cheer you up." Leo handed me a cupcake with a candle in it. "Happy birthday!"

I burst into tears.

"Well shit, I take it back."

I shook my head. "No, it's not anything you did. I can't seem to stop thinking what if, ya know?"

Leo blew out the candle on the cupcake and set it on a T.V. tray. "Not following here."

"Well, what if I hadn't walked in on The Jackass. We'd have been married by now and I wouldn't be all alone!"

He rolled his eyes. "Don't make me smack you. Do you really think he would have actually married you? Maggie, he was bilking you for your parents' insurance money. If you hadn't walked in on him, you'd still be living in a borrowed apartment while he paid you next to nothing to be his indentured servant. Even if you were in a relationship, there's no guarantee you'd be living it up tonight. Cripes, look at me. I've been with George for eight years and I still spend most of the important days alone."

I sniffled. "You're right, as always."

"Keep that in mind and we'll get along fine. Now, are you ready for your present?"

My gaze flitted to the cupcake. "There's more?"

"Don't be a moron. This is your present." He handed me a little pink bag. Inside the wrapped package was roughly the size of a shoebox. "Really Leo," I said as I tore open the paper, "You shouldn't have done this...."

My voice died as I took a closer look at the present. "Is that—?"

"Top of the line, batteries not included." Leo shook his head. "If only I'd brought a camera because girl, you need to see the expression on your face!"

It must have been fire engine red and shiny. "Well excuse me for not knowing the protocol, but no one has ever given me a vibrator before!"

"Think of it as a battery-operated boyfriend. BOB for short."

I glanced from him to my gift and raised my eyebrows. "Not sure how I feel about you naming it."

"Oh, give him a whirl. The store has a no-refunds policy anyhow."

"Gee, I wonder why." I scanned the advertising. "I don't care how well it's sealed, I'd worry about infections."

Leo took the package out of my hands. "So sterilize it first. Says here it's dishwasher safe, top rack only."

He tore open the packaging and paced into the kitchen, I followed like a lamb to the slaughter. "Um Leo, I don't think—"

He ignored me and plopped BOB in the top rack between the baby bottles and sippy cups then cocked his head to the side like a robin eyeing a worm. "Oh now, that's wrong on *so* many levels."

We cracked up. I wheezed from laughing so hard and slid down the wall.

"Hello?" another male voice called out. My gaze met Leo's. He shook his head solemnly; it wasn't George looking for him. "Neil," he breathed.

"Hey," I called brightly, planning to keep him out of the kitchen at all costs.

Leo slammed the dishwasher shut. I guess it was better than waving BOB around under Neil's nose but...

"Josh is feeling much better and I put Kenny to bed a little while ago. They're both asleep upstairs if you want to go check on them."

"I will in a bit. Got a beer?" He looked exhausted like he'd aged a decade in the last seven days.

"I'm the nanny. You'll have to ask the owner."

Neil winked at me. "I'm sure he's cool with it." He physically picked me up and moved me out of his way. My inner skank ho swooned at the manly display of strength and I caught Leo fanning himself with a T-Rex placemat. Yeah, God didn't make 'em better than this man, especially dressed in uniform. I cleared my throat and made a pointed face at Leo, sending him the telepathic signal for "Don't be a groupie." He put the placemat down when Neil caught sight of him.

"Hey, are you Maggie's...er...boyfriend?" He scowled as he caught sight of the belt.

I snorted in a most unladylike fashion. "This is my friend, Leo. He lives across the street." For discretion's sake, I didn't mention with whom. Stupid don't ask, don't tell. Not like Neil would give a rat's hairy ass who George dated—he had enough drama of his own.

Neil immediately extended a hand. "Oh, I apologize, I haven't been around much."

"Not a problem. Nice to finally meet you." There was an awkward pause. "Well, then, I'd better go. Maggie, happy birthday again."

Normally I would have walked him out but no way was I letting the dishwasher out of my sight. "Thanks again for... uh...stopping by!"

With a jaunty wave, Leo was gone and I was alone with my fantasy.

"So how was...er...it?" That sounded ominous and dirty, but I was the girl with a BOB in the dishwasher. How did these things happen to me?

"What's with you, you look nervous." Neil popped the cap off his beer and took a long swallow, leaning against the dishwasher as he did. "Man, I've been dreaming about this all week."

Apparently, he'd been someplace with a smaller citizen to bar ratio than a Navy town. The protocol in this situation was beyond me, not like he'd been desk-jockeying for a week. "Was it horrible?"

"One being a day at the beach and ten being the end of life as we know it, I'd give this week a solid six." He set the empty bottle down. "Knowing you were here was a huge relief."

"Really?" Hope inflated like a hot air balloon in my rib cage.

"Yeah, even with Amber here, I was always worried about the boys. Having you taking care of them really helped."

Oh, he'd been talking about my role as the nanny, not as the hot lusty wench he was planning to take to bed. I eyed the dishwasher. Just me and BOB tonight.

Neil was back to trolling through the fridge. "Anything good in here?"

Damn it, what was his deal anyhow? He'd been on the verge of a major revelation before he'd left and now he was sliding back into the friend/employer role. I couldn't downshift so fast.

"Maggie?"

"I'm tired, goodnight." Heart beating like a tribal drum I left the room and marched upstairs. After I climbed into bed I remembered BOB. If Neil said anything, I'd tell him where to stick it.

CHAPTER SIXTEEN

The yelling woke me. I blinked away the sand in my eyes and turned to face the clock radio. Two in the morning. Thunder rumbled outside, and I was momentarily blinded by a flash of lightning. Weird, we hardly ever had storms in October.

The anguished cries came again as my feet hit the floor. I cinched my bathrobe before my brain acknowledged it wasn't Kenny or Josh having a nightmare.

Neil.

I shut the door to the boys' room to muffle the sounds of terror and made sure the gate was secure at the top of the stairs in case they did wake up and I was pinned to the floor.

Safety first. My mother's voice was slightly hysterical in my head and I ignored the desperate note. "Neil," I called out and made my way down the stairs.

Moonlight spilled through the half-circle window above the door, but otherwise, the room was dark. Was this another one of his flashbacks? I couldn't tell anything other than the fact he was in genuine anguish. Each one of his tortured moans and guttural shouts awoke something instinctive in me, a drive to soothe.

What if he had a gun? I grunted and knocked the errant thought aside. Like Neil would really sleep armed with Josh and Kenny in the house. Come on, brain! Help or get the hell out of the way.

My boss was a large, writhing mass on the couch. Why he'd decided to camp out here, I had no clue, but not like I would be able to ask him until he was calm and alert.

"Neil." Without touching him, for fear of being sacked like a starting quarterback again, I bent low over the dark lump which I guessed was his upper body. He thrashed and cried out and I shoved aside my fear and gripped him in a bear hug —he couldn't pin me if I got him first. At least I hoped not.

Naked from the waist up and shaking, he sat up, but I held on to him. Awareness would return eventually, with any luck before he hurt himself, or me.

"It's okay, Neil, you're home. You're safe." The mantra fell from my lips as I clung to him, practically sitting on his lap to maintain my grip. Lightning charged the air outside and the hair on my arms stood up as the bolt struck nearby and he started, his skin perspiring, his body quaking.

"Here, let me get the light." It was a calculated risk, but I figured being able to see would help snap him out of this trance.

"No," he gasped. One minute the embrace was one-sided —my feeble effort to ground him to reality—and in the next his arms went around me. His grip was solid, even as the tremors continued to rack him. The boom of thunder made him jump and I could feel his heart pound behind his ribcage.

"Sssh," I soothed. "Yeah, I'm here, everything is all right now. It was just a dream."

He sucked in a shaky breath and buried his nose in my

hair. Was I an idiot for charging in when someone who had a solid thirty pounds of muscle on me wasn't in control of his faculties? Probably, but as I reviewed all the things which might have gone wrong I swallowed the understanding that it wouldn't have mattered.

Rain pattered down against the window but the fury of the storm was over. I stroked his back, all too aware of our intimate situation. His night terrors had ebbed—there was no reason to hold him this way. The powerful drive to soothe ramped down, only to be replaced with another primal need, one that didn't belong in the moment.

"How are you doing?" I pulled back, but his arms didn't loosen and fall away as I'd hoped. They moved to grip my sides, his thumbs beneath the swell of my breasts. Now I was the one trembling. Time to retreat.

"Neil, I—"

"I need you," he breathed and pulled me close again. "I need you so much."

A pained whimper escaped my dry throat. Cripes, there was no way I could say no to him. Choice evaporated as his lips took a hold of mine in a hungry kiss. My hands returned to his bare skin and instead of soothing, I stirred the embers of attraction. This was incredible, the unapologetic intensity that wound around us. We reveled in each other.

"Neil," I gasped as he laid me back on the couch, fingers battling with the ties of my bathrobe.

Sometime in the last few moments, my eyes adjusted to the dim lighting and I watched in awe as he unwrapped me like a present, undeterred as my hands traveled up the lean muscles of his chest. The robe parted and I struggled to get my arms out while he explored the territory he unearthed through my thin sleep-shirt with the coffee cups.

"Too many clothes," he grumped.

Shifting my weight I yanked the back of the shirt free

then over my head and dropped it to the floor. I faced him, too turned on to be embarrassed at my abrupt unveiling. "Better?"

His hands roved over my bare body and I caught his smile before he leaned in to kiss me again. "Much."

The feel of his skin on mine, the taste of him, I was unable to decide which I enjoyed more. One hand cupped my breast and a callous on his thumb scraped over the nipple. I arched against him for more.

"You are so beautiful," he whispered as he kissed a path down my neck to a sensitive spot on my collarbone. Those weren't words meant to seduce. Well, they might have been but the awe in his voice told me he meant what he said. I shivered as he studied me fully, his gaze leaving a warm trail in its wake.

He teased my breasts to full arousal, and I opened to him, parting my thighs around his lean waist. My underwear to his boxers was no real barrier and we both made a pained noise of frustration as his hips aligned with mine.

"Please Neil." Begging wasn't an option I'd ever resorted to before but desperate times….

He backed up off of me and shoved his boxers down past his knees. I licked my lips, more than ready to get the show on the road. He stood up to take them off, and almost fell as my hand shot forward to touch him, stroke him. His eyes closed as I explored his body and studied his face. This man was exquisite fully clothed. Naked, he was a true master-piece. Happy birthday to me.

"Need you now." He knocked my hand away and pinned me to the couch.

"Yes." I made room for him, belatedly aware I'd never shucked my own underwear. Neil realized it at the same moment and before I could suggest switching positions, he ripped the fabric on either side.

How I adored a man of action.

He touched me then, no obstacles between us, and I stuffed a fist in my mouth to stifle the cry. Every cell in my body screamed for him to be inside me, to merge with me.

Then he was.

Though I'd been sure my body was ready, he was bigger than I'd realized and I flinched as he stretched me past the point of comfort. His eyes were closed and he didn't notice my distress. I'd have to say something.

"Neil—"

"I love you." His words shocked me into silence and then he moved. The pain vanished, whether because my mind leaped for joy or because I'd grown accustomed to him, I didn't know. Words bubbled up as he claimed my body, words I never thought I'd say out loud.

"I love you too, Neil,"

Spurred on by my declaration, his pace increased and tears spilled from the corners of my eyes, I was so overcome with feeling, physical and emotional.

He hit his peak and while I wasn't able to climb it with him, I held him close as he shuddered in his release.

He sighed and settled more comfortably beside me. It was a tight fit on the couch. Tucked under his chin, I listened to the beat of his heart and smiled. We had time to fix this part of our relationship. The affection, the genuine caring bound us together. The situation had been intense. Later, when he wasn't suffering from the aftermath of one of his PTSD attacks we'd—

"Love you, Amber." He sighed and settled into sleep, no idea of the devastation he'd wrought.

❆

"WAKE UP, MISS MAGGS." Josh, the angelic little devil, picked up the corner of the blanket so he could poke his head in.

My heart ached and I was still unprepared to face the harsh reality of day. But Josh didn't know what had happened and for his sake and Kenny's, I needed to get my sorry hide in gear.

"Morning, Scamp." I turned my head and groaned. Man, he was developing a severe case of dragon breath.

"Daddy made choco chippie cakes for breakfast." He smiled and I saw dark brown smears across his front teeth. Lovely.

Hell, Neil was up before I was and he'd made breakfast too. "Better go brush," I told Josh. "You don't want to get a cavity." Or set the little girls' nose hairs on fire at the park.

He offered me one last grin and ran out of the room, heavy feet thundering down the stairs. Having Neil here made all the difference in Josh's disposition. Mine too, in a different way.

It galled me that Neil had been right, our having sex had made everything horrible. I didn't want to face him. The jury was still out about whether I could face *myself* in the mirror. I hadn't been able to last night after I'd slunk away to clean up.

With no one to blame but my own stupid self, I dressed and tied my hair back, ready to get this over with. Doubtful he'd fire me. Knowing Neil, he'd be embarrassed and apologetic and I'd force a smile as we ate pancakes together. People had sex all the time, for crying out loud and the world kept on spinning.

So why did I feel dead inside?

Neil must have gotten Kenny up already. I unlatched the gate and trudged downstairs, sucking in a deep breath for courage.

Sumo baby was strapped in his highchair, still dressed in his pajamas. Neil's back was to me and for an instant, I pretended he hadn't said his ex-wife's name last night. That it was Maggie he really complimented and adored while he made love to me.

Utterly disgusted with myself for being such a sap, I called out in an overly cheery voice, "Morning,"

"Hi there." He glanced over his shoulder and grinned at me. "How'd you sleep?"

I blinked. Was he kidding? "Um, not too well, actually."

He offered me a sympathetic smile. "Sorry to hear that. I slept like a rock, even on the couch. There are pancakes in the kitchen if you want."

Maybe he was playing it cool for the boys' sake, but his posture was all wrong. His shoulders were relaxed, his movements fluid and stress-free. Where was the sheepish look, the lack of eye contact?

Needing time to regroup, I headed into the kitchen. I checked the dishwasher but BOB was gone. Great, more ammo in Neil's arsenal for when we engaged in the most humiliating discussion of my life. At least I could blame Leo for something.

What was Neil waiting for anyhow? Maybe he'd bring it up to me later when the children were distracted or asleep. Though Josh was in the bathroom and Kenny had food so he wouldn't give a fig what else was going down. My eyelids slid shut and I swayed on my feet, wishing it was twenty-four hours earlier when I still had hope.

"Hey." Neil poked his head around the doorframe. "I guess I owe you an apology."

"Ya think?" I winced at my bitter tone.

Neil appeared unfazed as he continued. "I'm sorry, I didn't remember yesterday was your birthday, or I would have arranged for someone else to come stay with the boys."

I didn't move a muscle, just stared at him stupidly. *That's* what he was sorry for? Was he trying to pretend I hadn't stripped for him, begged him to have sex with me, and then declared my undying love for him while he envisioned his ex-wife? Could I possibly *be* more pathetic?

Ready to quit to protect my last remaining shred of pride, I opened my mouth and met his gaze. His utterly innocent gaze. The light dawned.

Holy crap, he really didn't remember!

"Maggie, are you all right? You look a bit shell-shocked." His handsome face was etched with genuine concern.

Why didn't this occur to me sooner? It was the same situation, well, not the same scene he'd relived but chances were the last time he'd been plagued with nightmares, it was Amber who'd comforted him after. He'd been lost in the flashback, like when he thought I was the woman who'd been shot. I'd needed to explain to him what happened the first time.

I swallowed, torn about what I ought to do next. The right thing would be to bring him up to speed, let him know what happened.

Why? The voice in my head wasn't my mother's. *So you can have an incredibly awkward scene where he stutters and apologizes? Give the guy a break.*

It wasn't his well-being I was thinking of though, but mine. Maggie's comfort vs. hiding the truth from Neil. No contest.

"Well, um Neil, you should know, um you had another incident last night."

He deflated like a balloon, dropping onto a barstool as though his bones had turned to jelly. "Shit, really? What happened?"

Lie, damn it! The voice insisted.

"Well, um, do you remember the storm?" If I was stalling, I could be excused for not wanting to blurt out the mortifying truth.

He shook his head, his eyes miserable. "I fell asleep, around midnight I suppose, and then the next thing I knew it was morning."

Kenny squealed from the other room and Josh tore past the doorway, still in his spaceman pajamas. Did I really want to disrupt this morning of domestic bliss with the ugly truth?

Inhaling until my lungs were full, I blathered out what I could. "Yeah, so anyhow, you were screaming and you woke me up and I came downstairs to try and rouse you and calm you down, you know?"

He'd gone pale beneath his tan. "I didn't attack you again, did I?"

I knew what kind of attack he meant and shook my head. "No, I kind of pinned you down until it passed."

"Sorry." His eyes slid closed, all the relaxation totally gone from his posture. "Maggie, jeez, I don't know what else to say. Sorry doesn't seem to cover it."

Guilt radiated off him in waves. And he hadn't heard the worst part yet. Did I really need to relive everything?

"Daddy, are you coming to the farm with us today?" Josh chirped from the doorway. Shoot, I'd forgotten I'd promised to take them to the petting zoo/pumpkin patch this morning.

Neil glanced at me, seeking my permission. "All right with you?"

He's already embarrassed, let sleeping dogs lie!

I put on my happy face. "Of course."

Josh squealed and ran to get dressed. I turned my back to give myself a minute to think this through. I would tell him, abso-fricking-lutely I would man up and tell all.

Later.

CHAPTER SEVENTEEN

My mother had stopped talking to me. I thought it was petty of her to give me the silent treatment from the great beyond, but my ire at her juvenile actions didn't make a difference. We'd been at the petting zoo all morning and no matter how I let my thoughts stray, Mom didn't pipe up once. Not even when I imagined converting to Judaism. Yup, mom's ghost was downright P.O.ed at me.

Apparently, the rain from the previous night hadn't been as torrential here since the ground was bone dry. Josh was in three-year-old heaven. He'd fed the goats numerous times and hay stuck in his hair from where he and Neil rolled around in the loose piles set up for that purpose. Kenny sat in his stroller and watched their antics like a prince from his throne. I alternated between valet and royal photographer, capturing the family's moments on the old Nikon camera Neil had unearthed.

If this had been yesterday, I might have enjoyed myself, what with the leaves turning colors and the fat orange pumpkins ready to carve or cook. Today, I observed it all without experiencing any real emotion.

"You've been so quiet all morning," Neil said while he held Kenny's bottle, his royal highness propped up and sucking down his midmorning fix. Joshua wandered among the rows of pumpkins, making the impossible choice about which one he should take home to carve.

"I guess I'm having an introspective day." It wasn't a lie, since I'd been churning over the events of the previous night in my mind, looking for any way Neil might uncover the truth.

"Anything you want to talk about?" He raised an eyebrow when I shook my head. "Well, I'm here if you change your mind."

I sighed. "It's been a really messed up couple of weeks. My life is the epitome of chaos."

Kenny glugged down his eight ounces in record time and Neil shifted him to his shoulder to assume the position. "Not all bad, I trust?"

I wasn't able to look him in the eye as I thought of how happy I'd been, lying in his arms. I stared over his shoulder at Joshua instead. "Some parts have been truly spectacular." Unfortunately, I didn't know how to change my address to the Land of Make Believe without a straitjacket.

"Your cooking, for instance. I don't think I've eaten as well in my whole life as I have since you've been around. I don't know what half of it is, but it's excellent."

I nodded, accepting the praise as my due. "Runs in the family, I guess. My mom was the lunch lady at our elementary school. It was the only cafeteria in our county where people actually enjoyed eating the daily fare."

Kenny burped like a three hundred pound contestant in a hot dog eating contest. "That's my boy." Neil shook his head at his son, but I spotted a glimmer of pride and my heart clenched up mid-beat. They were so perfect together and here I was, the stand-in, Amber's frigging understudy. Last night had underscored that fact so even my dumb ass received the message.

I took Kenny from Neil and he began to fuss immediately. Neil gave me an inscrutable look and took him back.

"You don't talk about your past much."

"What do you want to know?" I couldn't help my wary tone.

He grinned. "Don't sound so defensive. This won't hurt a bit."

"Should I get the rubber gloves out of the truck?"

Neil laughed. If joy was a color, it would be the sparkly yellow I always imagined when he really let go and had fun. His boys had inherited the same bubbly chuckle, turning the sound of their delight absolutely palpable, lacing the air with spice and excitement.

"Tell me about your childhood. You seem so…"

"Old?" I supplied, my expression dared him to agree.

"World-weary," Neil corrected. "Battle-hardened would also fit. Were you like that as a kid?"

"The extra-crunchy exterior didn't come about until after my parents died. I needed all the bitchiness I could muster to deal with Marty's sorry hide."

"Is he really so bad?"

"I like you too much to expose you to him anymore." I glanced away, a blush staining my cheeks.

He'd put Kenny back in the stroller where the little imp sucked on his own fist.

Neil strapped him in and I watched his back muscles flex, remembering how they'd felt under my hands. Bad Maggie, bad. My gaze drifted to Josh who hadn't moved. "Is he having a staring contest with the pumpkin?"

"Joshua, pick one already!" Neil shook his head. "Nice segue, but I'm still waiting to hear about your childhood."

I shifted on the bench. "Typical, I guess. Marty and I were constantly at war but we had each other's backs. I remember this time when a bully was snagging his lunch money every day. Since our mother was the lunch lady, she knew if he didn't buy lunch so I lent him my allowance."

Neil smiled. "Nice of you."

"No, Marty didn't want to involve Mom in the mix because her stern finger shaking lectures to the other kids were a source of torment to both of us. So, after several weeks of lending him my allowance, I took it upon myself to thwart the fiend. Since I didn't want Marty to be known as the kid whose sister had to fight his battles, I traded my purple Pegasus *My Little Pony* for a favor from Ruthie."

Neil grinned. "What we do for those we love."

I dug in the diaper bag for my sunglasses so I could hide my eyes. "Ruthie confronted the bully during second lunch. We had each taken bathroom passes from our teachers and sneaked down to the blacktopped courtyard which served as a playground. Dexter stood beneath one of the two net-less basketball hoops, surrounded by his group of cronies who had *do you want fries with that* imprinted on their DNA.

"From my hiding spot behind the trash can, I watched Dexter turn pale as he faced Toothy Ruthie. No prepubescent boy wanted to be seen with Ruthie. Her record for the most wedgies given in a school year still stands. Nothing can shatter a fragile male ego like being beaten up by a girl, especially a butt-ugly girl."

"Amen," Neil said.

"Ruthie stopped in front of Dexter and stared him down through her lank brown hair. 'I hear you've been collecting money from some of the other kids. Good job.'

"Dexter squinted at her, his expression wary. He had the

presence of mind to ignore her compliment. Ruthie could take him in point five seconds and he knew it, so he kept his mouth shut. She looped her arm around his neck and I saw him wince as he discovered Ruthie's mom didn't believe in wasting her pole-dancing money on deodorant."

"You really know how to spin a yarn." Neil shook his head. "We ought to get going."

We ended up with four pumpkins, two to carve and two to cook. Everything was back to normal, at least on the surface.

"Tell me the rest of the story," Neil prompted as we drove back to the house.

"You really want to hear this?"

"Well, you left Dexter standing there sniffing Ruthie's armpits. So yeah, inquiring minds need to know."

"Whatever makes you happy, slick. Well, Ruthie was really sly about the whole thing. She said, loud enough for us all to hear, 'I admire your initiative, Dexter, but you see this here is my turf. Now maybe if I take a liking to you I'll leave you my empire when I move on to Junior High, but for now, I need to enforce a few taxes.

" 'Taxes?' Dexter's Adam's apple bobbed in his turkey neck.

" 'Yup, ya see Dexter, it's my school yard and I'm entritled to forty-two percent of whatever you collect.'"

"Other than Ruthie's word confusion over entitled, she put on an Oscar-worthy performance. Dexter shuffled his feet and even from my perch behind the garbage can, I could sense his nervousness. It was obvious he didn't want to lose face in front of his pockmarked posse, but he didn't want to tangle with Ruthie either.

" 'Who died and made you Darth Vader?' he asked in a last attempt at bravado.

Ruthie, who could smell weakness like a dog could smell

a ham bone, went in for the kill. " 'I guess I could cut you a break if you gave me a kiss.'"

"All the color drained from Dexter's already sallow complexion. 'No way!'

" 'Come on, you know you want to.' Ruthie's sing-song tone and the age-old challenge of peer pressure spurred Dexter to react.

"I'd rather kiss the lunch lady than your crusty face, toothy Ruthie!'

"Ruthie curled her lip, exposing the buck teeth which had inspired her nickname. Dexter's bravado melted under her black scowl. She said "Then I'll see you at the corner of Oak Summit drive and Fifth at three.'"

"Oh, showdown time." Neil flashed me his killer grin as he navigated the truck into the development. "She presented Dexter with the no-win scenario"

I nodded. "The corner of Oak Summit and Fifth was our elementary school version of Thunder Road. Every now and then, some stupid fool would try to usurp the Queen of Crap and Ruthie would challenge the offender. Instead of street racing though, Ruthie beat the snot out of whoever was on her shit list for the week. A very successful way to maintain the balance of power.

"Dexter's face crumbled. His older brother Mark had once had a run-in with Ruthie, who towered over every boy in the elementary school. Ruthie's power lay in being a girl and as mean as a rabid badger. She gleefully abused the situation since the boys were reluctant to hit her. She went for the family jewels every time. So then Dexter pulled out a crumpled wad of bills and held it out to Ruthie. 'Nice doing business with you, Dexter.' Ruthie stalked off to the lunchroom, the tatters of Dexter's pride bouncing across the blacktop in her wake.

"Rules of the school yard, Dexter was never taken seriously again, at least as a bully. He'd been had by Toothy Ruthie. Marty was inexplicably grateful and promised he would save up his allowance to buy me a new Pegasus, but then he got into baseball cards so that was the end of it. I didn't mind, he was my brother, and besides, I stole Pegasus back from Ruthie at the next sleepover after she ran my underpants up the neighbor's flag pole. *I* wasn't afraid to hit her."

Neil shook his head. "What happened to them?"

I shrugged as he parked the truck in the driveway. "Dexter grew something akin to a spine and Ruthie got braces and discovered deodorant. Their wedding is next June."

He shook his head. "I hope you're a bridesmaid or something since you were instrumental in bringing them together."

With a mock shudder, I opened the door. "You have a habit of giving me credit for things so far out of my sphere of influence, I can barely even see them."

I made lunch while Neil dipped Josh in the tub to get rid of the farm smell. Kenny ate his lunch in record time and started to drift off in the high chair. He squawked while I wiped the gunk off his face, but his eyelids were already drooping by the time we made it up the stairs.

Josh ate peanut butter and jelly and then Neil took him outside to ride his tricycle. Restless, I paced the house searching for something to do. My gaze landed on the couch. Neil's blanket was folded neatly at one end but a scrap of peach lace stuck out from between the cushions.

Shit, my underwear! I'd left them there last night. I picked them up and couldn't help reliving the intense pleasure when he'd ripped them off me.

How did he not noticed these when he folded the blanket? I'd seen them from across the room. For that matter, why didn't he question how he had gone to sleep wearing boxers and woke up without them?

I closed my eyes as Amber's words came back to me. *He'll seduce you, convince you to stick around one way or the other, and then go do whatever the hell he wants while you sit by the phone and wait. He'll take and take until you've got nothing left to give and then he'll move on.*

No, no way, he wasn't...playing me?

Was he?

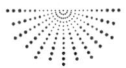

CHAPTER EIGHTEEN

"**W**hat do you want to be for Halloween?" Leo asked Josh.

"My daddy." Josh didn't look up from his Mega Block fire truck.

I smiled at Leo, hoping it was the genuine kind and not the brittle shaky smirk I'd offered Neil the last few days. Crap, why couldn't I be one of those shy, mysterious women who didn't wear her feelings on her sleeves?

"Well, I can't make you into your daddy, but I might be able to turn you into a sailor. Would you like that, Joshua?"

Josh's attention span had run out. On the floor next to him Kenny flipped himself like a pancake and slithered for a stray Mega Block. I snatched it away before he stuffed it in his mouth.

"Leo, could you get me the teething ring in the fridge?"

Leo maneuvered around the obstacle course on the floor but stopped at the doorway. "Only if you tell me what happened."

"Leo," I growled.

"Fine, holding the kid's teething ring for ransom might be

below the belt," he admitted. "But I will find a way to make you tell me."

Not in this lifetime, bub. More than my pride was at stake here, my job, my connection to Kenny and Josh, and yes, even Neil. Last night I'd woken up in a cold sweat, feeling like I'd somehow victimized him. Like he was a drunk I'd picked up at a bar and had my nasty way with him under false pretenses.

I honestly didn't know which was worse, thinking he might be toying with me, or that *I'd* duped *him*.

Talking it out with Neil wasn't an option, too much time had passed. Then, Neil disappeared two days ago, though there was a message on the answering machine when I brought the boys back from story hour at the library.

"Hi, Maggie, I'm going wheels up in about twenty minutes. I'll see you when I get back. Kiss the kids for me."

There'd been a pause before he'd whispered "talk to you soon." My crazy brain had gone over and over that pause, what it might mean in the grand scheme of things. Was he wondering why our flirting dynamic had suddenly ceased? Or maybe, his mind was on the mission ahead and he was worried he'd never see his children again. What *the hell* did he do while he was gone? Stupid, thought-provoking pause.

I put my head down between my knees. Leo knelt on the ground next to Kenny and helped him hold the teething ring in place. "Don't worry little man, she's just having another one of her episodes."

Kenny gurgled as he noshed.

"What am I, frigging Blanche DuBois?"

Leo batted his eyelashes at me. "I have always relied on the kindness of strangers." Southern honey dripped from his mock effeminate voice.

"Bite me."

"Bite me, bite me, bite me," Josh mimicked.

Leo shook his head. "See what you've done now? How are you going to explain that to Neil?"

"Easy, I'll blame their mother." Call me petty, but someone needed to fault her for something.

Leo scrutinized my face. "You mean Amber?"

I flinched. He snapped and then pointed at me. "You think I haven't noticed you stopped using her name? What did she do, call and beg Neil to take her back?"

"Not to my knowledge."

"She's still on your—" he stopped, glanced at Josh the parrot, and spelled, "S-H-I-T list, right?"

I closed my eyes. "Can we talk about something else? How's Peter doing?"

"Don't you want to know about your brother?"

"Nope." Marty was one of my problems and I couldn't dwell on him right now. He'd gotten his wish. I'd spoken with the ADA in Richmond and a case was being assembled against the Jackass for larceny. No word yet on when anything might happen on that front. Marty had been mowing lawns to pay for his room and board with Leo, his life on hold until the mighty lawsuit ship came in. Or until Leo and George tossed him out on his keister.

Leo stretched out his legs and Kenny got all the way up onto his hands and knees.

"What should we dress this guy up like for Halloween?" I asked as we watched his effort. Any second and the kid would crawl. My gut told me he was ready to be on the move. Much like his Dad, Kenny was a man of action.

"Wait, I have to make both of their costumes as well as Peter's?"

My eyebrows met as I scowled at him. "Peter's dressing up for Halloween?" Didn't sound like Mr. Whatever to me.

"Costume party for his class." Leo tickled Kenny under

his chin. "They have to dress up as their favorite figure from American history."

"So what he's going as an astronaut or a war hero or something?"

"I wish," Leo said and mock shuddered. "The guy who invented Pop-Tarts."

I threw my head back and laughed. "I could have invented Pop-Tarts. They taste like iced shingles."

"Shit on a shingle to be precise. I make gourmet food and the kid eats Pop-Tarts like he holds stock in Kellogg's."

"Cheer up. One of these days he'll wake up and realize what he's been missing and in the meantime, I'm always happy to provide a home to the fine pastry. What did you bring today?"

"Cannoli."

"Stop talking dirty." One of the nice things about not being engaged anymore was I didn't have to worry about what I stuffed in my face for fear of bursting out of my wedding dress. "I love Italian pastries."

"Actually, cannoli is Sicilian."

"Never go up against a Sicilian when death is on the line!" I cut my gaze to him. "Name the movie."

"Pshaw, that's not even a hard one. *The Princess Bride*."

"You sure we weren't separated at birth?"

"The accents say otherwise. Anyway—"

Leo paused as the front door opened. I stood up, ready to face Neil, but a different sort of nightmare awaited me.

"Oh, I see you're still here." Laura Phillips frowned at me then called out over her shoulder. "It's the same girl, Ralph!"

"I'm not deaf, Laura." A man with salt and pepper hair styled even more than Leo's and a charcoal gray business suit pulled his sunglasses off his face in a move I was sure he'd practiced. Another generation of those intelligent hazel eyes studied me.

"Well, now, here you are. Ralph Phillips, at your service."

Laura made a disgusted sound.

"Gwampa!" Josh vaulted over his tower to greet the man. Ralph scooped the boy up. "Aren't you getting big? What have you been eating?"

The question was poised casually but it was clear he waited on my answer.

"A little bit of everything these days. Chicken, as long as he has ketchup with it, pasta, and even a few real vegetables once in a while."

Ralph nodded at me and then turned on his wife. "She seems competent enough to me, Laura."

My smile grew brittle. "I'm afraid Neil's not back yet—"

Laura shooed me away like an insect. "Yes, yes, we know. He sent his father an email stating he would be gone for at least a month."

I choked on my own saliva. Oh my God in Heaven, a month? Why hadn't he told me?

Because you weren't talking to him, smarty.

The horror didn't end there, however. "We're here to keep an eye on the boys while he's away. Neil insisted you had personal matters which needed your attention. We've brought Hilda to cook, so don't worry about preparing our meals."

They were going to stay for a month? I looked to Leo.

"I need cannoli, stat."

HILDA WAS a large woman of German heritage who wore support hose, orthopedic shoes, and a dour expression. Leo hated her on sight and from the sharp angle of her unibrow, I felt sure the feeling was mutual.

"You call zat a pastry?" She sniffed at Leo's cannoli like a bloodhound. "Itz, too crunchy."

Leo gave her the squinty-eyed glare of death. "It's *supposed* to be crunchy."

Forget the cannoli, I needed a stiff drink. "Um, so where will everyone be, um, staying?"

"Ralph and I will take the master suite, of course, and Hilda will have to share your room."

A whimper escaped. I shot Leo a panicked look, but he shook his head. "Sorry kid, no room at the inn until Peter's mom gets back next week."

"Who are you?" Laura zoomed in on Leo like a SCUD missile.

"The neighbor, who must be on his way." He hugged me and whispered. "I'll keep Peter home this afternoon."

"Good, I'd hate for him to be the one to find my corpse after I hang myself with the cord from the blinds."

"Chin up kid, it's only a month." In a louder voice he sang out "Toodles," and with one last sneer at Hilda, made his exit.

"I know you weren't expecting us so we'll wait down here with the kids while you prepare the room." Laura sniffed and sat on the couch where her son had thoroughly defiled me. Yes, thoughts like this were going to make the next month bearable.

The reality of the situation sank in. "Prepare the room?"

"The master suite, sweetheart," Ralph spoke slowly, to overcome my obvious mental handicap.

Oh hell, I was supposed to prepare the master suite for them to stay in? From the expectant looks, it became clear that yes, indeed, I was supposed to hop to it.

I trudged up the stairs, hoping the room wasn't as bad as the last time I'd been in there.

The door creaked open like the entrance to a haunted house. Nope, it was worse than the last time. Shit, I was fresh out of holy water and flamethrowers. How was I supposed to prepare this room for them?

"I don't even know where to start." Panic welled up, and I sat down hard on the floor. This wasn't a quick change of sheets for the company. They were asking me to dig through what had been Amber and Neil's personal space. And if I was a good girl and got the room ready for them, my reward would be sharing a bed with Hilda of the unibrow.

Nope, I couldn't do it. This was above and beyond the call. I spun on my heel and marched downstairs, back to the living room. I opened my mouth and Josh chose that moment to beam up at me.

"Isn't this great, Miss Maggs?"

"It sure is, Scamp." I headed out to the garden shed to find some boxes and trash bags.

CHAPTER NINETEEN

"Well, that, is, um…very interesting?" Leo stared and the wad of fabric was destined to be Kenny's costume. "A turtle, right?"

My shoulders slumped. "No, a caterpillar." Betsy Ross with a needle I wasn't, as evidenced by the mess on the dining room table. The early afternoon sun shone through the screen, illuminating my most recent domestic disaster. The sewing box had been one of those ready to go Wal-Mart purchases and I think I'd misused every single item in it at least twice, plus jabbed myself repeatedly with the needle.

He blinked and stared at the lumpy green thing again. "Oh, well, the rounded back threw me for a second. Hey, I could tell it was something small and green! At least I was in the animal kingdom because my second guess was a pea pod."

Under normal circumstances, I might find this situation funny. Instead, I ripped the tape measure off of my neck and tossed it onto the floor. "This is your fault, you know. If you'd agreed to make the stinking thing, Kenny wouldn't have to be dressed up as a mutant caterpillar for his first Halloween."

Leo folded his arms over his chest and gave me an assessing look. "You know my terms. I won't make another thing for you or the kids until you tell me what happened with Neil."

I picked a pin off of the costume from hell and extended it to him. "See this? I'd rather stick this pin in my eye."

Leo rolled his own peepers. "Fine then, drama queen. But it's not healthy to keep secrets. They back build until you explode from the pressure."

I ripped out a jagged seam and my elbow knocked the container of pins onto the carpet. "Shoot. Help me, please. I need to finish this before they get back."

Neil's parents had taken Josh and Kenny somewhere to "instill a little culture in them," and I politely declined Ralph's offer to join them, citing my appointment with the D.A. in Richmond at three as a solid excuse. Hilda had the afternoon off. A normal, non-psychotic person would be in a good mood, what with the autumn breeze, the scent of crisp leaves and applesauce from the batch I'd made with Josh this morning still thick in the air.

Leo knelt down and collected several pins. "Don't take this the wrong way, but you look like hell. Are you still sleeping on the couch?"

I nodded like my head might fall off. Instead of snuggling up to Hilda in the double bed, I'd given up my room and slept on the couch where memories plagued me in the dark of night. The best were the ones of Neil until the memory of mistaken identity surfaced. The worst included the Jackass, Marty, and the lawsuit. And then there were the things I'd discovered when packing up the master bedroom.

Three hours I'd spent making the room presentable, feeling like a psychotic bunny-boiling stalker the whole time.

After tucking away anything Amber and Neil—everything from their wedding album to a copy of the declaration of legal separation—I knew more about Neil's marriage than he probably did. It's amazing what one can learn about people from pawing through their stuff. By amazing, I meant nightmare-invoking. The veil of civility is totally ripped away, the blinders dashed into a thousand pieces as I used tongs to stuff her clothes into trash bags, along with her copy of the karma sutra and pleasure enhancement toys. Ick.

The items in the room gave me insight into Neil and Amber, the couple, whether I wanted the info dump or not. Their relationship appeared to be a total cliché, Navy boy meets slutty girl, they get married, he's deployed and she seeks solace elsewhere. Three years, from meet to divorce, and considering how often Neil was away, I'd wager they maybe had a year of face time.

To take my mind off the couple, I focused on the space itself. The carpet needed replacing, the walls would benefit from a fresh coat of paint, but I'd done what I could, including cut something stiff out of the carpet which I really hoped was candle wax. I'd flipped the mattress, changed the linens, and removed everything that looked even remotely like Amber, all the while wondering what Neil would think about my take on this task.

Neil's things, what few there were, remained in the closet. He had more medals than I had time to count, which for some bizarre reason, were kept in a bin full of other flotsam, like batteries, headphones, and stray buttons under the bed. I'd carefully dusted the awards off and put them on display on the dresser, where their wedding picture had been. That, I boxed along with other memorabilia and cutsie knick-knacks. Her remaining toiletries, I'd trashed with relish, rationalizing that anything she really wanted, she would have taken with her, the same way I did.

Amber had two shoeboxes full of letters addressed to her. One was from Neil, real honest to goodness love letters which set me off on a weeping fit. His handwriting, a bold blocky print that was as solid as the man himself detailed everything from hopes and dreams regarding their future, to all the ways he'd planned to make love to her on his return. There was nothing flowery or over the top and I think the raw honesty touched me the most. He wrote naked, every word used like a brushstroke to paint a picture of the shining future he desired. Though I knew I shouldn't have read them, I couldn't summon the will to stop. No matter what Amber believed, the man had given her his all.

Then there was the other box.

"Are we allowed to burn things outdoors in this development?" I asked Leo.

"Things like what?" He didn't look up from his search of the rug.

"The usual stuff, leaves, yard clippings..." Notes from Amber's slew of boy toys. It made me sick to think she might have received one of those nasty-grams in the same batch of mail as one of Neil's tender missives. The notion seemed almost sacrilegious.

Heaven forbid he ever found those letters, it would mess with his head even more. The letters proved Neil's PTSD had nothing to do with Amber's affairs—his affliction was just her out clause. While most of the notes hadn't been date-stamped, the oldest one I'd come across was still in the enve-lope and postmarked six months after their wedding. When she'd been pregnant with Josh. The tone sounded like some-thing the Jackass would think was romantic. "Thanks for last night, baby. That thing you did rocked my world." Gack.

"What's with the face? " Leo asked me. "You're sneering like Elvis."

The phone rang. "Sorry, I'll be right back." Though I had

no intention of explaining the venomous spiders crawling through my mind. "Phillips residence, Maggie speaking."

"Boy, my mother has trained you well. I hope she's giving you Scooby Snacks for your efforts."

Neil. I closed my eyes and leaned against the wall, searching for something light and banter-esque to toss at him. After a few moments of silence, I gave up. "How are you?"

"All in one piece. I'm really more concerned about you. You were acting so weird when I left and then I got my father's email. I swear, I had no idea they were going to drop in on you. On a scale of one to ten, how bad is it there?"

"Josh is happy. Kenny's ambivalent," I said.

"How about Maggie?"

Maggie's miserable. Maggie misses you. "Maggie's has Hilda sleeping in her bed and she's still treading water, Leo's here. He's helping me with Kenny's Halloween costume."

"Nuh, un. You're not laying that on my shoulders, sister." Leo called out.

Neil laughed, and the sound wrapped around me like the warmest quilt. God, I missed him.

"Take pictures for me, okay?"

"Will do, boss."

There was a pause like he was waiting for me to say something else. "I was worried you wouldn't answer the phone. That you might have left."

My gaze fixed on the refrigerator, on Josh's latest nature collage. The kid loved glue the way I loved cheesecake. "Why would you think that?"

"Just a feeling." His voice was quiet.

Shoot. Here I was dwelling in misery city and it sounded as if Neil had a room in the same hotel. He really didn't need to know I had almost bailed. "Well, I'm still here."

The smile rang clear in his voice. "I'm really glad. I'm

going to take some leave when we get back, spend some uninterrupted time at home. Could I speak with Leo for a second?"

"Sure." I raised my eyebrows at Leo and extended the phone. "He wants to talk to you."

Leo took the receiver. "I didn't do it."

I grinned and shook my head, then turned back to the table so I wouldn't be so obvious in my eavesdropping. Why did hearing his voice make me feel so damn good?

"Yeah, I think I can arrange something. If her head doesn't explode first."

Warning bells clanged in my head as Leo handed the phone back to me. "I have to go get Peter off the bus."

"What was that all about?" I asked Neil.

"I needed to ask him for a favor."

Mystified and a little hurt I asked, "You couldn't ask me?"

"Nope." His tone sounded smug.

"Can you tell me where you are?"

"Nope."

"Well, what can you tell me?"

"I wish I were home, with the boys. Home with you."

I sucked in a breath. "Neil—"

"Maggie, I need to go, about nine guys are breathing down my neck, waiting to phone home. Promise me we'll talk when I get back, that you'll still be there."

I imagined him fretting over me. Worried I'd take off in the middle of the night and abandon his sons. What if he was so distracted that something awful happened to him? I glanced at the pinholes in my sore fingertips. That was the worst I needed to worry about. Neil might get shot, or blown up if he lost sight of the task at hand. "Neil, don't waste another second thinking I'm going to leave, all right? I promise I'll be here when you get back. No matter what. Okay?"

"Thank you, Maggie. You're the best."

I said goodbye and hung up with him, though I couldn't make myself put the phone down, the connection to him too precious to break.

"What in the hell are you wearing?" I eyeballed my brother's ensemble and shook my head. "No freaking way, Marty. I am not going anywhere in public with you while you dressed like the drummer from a grunge band."

Marty looked at his dirty jeans and plaid shirt worn open over a grubby T-shirt and shrugged. "Stop being such a Miss Priss and get your ass in the car. We're going to be late."

My eyes begged Leo to say something but he mouthed "I tried," and turned back to supervise Peter raking the leaves in both yards.

"Your jeans have holes in them, what would Mom think?" I huffed.

"I'm playing a part here. We were victimized, remember. If the jury sees me looking like a bum, we'll get the sympathy vote."

"There is no jury yet. We're meeting with the District Attorney." Not to mention the Jackass and his lawyer. I felt sick and thought *great, something new and different for me.* "Besides, we don't want to show up looking like victims, we want to pretend we're upstanding citizens who were fooled. Like we could be anyone off the street. That's why I wore white, so I appear innocent, virginal."

Marty snorted. "Good one."

I smacked the back of his head. "Change, now."

Mumbling something foul about overbearing sisters, Marty schlepped back to Leo's house. I gazed heavenward. *Could really use a pep talk down here, ma.*

Tell Neil the truth.

I blinked. It was the first time she'd actually responded in days. You know your life is on the skids when the return of hallucinations is a plus.

I can't right now, Mom, I have no way to get a hold of him.

Nothing. I blew a wisp of hair out of my eyes and waited, but I knew my mother, she was never one to accept or make excuses. Mom wanted things done, stat.

Grumbling, I stomped up the porch to Leo. "I need a piece of paper and a pen."

"Check Peter's room."

I nodded and headed into the house.

"Hey, Maggie!" Leo called out.

"What?" I turned back to face him and was momentarily blinded as a flash went off in my eyes. "Jeeze, Leo! You could have warned me!"

"And you would have ducked and hidden like all the other times."

That's the trouble with having an artistic best friend. Leo wanted to turn messy me into art. I shot him a dirty look and continued into the house.

Though I couldn't find Peter, I spotted a notebook on his dresser and ripped a page out of the back.

"Dear Neil," I said as I wrote, then stopped. Now what?

Go on. My dead mother prompted, nagging from beyond the grave.

"I owe you a really big apology," I said and waited. Mom didn't reply, so I guessed she needed more. "Remember that night after the last time you got back? Well, I didn't tell you everything…."

I dictated it all to myself and when I was done, had a very apologetic letter that made me feel like scum.

"Ya happy now?" I asked.

"Holy crap!"

I whirled around and Leo stood in the doorway, his eyes as big as beach balls.

This was not happening. "Look, Leo, I can explain—"

"You just did, and it's bad. You should have told him right away."

My gaze fixed on the carpet, shoulders hunched. "I know."

"You are such a train wreck, carnage as far as the eye can see. I think he was actually falling for you, but now this…."

What was up with all the judgment from Leo? Hadn't he been rooting for team Maggie and Neil all along? "Look, he was a willing participant! I wasn't aware until well after the fact that he was in the middle of a flashback! He seemed lucid enough."

"You mean lucid enough for your purposes?"

I recoiled from his harsh words. "Not fair, Leo."

"If you think this is bad, wait until you actually tell Neil! How much better do you suppose he will take your little revelation?"

"You're acting like I assaulted him or something! He might be manipulating me, did you even consider the possibility?"

"What, you think he's *faking* PTSD? Why would he do something like that?"

I crumpled up the note and stuffed it in my purse. "You wouldn't understand."

He grabbed my arm and spun me around. "No, I don't. I thought you were a good person but look at you, sneaking around, lying to him, exactly like Amber. "

My eyes filled with tears. "Well, if that's what you think of me, I won't bother you anymore." He didn't say anything as I shoved past him and pounded on the guest room door.

"Marty, let's go."

From the look on my brother's face, I knew he'd heard every word.

"Pack your bag, you're staying in Richmond."

"What about you?"

I glanced over my shoulder to Leo. "I would, but I have a promise to keep."

CHAPTER TWENTY

"So, Ms. Sampson." The assistant district attorney, Paula Stone, stared at me over the rim of her coffee cup. "Would you please tell us exactly what happened with the defendant?"

I'd tried the java and been delightfully surprised at its quality, but my cup remained full. My nerves were already stretched to the breaking point. I didn't need the caffeine rush right now. "Could you please repeat the question?

"Would you please tell us exactly what happened with the defendant?"

Marty and Norman Yates shared the beige sofa, both watching as Pamela and I went through the question and answer session in her office again. Each round was harsher than the one before and I was ready to call it quits at any time.

As Ms. Stone had explained, this was a trial run to see if I could stick to my story under verbal attack from The Jackass's lawyer. Attack me they would, in every way imaginable. While Norman Yates was pretty much worthless as a lawyer,

Paula Stone looked like she could rip a criminal apart with her expensively manicured hands.

It was freaking hot in the cramped little office, and sweat trickled down my cleavage. The air conditioning must have been shut off for the season and the lack of circulating air made it hard to breathe.

Ignoring my general discomfort, I folded my hands in my lap and crossed my legs at the ankle, practicing the demure look, a new one for me. "Well, after my parents died—"

"How did they die exactly?" The ADA cut me off sooner than the last time.

I blinked at her abruptness and stuttered "There was a gas leak, an explosion—"

She made a hurry-up motion with her hand. I did my best to disregard her rudeness and continued. "He went with me to settle the estate."

"So, you trusted him enough to bring him into family business right from the start?" She raised an elegant eyebrow at my naïveté and I shifted my weight.

"He was the brother of my childhood friend—I had no reason not to trust him."

"Didn't you?" Her tone was disbelieving.

My eyes narrowed to slits as I took in her tone. "What's that supposed to mean?"

"Remember, don't lose your temper, because you'll only look like a woman scorned," Paula lectured.

"Right. Sorry." I fanned myself with my hand, wishing she'd open a window. It was hot as the fifth ring of hell in here.

"The State no longer recognizes breach of promise, and the last thing we want to do is make it seem as if you are going after him for abandoning you. Focus on the money he stole, someone you'd known since childhood deceived you in a time of mourning."

"I'm pretty sure the swindling didn't happen until later on. I mean, he was like a financial advisor—"

"Did you pay him?"

I shook my head. "No, after graduation he set me and Marty up in Darcy's condo and gave me a job as his personal assistant, so I could provide for my brother until he finished high school."

"And the money?" Paula stood up and circled the room. Following her made me nauseous, so I fixed my gaze on an overflowing bookcase instead.

"I trusted him to invest everything we'd received from the sale of my father's hardware store and the insurance on the house as well as their life insurance policies."

"How much money, approximately?" Her tone was deceptively mild as she faced the "jury".

"After the funerals and hospital bills, about 250,000 dollars."

She nodded and continued her orbit around me. "Did you keep track of where he put the money?"

"No, it didn't seem necessary at the time."

Pamela Stone stopped and blinked at me, her mouth open. "You let him take care of everything for you and you never gave his motive another thought? Were you sleeping with him?"

I blushed. "Not at first."

"So when exactly did you start sleeping with the defendant, Ms. Sampson."

From his seat off to the side, Marty squirmed and spoke up for the first time. "Is this really necessary?"

"Yes," we said in unison. I scowled at him for extra measure. He didn't say a word when the ADA circled around me the way a buzzard does fresh road kill, but the mention of my sex life was a reason to object? Of course, this was the

WHO NEEDS A HERO

second mention of some guy shtupping his sister in one day, so maybe it was the frequency that bothered him.

"We didn't become personally involved for over a year after I started working for him. He dated other women and I was busy taking care of my brother, so a romantic relationship wasn't on my to-do list."

Paula nodded her approval. "Good, say it exactly like that. We want to make sure the judge and jury are all keenly aware of how much pressure was on you. As the guardian for an underage sibling, you didn't have a chance to develop normal attachments. We'll paint the picture, cast him as the villain who used your lack of opportunity for a real relationship to his advantage."

I frowned. That wasn't right. Sure, I'd had a crush on him, what girl wouldn't after he'd ridden to the rescue, swooped in, and made everything all better? He'd given me the job, but I'd excelled at it, organizing his life so it ran well, throwing myself into building a new existence after everything had fallen apart....

Like I'd done with Neil. As the light dawned, the room spun.

"Are you all right?" Someone asked from what sounded very far away. I turned my head in the direction of the voice but saw only a blur of color. A fuzzy buzzing started in my ears before everything went dark.

"Maggie?" Marty sounded frantic. Wanting to reassure him I turned my head and struggled to open my eyes. The world flickered a few times before slowly coming back into focus.

"Hey, welcome back," another male voice said.

I blinked a few times, wondering why I was on the floor.

Something covered my face and I lifted one hand to investigate. An oxygen mask.

"Neil?"

"Nope, I'm Joe," the man said and I squinted at his blurry outline.

"Why am I on the floor, Joe?"

"You fainted," Marty supplied.

I shook my head. "You must be thinking of someone else because I don't faint."

I struggled to sit up but Joe held me back. "You need to stay still, Maggie. I'm going to take your blood pressure and ask you a few questions, all right?"

"Sure."

"Are you currently taking any medications?"

"Nope, fit as a fiddle," I said from my prone position.

"When was the last time you had anything to eat?"

"Um…" Jeeze, I was gonna fail this little pop quiz if I couldn't answer that one. "Last night I think? I haven't been hungry lately." Probably had something to do with Hilda's mediocre cooking, she used too much spice.

"Any chance you are pregnant?"

I opened my mouth then closed it with a snap. Was there a chance? I had told him I wasn't on any medication, which included birth control pills. Neil and I had unprotected sex. Shit, there was a chance, a pretty good chance. "I'm an idiot," I told Joe.

Marty made a pained sound, obviously distraught at being cast as the responsible Sampson sibling for a change.

"We'd better take you to the hospital and run a few tests."

The mention of the hospital made a cold sweat break out on my forehead. "No!" I shrieked, fighting anew to sit up, hysterical and bargaining for my freedom. "I'll eat something, get one of those over-the-counter pregnancy test deals, but I refuse to go to the hospital. People die in hospitals!"

"Maggie, you ought to go," Marty tried but I shook my head.

"No, I have to get back to Virginia Beach. I promised him, Marty!"

My brother and Joe exchanged looks. Joe shrugged, clearly unwilling to get into this fight. "I can't make her go and she appears well enough. Her blood pressure was a little low, but that could be caused by several different things. Just promise me you'll eat something and see your doctor soon."

I nodded vehemently. "You betcha. Thanks, Joe."

He and Marty pulled me to my feet and I focused on remaining upright under my own power. After assuring himself I wasn't about to fall on my face, the paramedic packed his bag of medical tricks and left. Paula Stone breezed in as soon as he departed.

"Are you sure you don't want to go to the hospital?" Lines of worry stretched under her eyes.

"Positive. I'll be fine. Are we finished here?" It was only polite to ask, even if I didn't give a crap what she said. I was done, regardless.

She nodded. "I'm going to do some digging, see if I can come up with a solid enough case without you. You said you overheard him mention trouble with the IRS?"

"That's what he told Darcy."

"I'll start there. You have enough to deal with and I don't think your testimony would help much in the criminal case." She cast a black look at Norman Yates, who'd skulked in after her like a whipped dog. "I'd seriously rethink the civil suit, at least with Ms. Sampson on the stand."

We left her office and I stared ahead as we proceeded down the hall to the elevator. I didn't want to see the stares of all the people who knew I was the fainting girl. It'd be hell on my badass reputation.

"There are other tactics we can take," Norman started

once we were all alone in the elevator. I focused my gaze on him and he cowered, but continued, "If the IRS has frozen his assets—"

"Norman," I spoke over his burbling. "Where do you honestly think our inheritance is at this moment?"

The lawyer deflated like a balloon. "Re-circulating."

I turned to Marty. "You hear what he said? The money is gone. I screwed up, trusted the wrong guy and we have nothing left. So blame me, yell at me, call me names if you want, but you need to accept the fact we're broke." I dismissed them both and staggered out to the parking area.

The lawyer skulked off into the night and Marty grabbed my elbow.

"Maggie, I—"

"There's a diner up the road a spell. Do you think we could stop there on our way to the bus station?"

My brother started at me for a minute. "Sure, whatever you want."

The diner was one of those retro deals, chrome exterior, black and white and red color scheme inside, complete with torn vinyl bench seats and rotating desert display.

Ignoring the *please wait to be seated* sign, I grabbed a menu and slid into a booth. The waitress was outside on a cigarette break and I thought I might fall over if I didn't sit soon.

"Do you really think you're pregnant?" Marty whispered.

I met his eyes over the menu. "There is a possibility."

He let out a breath. "Shit, Maggie, just shit."

I slapped the menu down. "Look, I'm sorry if this screws up your plans to be the biggest baby in the Sampson family—"

He grabbed my hand and squeezed. "No, it isn't that. I mean, a baby is a *really* big deal. You don't even have a car anymore and I doubt you'll have a job or a place to live when you tell Neil." He hesitated. "It's his, right? That's what the huge fight with Leo was all about?"

The waitress came in, reeking of unfiltered Camels. I must have turned green because Marty stood up and ran interference. "Hey, could we get two burgers and chocolate shakes? That would be great, thanks."

She glanced at me and rasped, "If you're gonna puke, take it outside."

"Will do," I said and closed my eyes, wanting nothing more than to sleep for the next month, maybe longer.

"What are we going to do, Maggie?" Marty's voice was small and scared and he looked as vulnerable as a twenty-year-old man could manage.

"Take care of ourselves, like we always do, Marty. Sampsons are like roaches. We're nature's best survivors, even if no one wants us around."

"Good one," Marty laughed.

"Seriously, I know Neil. He's going to be upset with me no matter what, but he's a good guy, he won't throw me out on the street." A tear escaped and I turned to face the window so Marty wouldn't see it. I believed every word I told him, but at the same time couldn't help but feel as though this possibility crushed something precious. A future which included me and Neil and the boys—one too distant to see in the darkening night.

Of course, he was going to be upset, the rebound girl wasn't supposed to get knocked up, for God's sake. He'd been adamant about us not taking that road because of the impact a romantic relationship would have on his children. My guess was this would come as a huge shock on top of his recent mountain of misery, especially when he didn't remember the sex itself. The poor man deserved at least the memory of the deed. He didn't need this, didn't deserve this kind of welcome home.

The realization I'd had in Paula Stone's office came back to me. Leo had been right; I was exactly like Amber, a victim of my own hopes and dreams. I'd tied my financial and emotional future down to men, first to the Jackass, then to Neil instead of taking care of myself first. I'd been so caught up saving everyone else, I didn't even notice how turned around my priorities had become. Marty, Josh, Kenny, and even Neil made everything so easy for me. Playing house, focusing on the day-to-day needs of everyone else, losing myself in the mom role, the same way my mother always had. All I'd ever really wanted, but it wasn't real.

Our food arrived and we ate in silence. While I wasn't hungry I had promised Joe and if nothing else, I was a woman who kept my word.

CHAPTER TWENTY-ONE

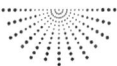

Despite my protests, Marty insisted on driving me home. I stared at his profile as we zipped through the construction area of I-64. "So what are you going to do now?" I asked him. My brother had so much potential, unbelievable amounts of this indefinable quality which shouted, *look at me, I can do anything*! Too bad he buried it under sloth and greed.

Marty shrugged. "Maybe I'll join the military."

"Not a commitment you can take lightly, Sprout. You can't say "do-over" or "my bad," when you decided to bail."

His lips twisted as he shot me a scathing look. "You really don't think I can do it, do you?"

"No, I believe you can do anything. It's *will* you do it that's in question."

"Joining the military would take care of my lack of housing situation since you ordered me out of Leo's house."

"Leo's angry with me and too generous for his own good, so I'm watching his back to make sure no bottom feeders latch on and bleed him dry."

"Bottom feeders like your only sibling?" His tone carried more amusement than resentment.

"Exactly like my only sibling." Red and blue lights broke through the dimness of the night and the wail of the siren drowned out the radio. "Slow down, Marty. If you get a speeding ticket in a construction zone, it'll cost twice as much."

Marty eased off the gas and the cop car sped past us. More lights lit up the night ahead of us in the westbound lane. "What the heck is going on?"

"DUI check maybe?" Marty rubbernecked but thankfully the road was straight. I changed the radio station, sick of the overplayed band bleating from the speakers.

An Amber Alert has been issued in the Hampton Roads Area for Joshua Phillips, age three years, and Kenneth Phillips, age seven months."

"What!" I shrieked. My ears must have been playing tricks on me.

Marty's gaze locked with mine as the announcer's grave voice continued. *"The boys were last seen in the custody of their grandparents, Ralph and Laura Phillips. They have been missing since two this afternoon. Father Neil Phillips is an enlisted sailor, currently station at the Naval Amphibious Base at Little Creek. Their mother, Amber Phillips has not yet been located and neither has their nanny, one Margaret Sampson. Both women are wanted for questioning, listed as persons of interest in the investigation."*

"Holy flaming monkey turds!" Marty cut off the broadcaster's diatribe on whom to call with information. "This is bad Maggie, really horribly bad."

I barely heard him as I stared at the clock. Quarter after seven. The boys had been missing for more than five hours.

"Do you want me to stop so you can call them? Should I turn around, go back to the cops?" Marty asked.

I considered it and shook my head. "No, the investigation

is at or near the house and they'd have to bring me to whoever is in charge there. Let's not waste time."

Marty drove as I twisted the radio dial to see if I could glean anything more.

One out of three radio stations played the information. A few referred to the divorce and custody hearings and one mentioned Neil was not stateside at the moment, but nothing more about the boys.

Panic welled up, but I refused to give in to raw fear when I might be able to do something. We lost radio transmission in the tunnel between Newport News and Norfolk and I made small crescent shapes divots in my palm where I'd dug my fingernails into the fleshy part, waiting for news, afraid to speculate.

Imagination was not my friend.

Weekday traffic after seven wasn't horrible at this time of year and Marty navigated us back to the house in record time without getting pulled over. The red and blue emergency lights were visible blocks away, casting weird creepy shadows over the cold evening. My heart pounded as we turned onto the street. There were people everywhere, uniformed police officers, as well as curious neighbors, clogging the cul-de-sac like cholesterol built up in an artery. Marty couldn't park any closer than three houses down without blocking through traffic. He'd barely pulled to a stop when I launched myself out of the car, tripping on the curb and going down on one knee.

"Ma'am I'll have to ask you to—"

"I'm Maggie Phillips, the nanny," I gasped. Those were the magic words because he hauled me up and navigated me through the crowd in a direct line for the house.

"Maggie!" Leo called out from across a sea of spectators. I broke the officer's grip with a self-defense maneuver I'd seen on television, surprised when it actually worked. I sprinted for Leo and pulled him along with me, needing a friendly face nearby. The cop had given chase and stopped in his tracks when he saw me coming back toward him.

"Where the hell have you been?" Leo hissed at me as I dragged him in my wake. "Cripes, woman. You really need a cell phone."

Too focused to quip back, I shoved my way through the crowd and onto the front porch, the eye of the hurricane as even more people were crammed into the house.

Laura spotted me first. "There she is!" Her finger jabbed at me like a hound pointing out a fat duck to his master. I ignored her and glanced around, frantic to find who might be able to do something.

A woman in a sleek business suit stepped forward. "Are you the ex-wife or the nanny?"

"I'm Maggie Sampson, the boys' nanny. What happened?"

She ignored my question, steering me by the elbow out of the living room and into the kitchen. Two cops had been sitting at the counter but one look from her and they'd scuttled out like whipped puppies. She closed the pocket doors and focused on me. "When was the last time you saw Kenneth and Joshua.?"

"This morning, when they left with their grandparents. I dressed them and packed lunch before they left. Joshua is picky and I was afraid the grandparents wouldn't find anything he wanted to eat. They're not exactly regular patrons of McDonalds. Plus Kenny really enjoys his snacks." Yes, I had a severe case of verbal diarrhea, but better to blurt out everything than forget something crucial.

"I need an account of your whereabouts, Ms. Sampson."

I spewed up the events of my day, including the phone call from Neil, the visit to the D.A in Richmond, and the burger with Marty. The woman in the suit wrote it all down.

"Ms. Sampson, are you aware of any hostile feelings between Mr. and Mrs. Phillips?

"Well, she's kind of an uptight prig and he's a bit of a randy old goat—"

The detective looked at me oddly and I realized she'd been talking about Amber and Neil, not Laura and Ralph.

"Sorry, um Amber is a free spirit and she really resented Neil for everything that happened. He still loves her though, even though she's humiliated him and virtually ignored the boys."

The detective surveyed me again. "How do you know that?"

Full disclosure. I couldn't hold anything back now, not if Josh and Kenny's lives might depend on it. "Because he called me by her name when we had sex."

EVERYONE KNEW. I could tell from the look in the cops' eyes, Ralph's knowing smirk. Laura's deepening frown lines. Every single person in the room had heard I'd slept with my boss. Everyone except my boss.

Of course, the suit had to grill me like a T-bone after I'd dropped my little bombshell. Yes, I'd been hired by Amber, no, Neil was the one who paid me, yes, I spent time alone with the kids, yes, I was as broke as the day was long.

From the police detective's perspective, I had motive and opportunity. I also had an iron-clad alibi, but that didn't mean I wasn't being watched. According to the detective, I might be in cahoots with someone else, someone who would contact the Phillips family and ask for money in exchange for the children. My gorge had risen at the supposition but I said nothing, unwilling to defend myself if arguing took the focus off finding the children.

Marty, hauled in off the street, was also being watched, I guess because he was my destitute brother. Leo had tried to apologize earlier, but I'd ignored him as I paced the house, thinking.

It had to be Amber. It must be, but why? As far as I knew, she had joint custody and no interest in the children. It was less than two weeks ago when she'd left and I'd sensed no regret or doubt from her. She really was that self-centered. The boys had been leverage to her, props for when she needed to play the mommy role, things to be stored, not cherished. I really despised her.

No one had been able to contact Neil. He was on a mission, with no phone number or forwarding address. Military protocol needed to be followed and by the time the i's were dotted and the t's had been crossed, he might be home already. Fricking red tape.

I stared out the window in the kitchen, watching as uniformed police officers dug through the crap I'd hauled out of the master suite, searching for clues to where Amber might have gone. From what I could tell, her boss had not been very helpful, telling them she'd quit with little notice. He assumed she was nursing a broken heart over the failure of her marriage and would check in when she was back up to snuff. Sucker.

Leo came up behind me. I knew it was him because I could smell his cologne, something with a musky base that screamed hip and modern. "How are you holding up?"

I turned to face him. "Did you think I took them?"

His appalled expression was genuine. "No! Of course not, how could you even imagine—"

"Well, you didn't think too much of me this afternoon, so apparently my character was in doubt."

Leo gave me a hug from behind, resting his cheek on my

hair. "I overreacted. Your confession caught me off guard. I'm sorry I was such a dick."

I didn't move, just stared out into the night. "Who lied to you?"

He went very still. "How do you know someone did?"

I stepped away from him. "Reactions like those don't pop out of holes in the ground. You don't turn on a friend because you're annoyed or disappointed."

Leo slumped against the sink. "My sister."

Not what I'd been expecting. "Come again?"

He shook his head. "Peter's mother, my sister, she went after someone I'd been dating. We had a fight, he was still in the closet at the time and his denial pissed me off. She got him drunk, tried to straighten him out." He made little air quoted with his fingers. "She forced him to try to be something he wasn't. Or maybe he was, hell, I don't know. The point is she took advantage of him when he was confused."

It didn't take a Mensa candidate to connect the dots. "Like I did with Neil." I leaned back against the cabinet and thunked my head on the door.

"No, honey, not like that at all. Neil really does want to be with you, I know, I've been watching the two of you together. You are the real thing."

I accepted his words with my head, but not my heart. Time to deflect. "I'm surprised you still talk to your sister."

Leo looked sheepish. "Well, I didn't until a few months ago. I was very angry. It didn't help that the man I thought I loved cheated on me with my sister, emptied my bank account, and split."

I blinked. "Seriously? And here I'd been whining about Darcy and the Jackass."

"Yes, but you *did* something, quite a few things actually, to show your displeasure and vent some steam. I just... imploded."

I swallowed. "This is the part where you tell me you met George and started your own happily ever after."

Leo didn't meet my gaze. "George is a good guy, he really is and he inherited a mess with me. If you think you've got baggage...." Leo let out a low whistle.

"Yeah." When in the hell was I going to learn there's no such thing as a real fairy tale finish? Life was more of a contest—he who made it through with the fewest scars won.

We were quiet for a bit, listening to the buzz in the other room, each of us lost in our own thoughts. Tears rolled down my cheeks as I realized this was about the time I usually read Josh a final story and fed Kenny his last bottle for the evening.

"I need them back, Leo. If anything happens to my boys...." Unable to finish, I sobbed on Leo's shoulder, allowing myself to get good and upset with worry I could no longer bottle up.

The phone rang.

I jumped to answer it but Detective Suit beat me to it. "Keep whoever it is on the line, in case there's a ransom demand."

I nodded and picked up the receiver. "Hello?" I saw Laura frown at me and turned my back before I gave her the finger. Phone etiquette and Miss Manner could kiss my lily-white backside.

"Maggie?" The male voice was hesitant but all too familiar.

"What do you want?" I snarled at the Jackass. "Look, this isn't the best time. I have something of a situation—"

My jaw snapped shut, but it had nothing to do with the police detective's frantic arm-waving that could have helped land a 747. "How did you get this number?"

He cleared his throat. "I've been keeping tabs on you, Maggie, you made some wild accusations when you left and I needed to know what you planned to do." There was some noise in the background, like thudding feet, followed by a child's cry.

My knuckles turned white as I gripped the phone, dread constricting my lungs like a python. "You took them, took the kids."

The detective mouthed "Who?" at me and tossed me a pen and notebook. With a shaking hand, I wrote my ex's name, his social security number and home address, and place of business.

"Miss Maggs?"

Oh, God, I was right. "Hey, Josh how are you, Scamp?"

"I'm tired and I want to come home. Are you coming to get us soon?"

The tears flowed freely. I'd done this, brought this man to Neil's doorstep, and now he had taken Josh and Kenny. "As soon as I can, okay Josh? Promise. I love you, buddy."

More scuffling and I heard Kenny's pterodactyl shriek. My heart was making the same sound. "Please don't hurt them," I whispered.

The rat bastard sounded affronted. "I won't, they've been treated well all day. I hate resorting to this, but I need money, Maggie. Your new boyfriend seems to have plenty to burn. And considering how we left things, I didn't reckon you'd put in a good word for me."

"How much?" I asked, vowing I'd kill him with my bare hands before giving him a dime. For the boys, I'd play his game though.

"Three million dollars."

I wrote the number down. "How do you want to do this?"

There was a hesitation like he didn't know what his next move ought to be. The Jackass never saw further than the end of his own pecker. Finally, he said, "You, bring it alone."

"Where?" The detective mouthed at me. I repeated the question.

"I'll call you with details tomorrow morning. Come alone, Maggie. If I see any sign of the police, you'll never see these kids again."

The line went dead.

CHAPTER TWENTY-TWO

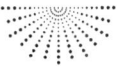

I spent the next three hours with the police, answering questions and going over every single tidbit I had on the Jackass. As his former secretary, I was in the know about business associates and assets and as his former fiancée, I could list names of family, friends, pretty much anyone who'd ever breathed in his general direction. Maybe at some point in the future, I might feel guilty for bringing up his sister, my friend Justine, or his mom the boozehound who spent most of her life in an alcoholic stupor, but I couldn't dwell on them.

"Ms. Sampson, are you sure he won't hurt the children."

I accepted a mug of coffee someone had pushed into my numb hands. "Almost positive. He doesn't like children, didn't want any, but he isn't a monster, just a rat bastard."

What the hell had possessed him to stoop so low? Not that he'd had far to go, but kidnapping? It didn't make any sense. I probably needed to grow up and stop looking for life to form a logical pattern. I couldn't understand why he'd followed me, other than to get his ring back. But I'd sold it, there shouldn't have been a trail for him to follow unless....

My gaze slid to Marty. "Did you tell him where I was?"

He took serious umbrage to the question. "What, you think we were hanging out together at the local Waffle House every night? You know I never liked the smarmy SOB. Get real."

"Did you tell anyone else?" I probed.

Marty shrugged. "A few of the guys, Gloria. Does it really matter now how he found out you were living with some guy who has serious family scratch?"

No, it didn't but thinking about how gave me something to do other than spin my wheels.

Leo had gone home to George and Peter and the police were off chasing down the leads I'd supplied them. Laura and Ralph invaded the other room, talking about whether they should look into hiring a negotiator to do the exchange so everything ran smoothly.

"Maybe you should try and catch a nap, you look like reheated death," Marty commented.

My expression soured as I took a swig of the now cold coffee. "I won't be able to sleep. I did this, Marty. I'm responsible for those boys. If the guilt doesn't do me in, Neil will when he gets back."

My brother pried the mug out of my hands. "This is not your fault. You really need to stop taking the weight of the world on your shoulders. Did you set him up to take those kids? Hell no, so knock off the blame game."

He was right, though I wasn't going to admit that out loud. "When did you get so smart?"

"Must run in the family. Go lie down, if not for yourself, then for someone else." His gaze went pointedly to my mid-section.

I closed my eyes. "I'd forgotten about that."

Marty helped me up the stairs but instead of going to my room, I curled up in Josh's bed and held his stuffed dolphin which didn't absorb my tears at all. Eventually, the well ran dry and I used my sleeve to wipe the moisture off my face. The stars and planets on the ceiling glowed in the dark as I thought about how I'd hit Neil with the diaper bin on my first night here. My eyes filled again as the memory acted as a divining rod and located an untapped source of misery. I couldn't think of him without major waterworks and turned on my side, focusing my unblinking stare at the door.

"Maggie?"

As if conjured from my musings, he crept into the room, the hallway light casting him in silhouette. Maybe I had fallen asleep. Curled on my side in the fetal position, I watched, wondering what form the first attack would take. He wouldn't hurt me physically, I was sure, but I almost wished he would. I deserved whatever he could dish out.

The waiting was killing me. He closed the door and then we were alone, under the night sky he'd painted for his sons. The carpet cushioned his footfalls and I remained still as he ghosted nearer with deadly grace. He sank to a crouch before me, reeking of old sweat and fear as well as his unique male spice. Heat more intense than the sun radiated from him, scalding my numb aura. I met his gaze without blinking.

His eyes told me everything. He knew it all. Whether from the police report or a phone call, or his own memory kicking into high gear it didn't matter, there were no secrets left between us.

My voice came out cracked, thick from crying. "I'm so sorry." Not enough, yet what else could I possibly say?

He didn't ask about what, only the boys mattered now. I waited for his righteous fury to rain down but he remained still, assessing me from every angle. As I owed him everything, I didn't flinch or shrink away though my instincts screamed at me to do something. He deserved better than my cowardice.

Without a word, he reached out, brushed some hair back from my eyes, then his thumb traced down my cheek, his gaze locked on mine like a heat-seeking missile. Between the physical and visual contact, I opened up to him, gave him everything, down to the darkest corner of my soul. The important and the useless, wisdom and whimsy flowed through the connection until I was nothing but an empty husk.

"You love my boys, don't you?" His callused thumb stroked my cheek.

"More than anything," I admitted.

"I'm here alone. The rest of my team is on a mission. Remember what I told you about having a swim buddy? I need backup. I need your help to get them back."

I sat up. "What can I do?"

"Go downstairs, tell everyone you're going for a walk. I'll meet you at your brother's car." He broke the tactile connection between us and went to the window.

"What about the police?"

He turned back to face me. "Do you really want to wait for them?"

Was it illegal to go around the law to right a wrong? "One condition, if we get into trouble, you let me take the fall, all right?"

"Whatever you say," he agreed and popped the screen out. I shut the window behind him and drew the blinds for good measure.

"Marty!" I clattered down the stairs. "I'm going for a walk!"

"What, now? It's one in the morning!"

"I have to get out of this house, or I'm going to lose my mind."

"Let me drive you somewhere then—"

"No, I want to be alone." The crazed look in my eyes must have done the trick because he nodded and backed off.

"Where do you think you're going?" Laura asked, but I ignored her as I slid my sneakers on and sprinted up the block. Neil was already sitting in the car, which he must have hotwired.

He slung an arm over the seat and backed up in a neighbor's driveway.

"Why didn't we take your truck?"

"Because we don't want to waste time losing a tail. You're still under suspicion by some."

"But not by you?"

He cut his gaze to me in the rearview mirror. "You're definitely suspect in my book, but I know you didn't take the kids."

I chewed on his words while he navigated back out to the highway. "Where are we going?"

"Your old apartment."

"Why?"

"A gut feeling. He had the key and Darcy is out of town most of the time, on business."

My eyes widened. "You really did check up on me?"

He sent me a small smirk. "Told you I would. Do me a favor and tell me everything about this guy on the way."

Neil planned to go in prepared. I took a deep breath and started at the beginning, feeling more confident by the mile. We could do this. Whether we ought to was a different story, but I was ready to do whatever it took to help reunite Neil and his boys.

Consequences be damned.

THE DRIVE from Neil's house in Virginia Beach to my old apartment in Richmond took less than two hours and the dashboard clock read two fifty-eight when he pulled to the curb. Marty's car still had the parking lot decal on the windshield, but when I pointed that out to Neil, he shook his head.

"The windows overlook the parking lot. We don't want to give up the element of surprise."

Made sense to me. "Tell me again why you're so sure he's got them here?"

Though I'd asked before, he didn't roll his eyes or make an exasperated sound. "He wouldn't risk keeping them at any of his own properties, and can't hide kids with his family. He's without the resources for a rental. So we're left with places he has access to, as in Darcy's condo."

"Yeah, but it smells like decomposing fish," I said. To his back, since he was out of the car and crossing around the front.

"Stay here, I'm going to take a quick sneak and peak. We don't want to scare someone's grandma to death when we bust down the door."

"It's five stories up and the fire escape is a death trap!" Surely he wasn't going to scale the building like Spiderman?

He flashed me his lopsided grin. "I'll be back in five."

I slumped down in my seat. Some backup. Betcha his real swim buddy didn't have to wait in the freaking car. This was Neil's show, though and I wasn't about to screw it up in classic Maggie fashion.

He returned in three minutes. "They're in there. They look all right, though Kenny's seriously pissed. He's in the throes of a major tantrum. We couldn't ask for a better distraction."

I closed my eyes in relief. "Thank you, God, I promise to

be good and go to church and donate blood as often as possible."

"You shouldn't make promises to God you have no intention of keeping," Neil said as he rummaged for something in his bag in the back seat.

"How about I promise I'll stay out of go-go bars then?"

"I think everyone would benefit from that one." He grabbed my hand and helped me out of the car. I intended to run to the building's entrance but Neil's grip kept me in check. "First, we need cover." He reached out and scrubbed his fingers through my hair.

"You're making a mess of it," I said.

"You already had bed head and we need cover. Put your arm around my neck and lean your weight on me. Try to stagger like you've had too much to drink."

"Couldn't we pretend to be the nice couple out for a stroll?" I griped.

"At three in the morning? This is about when last call is up and it'll keep people from looking too closely."

"So am I a happy drunk, a sloppy drunk, a mean drunk, or a total slut who knocks back the shots and brings random guys home?"

"Ladies choice, but don't get too loud. We want to blend, not get noticed."

I slung my arm around his shoulder and he stooped at what must have been an uncomfortable angle to wrap an arm around my waist. It took a few steps to align our strides so we were in sync.

"Let's take our time crossing through the parking lot, I want to get a good look at the cars, see which ones have car seats, and make note of the plates."

"Whatever you say, slick." I grinned up at him, working at smashed and besotted. Only one was an act.

He stopped right in front of the building and looked down at me. "God, I missed you."

I blinked, stunned. "Really? Even after everything?"

His answer was to pull me back against the wall and kiss me. Warm, firm lips crushed against mine. He tasted like coffee and need, a heady combination I couldn't resist. My fingers worked up his back and into his hair to hold him to me.

His hands traveled everywhere at a frenetic pace, lighting on my arms then my breasts, sliding around my back, cupping my ass. With my back against the wall, I had enough leverage to wrap my legs around his waist and did so with relish. My brain must have short-circuited because all it could form were one-syllable disjointed words like more and now. And Neil.

Air. That one came through as I broke away, gasping. He must have developed better lung capacity because he trailed kisses down my neck, nibbled on my earlobe. My head tilted to the side to give him better access and my heart thundered in my chest, pumping blood everywhere because I was on fire....

"Amber," Neil breathed in my ear.

My eyes slid shut. *Not again!* When would I fricking *learn?*

"Maggie, Amber at two o'clock," Neil whispered and I scowled.

"I thought you said it was after three?"

He pulled back enough and gave his head a quick jerk to the side. "Not time, compass point."

My gaze skittered to the lone figure in the parking lot. "What the hell is she doing—"

He kissed me again, though this time I knew the reason behind his actions. I needed time to think and not blurt out anything that would call attention to us. Just a couple of drunken idiots necking in the parking lot, nothing to see here, folks!

Because I was listening for it, I heard the distinct sound of high heels clicking on the blacktop, back toward the side entrance.

I pulled back so fast the back of my head connected with a cinderblock. "Ouch, stop kissing me, I can't hold a frigging thought when you do that."

Neil set me back on my feet and didn't say anything. He didn't need to, his eyes blazed in fury.

"She's the one who's planned it. Damn it, why didn't I think of this before? Josh is Mr. Stranger Danger, he's afraid of everyone and everything foreign to him. Amber would have walked off with a happy child, not a screaming one."

Neil nodded sharply. "She's gone too far."

While part of me was relieved that the kids were with someone they knew, another larger percentage was appalled at how a mother could be so cold and unfeeling. I stepped away from him and rolled up my sleeves. "This bitch is going down."

CHAPTER TWENTY-THREE

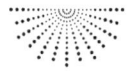

"**S**o, what's the plan, Slick? Knock down the door and start busting heads?" I crackled my knuckles and Neil shook his head at me.

"Call the police. It's the best we can do, now that we know the boys are here and safe." He gave me a rueful smile. "There will be no head busting."

"Well, what if they turn vicious when they discover their plan has been thwarted?"

"You really watch too much television." He glanced up at the building. "Does your ex have any violent tendencies?"

"No, he's pond scum, but harmless. The worst thing we'll face in that apartment is the smell." And yet, I still wasn't sorry about the fish.

"Okay, we'll call 911, give the operator a sit rep and hang tight."

As rescue plans went, it was neither bold nor flashy but it would do. "Kay, you make the call and I'll keep watch."

Neil frowned. "I don't like the idea of leaving you alone while I search for a payphone. Come with me."

"Where's your cell?"

"In my sea bag. I didn't want the GPS on me tonight, since I'm UA."

"Shit, Neil—"

"Now is not the time. Which direction?"

I pointed back the way we'd come. "Nearest phone is two blocks over, in the Getty parking lot. Go now, you'll be faster without me slowing you down."

"Stay alert, and do not take any stupid chances."

He kissed me again, a brief, yet intense brush of the lips that heated my blood and caressed my soul, before slipping into the night, taking the magic with him.

I shivered in the sudden cold and turned back to the building. Would it be better to keep watch inside? Maybe I could direct the police to the right apartment, once they arrived. Plus the Dumpster really reeked.

"Come on, let's go." I jumped as the Jackass's voice drifted across the parking lot. He carried what looked like Kenny's car seat in one hand and dug in his pocket for keys with the other.

The smart clickity clacking of Amber's heels on the blacktop followed right behind him as she dragged a sleepy-eyed Josh behind her with sharp, un-maternal tugs.

I closed my eyes, relieved to see him, but then jerked upright as I realized what was happening. They had waited until the plumber's butt crack of dawn to move the kids to wherever they would make the exchange tomorrow. This was bad.

"Hurry up." The Jackass loaded Kenny's seat into the car and faced Amber with a sour expression. In the glow of the streetlight, he looked pale and gaunt, his sharp blade of a nose more prominent than I remembered. He was dressed in his typical khaki-colored slacks and powder blue button-front shirt, ready for a day of scamming and wheedling.

If they got away, we would have to wait until he

contacted me again. Too much could happen and the boys were in spitting distance from me now. I needed to stop them, or at least stall them until the police arrived.

Block the exit. My mother's voice whispered. I surveyed the parking lot. Building on one side, guard rails blocking off access to a one-way street on two of the others. Dumpster right next to me, closing off the fourth side so the exit spanned the length of a mid-sized vehicle.

I sprinted for the car, praying I'd have enough time. That Josh would dawdle the way he always did. We'd lose the element of surprise, but they couldn't run with two kids in tow.

The door was unlocked and I slid behind the wheel, not bothering to adjust the seat. Crap, I'd forgotten about the key, or more specifically, the lack of one. Loose wires dangled from the steering column and as I grasped them in my hands I fought a wave of panic. Damn it, why hadn't I made the phone call?

Okay brain, simmer down and think. What had Neil done to stop the car? If I could remember, all I needed was to reverse the process to start the sucker back up. Closing my eyes, I pictured his hands, untwisting wires before the engine died. Sirens shrilled in the distance, and my eyelids snapped up like pull shades a split second before the lights came on in the parking lot. The cops weren't going to make it, there would be a high-speed car chase and Kenny or Josh might get hurt.

Okay, focus on the task at hand. Twisting the ends of two wires together did nothing. Frantic, I fumbled them and grabbed another set. A spark arced up and I hooked them together, giddy when the engine turned over.

I threw the car into first and stepped on the gas. The tire curb-checked as I spun the wheel to avoid the car parked too close in front of me, but then the front end was clear. Slamming on the brakes, I screeched to a stop in front of the parking lot access right as the Jackass hit the gas. The sickening crunch of metal and glass broke the stillness of the night and my head hit the driver's side window with a thud.

Seat belt! My brain screamed, too late to do anything about the lack. Their car was sturdier than Marty's, which appeared to be made of aluminum foil by the way it crumpled toward me.

Please, let the boys be safe in their car seats. The sirens were closer now and the lights flickered in my peripheral vision. I should get out of the car, check on the kids, but I couldn't figure out how to proceed. While I ruminated on the mechanics, someone yanked the door open behind me.

"Try not to move, ma'am." The voice was official-sounding and I glanced up into a familiar face.

"Hey, long time no see," I said to Joe the EMT.

"Jesus," he said and shook his head while giving me a medical once-over.

"Maggie actually. I'll be okay, Joe. Please go help the people in the other car, there are kids in there." I was proud of my calm tone.

"They're fine. Kids were strapped in and the airbags deployed. They were all out of the car and walking around when I got here. Do you remember the accident?"

"Wasn't an accident. I had to stop them before they got away."

"Right. How hard did you hit your head?" He didn't wait for me to answer as he put a neck brace around my throat. "Try not to move, we'll get you to the hospital in the ambulance.

Joe shined a flashlight in my eyes and I came up swinging. "No! No hospital!"

"Maggie!" Neil was back.

"Did you get them, did you get the boys?" I asked, trying

235

to turn my head toward the sound of his voice, and found it impossible in the stiff brace.

"Yes, they're right here. Slept through everything." Neil stood behind the EMT with a sleeping Josh on his shoulder, Kenny's carrier in his other hand. He was hauling at least fifty pounds of offspring and yet he looked fragile.

My eyes filled up. "They're all right?"

Josh stirred at the sound of my voice. "Miss Maggs?"

"I'm here, Scamp." I grinned up at Neil. "We'd did it! Go, team."

"Is this the father?" Joe asked me.

"Yes, I'm their father," Neil said. "Is she going to be all right?"

Joe cut his gaze to me "We need to take her to the hospital, run a few tests, but it looks like superficial damage."

"I don't want to go to the hospital," I implored Neil. "The kids need to get home."

"You trashed our wheels, so we'll do as he says until our ride gets here."

Joe peppered me with questions I didn't have the answers to, like had I lost consciousness, what was the last thing I remembered before the crash. Who really catalogs their thoughts like that anyhow?

After what seemed like an eternity, Joe and a female colleague transferred me to a gurney and from there into the ambulance.

"I'm fine really." I made another half-assed effort to talk my way out of a trip to the hospital, but knowing Neil was going to be there kept me from hitting the pinnacle of blind terror.

"I need to talk with the police, but I'll be there as soon as humanly possible," Neil told me.

"Don't take too long." I tried to look at him, but Joe *tsked* at me so I would lay flat.

"Look at the bright side," Joe said as he strapped me in for the ride. "At least now we'll know one way or the other if you are pregnant."

The ambulance doors shut on Neil's astonished face.

"Yes, Mom, they're really fine." I shut the door on my two sleeping little guys, but my mind was at the hospital, with Maggie. Who was fresh from a car wreck and possibly pregnant.

Swallowing the thought of Maggie with someone else was like choking down a mason jar full of rusty nails. Who could it be? Maybe her ex, the soon-to-be convicted felon? Or perhaps someone she'd met at the beach, some guy who was smarter and less emotionally eviscerated than me? Someone who took one look at her, threw her over his shoulder, and did all the things I'd imagined doing to her lush body over and over until she cried out his name in ecstasy?

"Neil, you're grinding your teeth so loud I can hear it from over here. Have a drink and relax, son. The worst is behind us." My father had procured a decanter of brandy and sat at the small desk, savoring his own glass.

The image of Maggie with someone else ate at me almost as much as the understanding that I could have lost everything that mattered to me tonight. Maggie and the boys. Amber, the selfish bitch, could have killed her own children, for what? Money? And Maggie would have been gone, without ever hearing me say how much she mattered to me.

My mother was more agitated than I'd ever seen her, which was really saying something because pissed off was her standard mode of operation. "I just can't believe Amber would do something like this! What in the name of God could she possibly have been thinking?"

"About herself, per usual," I gritted out. "I know you liked her, Mom. Maybe because she's as ruthless and manipulating as you are."

My mother sucked in a breath and my father rose to his full height. "Apologize to your mother at once."

"For what, speaking the truth? You were in charge of those kids, you let her take them right out from under your noses! Let me guess, you were on the phone with a very important client and didn't notice them wander off?"

"No." My mother held up her hand. "He's right, Ralph, if I'd been more observant she would never have had the opportunity." She rose and squared her shoulders with military precision. "I'm sorry, Neil. Ralph, let's go." I watched as they left, still too amazed to speak.

My mother actually admitted to making a mistake? Had Hell frozen over?

Without Kenny and Josh to distract me I paced, restless and itching with bottled-up energy. I needed answers, needed to see for myself that Maggie was really going to be all right. And if she was pregnant, well, I would fight for her. She already loved my boys, her actions tonight had proved that much. We belonged together, our lives entangled so effortlessly and I'd shamelessly use them to my advantage. I could be patient, stage a siege until she realized I'd do anything to have her for my own.

A knock sounded on the door and I strode to it. Maggie's brother stood on the other side.

"Dude, you have no freaking clue how much I want to beat the ever-loving piss outta you right now."

I sighed. This was not what I needed at the moment. "Sorry about your car—"

"Fuck the goddamned car!" Marty pushed his way past me, little more than a child, still somewhat gangly in the limbs. "You knocked up my sister!"

Shaking my head at him I pushed past him to pour myself a drink. "You're wrong. Maggie and I never—"

The little snot cut me off again this time by shoving a file under my nose. "Yeah, you fucking did."

Scanning the file I realized it was a police report on the boys' kidnapping. "Where the hell did you get this?"

"Does it matter? Read it!"

I did, a yawning chasm opening in my chest as I absorbed the words. Which was worse, the fact that Maggie believed I was still in love with Amber or that I'd had sex with her and didn't remember a moment of it?

Glancing up to her brother, this boy /man—the only family she had left, who was here to confront me on her behalf—I swallowed hard. "She didn't tell me. I didn't know."

Marty stared down at me. "Well you do now, so go fix it!"

THOUGH IT WAS DIFFICULT, I behaved while medical professionals stripped me, poked, and prepped my sore body like a slab of beef readying for barbeque. The diagnosis was minor lacerations, and shock. The treatment, stitches for the head wounds, and an overnight at the hospital for observation. Against my vehement protests, the doctors refused to release me. I stared out the door of my semi-private, moderately darkened room and watched the nurses scurry about. Tears rolled down my cheeks. Man alive, did I hate hospitals.

"Hey." Neil appeared in the rectangle of artificial light.

"You look exhausted," I told him. It was true, his skin had a grayish cast to it, like someone who hadn't seen the sun in months and his stubble had gone beyond ruggedly handsome into pirate scourge.

"Thanks, exactly the look I was going for." He sidled into the room.

"Where are the boys?"

"My parents drove up and checked them all into a hotel. They'll be by to bring you home."

Though I wanted to ask why he wasn't going to take me back, I chickened out. This might be the last time I saw him. "What happened with Amber and the rat bastard?"

"They're both in jail. I pressed charges against them and issued a restraining order against Amber. She's never to see the boys again."

"Good." I sat up and cleared my throat.

"Can I get you anything?" he asked.

"A drink of water would be wonderful."

He vanished through the door and I closed my eyes, doing my best not to think about what would happen next.

"Are you asleep?" His return had been silent, but since I'd been expecting him, at least I wasn't scared out of my wits.

"No, I won't be able to sleep here. I hate hospitals. People die in hospitals."

"People die everywhere. At least hospitals give them a fighting chance."

"Don't waste your breath talking sense to my phobia. Believe me, it doesn't make a dent."

He poured the water and stuck a straw in it. I reached for the cup, but he didn't let go while I aimed the straw for my lips.

"Thanks," I said when I'd had my fill. "I'm sure the Jackass did it for the money but did you find out why Amber was on board?"

"The same reason, just a less direct approach. She only wanted sole custody of the kids to bump up her alimony so she could quit her job. Apparently, your ex approached her with what she thought was a win-win deal. He'd get the fast cash and because the kids disappeared under my supervision and because of your ex, she would win full custody." He shook his head. "Amber never got it in her head that my parents' money was not mine. I think she was trying to break me so they'd have to step in and support her and the kids."

"Did they really expect to get away with it?"

Neil shrugged. "I don't know. Desperate people sometimes do stupid things, believing they will turn out all right."

I thought about the results of my pregnancy test.

"It was negative,' I told him, forcing myself to meet his gaze, expecting anger, bitterness, even disgust. All I saw was concern.

"Are you all right?" Somehow, I knew he wasn't talking about my surface wounds.

"Honestly, I'm not sure. Too much to process."

"Do you mind if I stay here for a while?"

I wanted nothing more. "Have a seat."

Instead of parking himself in the chair, he climbed into the bed next to me, wrapped his arms around me. "It's okay." His voice was soft, soothing.

Tears filled my eyes. "Don't be nice to me, I can't take it right now."

"I don't have a choice in the matter. I love you, Maggie."

The dam broke and I sobbed into his shirt. He held me and let me cry the way I really needed to, getting out all the fear and pain and anguish I'd stored in the cellar of my soul.

He stroked my hair and made soothing sounds while I mourned for something not meant to be, the picture in my mind's eye of a little girl with my curly dark hair and Neil's killer smile. *This is a good thing*, I told myself over and over. We didn't want another innocent life brought into the crazy mix. No matter how many times I repeated my mantra, I remained...bereft.

He tilted my chin so I looked into his eyes. "Tell me what happened."

"You still don't remember?" I sniffled.

He made a sound of frustration. "No. All I have are facts from a goddamned police report."

I flinched. "I'm so sorry—"

He kissed me, a gentle brush of his lips on mine, the gesture pure affection.

"I'm not upset with you, Maggie, just pissed at my lack of memory about what should have been special. I want to hear it from you."

"Okay." I took a deep breath and told him everything I remembered about that night.

I watched him absorb it all with the ultimate poker face. No reaction when I described how terrified he'd been, or how we'd shed our clothes and gone at it like hormonally driven teenagers on the couch. His arms tightened around me when I revealed his first declaration of love and he closed his eyes when I told him about him calling me Amber.

"Fuck," he said.

"Yeah, we covered that part." I buried my face in his shirt, sorry to have caused him so much anguish. "Do you wish you'd never seen me on the beach?"

He tilted my face up, locking his gaze on mine. "Are you crazy?"

"The jury's still out on that one." My tone was dry and though he still held my chin I glanced away.

"Maggie, look at me," he commanded.

Sucking in a deep breath, I did. His jaw was set, and his eyes blazed with raw emotions, too many to pinpoint.

"My heart stopped when I saw the wreck tonight. Not just because of the kids, but because I might have lost *you*, Maggie. For so long, those boys have been the only good thing in my life, but as soon as I knew they were safe, my thoughts were for you."

"You barely know me," I whispered.

He shook his head. "You make me laugh, charm everyone

around you, even the pissed-off adolescent next door. You picked me up at a go-go bar, turned one of the worst nights of my life into one of the best, and risked your life for my children. You drink coffee like an air traffic controller, talk to your dead mother and you are quite possibly the shrewdest money manager on the planet. I see you, Maggie, and I love the whole package."

My tear ducts were working some serious overtime tonight. "I love you too, Neil."

He held me and I forgot we were in the hospital, dismissed everything but the warmth spreading through my body. I had almost drifted off to sleep when he shifted out from under me.

"I need to go back to the base. My folks or your brother will be back in a few hours to drive you home."

The recollection that he was UA gave me a second wind. "Are you going to be in trouble?"

He grinned. "Nah, I know a few nasty lawyers. I'll meet you at home."

"I like the sound of that."

CHAPTER TWENTY-FOUR

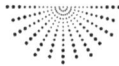

"**P**hillips, where the fuck have you been?" Lieutenant Commander Roberts barked as I exited the truck. The team was back, scattered throughout the parking lot. Most of the guys appeared as ragged and worn out as I probably did. Having your beating heart ripped from your chest twice in one night could age a man. First the boys in danger and then finding out I had sex with Maggie, possibly impregnated her, and I didn't even remember? Too much to assimilate.

I snapped to attention even as a bigger part of me wanted nothing more than to climb in the truck and drive back to Richmond to be with Maggie and the kids. "Sir, I had a personal situation which required my immediate attention and—"

Roberts closed in on me, eyes lit with an unholy light. "You were U.A. and in the U. S. Navy that is still a serious offense. What the hell was so fucking important that you'd abandon a training mission and risk your career?"

I stared him down, jaw and fists clenched. Roberts

244

wanted to do this here? Fine. "My children were kidnapped, sir."

For once in his life, Roberts had run out of noise to spew out of his pie hole. He scowled at me, ascertaining if I was making shit up. I held his gaze, letting my thoughts telegraph so he'd know I wasn't about to back down. He could still bust me down, send me to the Captain's mast, hell even toss my ass in the brig but he'd have to do it in front of the whole team. For a SEAL unit to work effectively, there needed to be a level of trust and respect and Roberts would risk the effectiveness of his team if he came down too hard on me. He glanced around and deflated like a popped balloon.

"My office in five."

"JEEZE, I've scraped gum off the bottom of my shoe with more color than you," Marty said as he pushed my wheelchair out to where the car was parked.

"Gee thanks, Sprout." I practically launched myself out of the wheelchair and onto the front seat of Neil's truck. I couldn't wait to get home and scrub the medicinal smells off me. Hospital funk, gack.

Marty returned the chair to the hospital lobby and I wrung my hands impatiently. "Have you heard from him?"

My brother looked at me blankly. "Who?"

I wasn't buying the clueless act. "The guy who's truck you're driving. Neil."

"Not directly," Marty hedged as he pulled out of the hospital parking lot. "He called Leo and told him you needed a ride home. He wasn't back from the base yet."

"It's after two!" Another reason I avoided hospitals, released in the morning on the East Coast meant morning on the West Coast, with at least a three-hour time difference.

"He's probably lying low since he busted up my ride."

I tapped the bandage on my forehead. "Actually, it was me who wrecked your car and I'm pretty sure Neil isn't the type to hide from confrontation."

"First he knocks up my sister then steals my wheels. Man is asking for trouble."

A lump formed in my throat. "I'm not pregnant and I'd trade your POS for Josh and Kenny any day of the week. Get your priorities straight, Marty."

He didn't say anything else to me until we crossed through the Hampton Roads tunnel. "So what happens now?"

I was really tired of that question. "I'm going to marry Neil and raise those kids."

Marty snorted. "Right."

"I'm dead serious."

"Did he ask you yet?"

"He will when the time is right." The thought of him brought a smile to my face until I remembered his dangerous career. He'd keep running off to save the world while I held down the fort. I bit my lip. Unless he was dishonorably discharged for last night's unauthorized rescue operation. Crap, I didn't know what to fret about, so I worried about everything.

Marty parked the truck and Leo was at my side before he took the key from the ignition. "I made you another cheese-cake. And Kenny's costume."

"Maybe I need to get in car accidents more often." He helped me hobble into the house. Nothing hurt really, but I was stiff and exhausted.

"You look terrible," Laura said to me arms folded across her chest.

Ralph was more tactful. "There's no way I can properly

thank you for saving our grandsons, so I'm going to pay for your hospital bills and buy you a new car."

"Hey! It was my car!" Marty said.

"Two cars then," Ralph said and his cell phone rang.

"Where are the boys?" I asked, more than ready to cuddle up with them under a blanket.

"Napping. Ralph and I have a flight to catch," Laura said and pivoted to face Leo.

"If you're ever looking for a job as a housekeeper, give me a call." She extended a white business card.

Leo blinked. "What about Hilda?"

"She met a sailor at the supermarket." Laura made a sound of absolute disgust. "Anyhow, give it some thought."

Leo took the card and nodded.

"Ready, my dove?" Ralph picked up the suitcases.

"Don't call me that," she snapped and marched out the door. Ralph winked and followed her.

I looked pointedly at the white rectangle in Leo's hand. "Would you really consider working for her?"

"Not unless I was totally desperate." But he pocketed the card.

The phone rang. Leo rushed to get it before it woke the sleeping kids. "Phillips residence."

I held out hands, palms up, beseeching him for information.

"Yeah, she's right here." He mouthed *Neil for you* at me and I lunged for the phone.

"How are you? Is everything all right?"

"That's my line." I heard the smile in his voice. "You can stop worrying, I got a slap on the wrist and probation. The bad news is I have to head out."

So soon? I swallowed. "When?"

"In like five minutes." My heart tore in two at his next

words. "I'm not sure when I'll be back. I'll give you a call as soon as I can though, okay?"

I said goodbye and hung up.

"You don't look happy," Leo observed. "Especially considering you were recently sprung from the hospital."

"Neil has to go overseas." *Please, God, keep him safe.*

Grasping for a way to change the tone of the conversation Leo asked, "So are you going to be moving into the master suite?"

"Yeah, about that…I need a hand from you guys."

"You and your big mouth." Marty elbowed Leo in the side.

"YOU'RE GOING to be gone how long?" I asked, clutching the phone to my ear as I lay back in the bed in the guest room, staring at the dark ceiling. Josh and Kenny were asleep for the night and I was alone and hating every minute of it. This was so not fair— I was more than ready for a happily-ever-after. And an orgasm.

Neil's voice rumbled in my ear, sending shivers down my spine. "I wish I knew, love. My request for leave was denied. I'm lucky they didn't bust me down in rank."

I bit my lip. "I hate this, this not knowing where you are all the time."

"I hate not being there with you. I had… plans." The innuendo was thick and I nearly groaned aloud at all the things I had wanted to do with him. To him. When the hell were we going to catch a frigging break?

"Can you at least tell me you're safe?" I asked, not knowing if I could deal with this nonstop worry. Though I was exhausted, my mind churned out all sorts of worst-case scenarios. Was there any way to avoid it after all the suffering I'd seen?

"I'm fine, Maggie, safe in a hotel for the night, just worried about you. The day after the scuffle is always the worst. I bet you're black and blue all over."

My gaze landed on an unmarred patch of pale skin on my arm. "Not *all* over."

He chuckled once. "It's probably better this way, me not being there. I want you too much to allow you the recuperation time you need."

"Really?" Would I ever get used to him saying he wanted me?

"Trust me, you have *no* idea. I've fantasized about you every night since I first saw you on the beach." The deep timbre of his voice was like a caress.

Still, I couldn't let that remark go unchallenged. "Not buying that one, slick. I was a total lunatic."

"A sexy lunatic I wanted to strip down to her skin and mount in the sand."

"You're a sick man." I didn't even try to keep the purr out of my voice. God, how different would everything have been if he'd done so? "Why didn't you? Not necessarily in the sand but at the hotel...?"

"You were hurting," he said simply. "And I was still technically married."

I closed my eyes. Those things mattered to him. He wasn't the kind of man who would take advantage of a woman down on her luck or cheat on his adulterous wife.

"Didn't stop me from jacking off to thoughts of your lips around my cock about five minutes after you ran off though."

I sucked in a breath. "I can't believe you just said that." I *loved* that he said it, that he'd done it—gave me a serious case of the shivers.

"Well, normally I prefer action to words but we're in an untenable situation here. So tell me, what are you wearing?"

249

"Are you propositioning me for phone sex?" And why did the idea appeal to me on a very basic level?

"Next best thing. Answer the question, Maggie."

Could I really do this without feeling like a total idiot? Glancing down at my stained coffee cup nightgown I said, "Nothing but a smile."

"Liar," he accused. "You're wearing something, you wouldn't be comfortable sleeping naked with the kids just down the hall."

"All the mystery has gone out of our relationship," I groused.

"Take it off, now. I'll wait."

I set the phone down and stripped the nightgown off. "I'm naked, you happy?"

"You have no idea. That night when I watched you strip, I thought I was gonna suffer a heart attack."

"You're laying it on a little thick here, Neil. Really, I know what I look like so there is no need to seduce me with phony words."

He let out what I was sure was an exasperated breath. "Why can't you ever just take a compliment? Your body is exquisite, you drive me out of my fucking mind with lust, my cock is so hard I could drive railroad spikes with it and you think I'm *faking it?*"

What could I say to that? "Umm…." Brilliant, Maggie. Really.

"The next time I see you I'm going to toss you down on the nearest horizontal surface, pin your knees up by your ears and screw your brains out."

His sailor was totally showing and I loved it, was reveling in the image he painted in my mind. "Yesss…" I hissed out a breath.

"Are you touching yourself?"

"No." Amazing, but true. I was naked and 100 % aroused

yet hadn't engaged in any manual stimulation. It was all mental.

Not for long. "Do it, touch yourself for me."

"Where?"

"You have to do some work here, too. Surprise me."

I swallowed, my brain fogged with lust with no clue as to how to please him this way. "Are you joining me in this?"

"Already way ahead of you."

"What are you doing?" I asked, a quiver in my voice, though whether it was from lust or fear, I had no idea.

"Right now, I'm lying on my back, knees bent up and sliding my thumb over my cock."

Something clenched deep inside me and my hand roved down to touch it there. "I want to see that, to lick you."

"Maggie." His breaths were ragged, delighting me. I loved to hear him say my name. "Where's your hand?"

I slid my index finger down into wetness and back up. So good. "Between my legs."

"What are you... thinking?" he grated out.

"I'm imagining it's you, rubbing yourself against me right before—"

"—I slide my cock deep inside you." He finished the thought for me.

"Yes!" I cried out, my hand working faster on my sex. So damn close, I could feel the tightening low in my belly, knew he'd feel the same.

"That's not how it's going to happen though," Neil admonished and my hand stilled. Had I done something wrong?

"It's not?" My breath came out in shallow pants. Needing the release I'd been denied.

"Nope, first I want to taste you, put my tongue right where you're touching, then lower so I can lick inside you."

My whole body trembled, legs falling wide as my mind's eye conjured him doing exactly that. "Oh, God...*Neil.*"

"Do you ache, love? Are you on fire?"

"For you." Whose 1-900 number voice was issuing from my mouth?

"Are you wet? Is your body ready for me?"

Words bubbled up, pushed out by emotion thick and unstoppable. "Yes, Neil, oh I want you so much!"

"Show me the way. Slide your finger in deep."

I did as he bade, thrusting my hips forward to meet the penetration. It was too much and not enough at once and I cried out my need, his name a benediction as it fell from my lips

"I can feel you around me, love, your wet heat gripping me tight. You set me on fire, Maggie."

I dropped the phone from my hand, body limp with relief.

"I love you, Maggie." Distantly I heard the words before the disconnected tone filled the quiet of the night.

As I emerged from the storage room, sat phone in hand, my body shook with unspent lust and self-loathing. Hell, I'd lied to her, to the woman I loved, told her I was doing the same thing. There'd been a moment there when I almost had come. Listening to her moans of sheer pleasure had me dangerously close to the edge. Hell, it might have been worth it.

It had started off as me wanting to please her, give her a little bit of satisfaction. What I hadn't counted on was that she'd be so adept at it, so open and honest with herself, her pleasure distinguishable in every gasp. Unless she'd been phoning it in, too.

Hardee har har.

My flawed reasoning that I owed her an orgasm didn't seem like enough when faced with the way she'd trusted me, what she'd shared with me as I knew she had no one else. She was so sweet and shy, fighting her baser urges, self-conscious in the extreme.

Would I ever be able to deserve her?

"Phillips, we're moving out in ten minutes." Roberts barked at me from across the camp. My head bobbed in acknowledgment.

I told her I was safe, and while that wasn't really a lie because SEALs were tough to kill, I somehow doubted Maggie would see sleeping on the sun-baked earth with scorpions and other fun little tidbits of nature crawling all over you as "safe".

She'd been through enough, deserved more than an extreme dose of cold hard reality.

I stowed the sat phone in my bag, which would remain behind. Only weapons, night vision goggles and MREs were being packed for this trip. We'd pick up the rest of our gear on the way back.

I sat down, needing to do something other than fucking think. Now that I had Maggie and the kids safe, I was terrified in a way I'd never been before. Of dying. It made nc sense but what the hell did anymore?

"Make your call?" J.T. asked on his way to the mess tent.

"I'm good," I lied.

J.T. wasn't an idiot. "You need to get your head in the game, Phillips or it'll get blown off."

CHAPTER TWENTY-FIVE

"So, how long has it been since you spoke to him?" Leo asked as we shopped swatches at the local home improvement store. Since I didn't like the question, I decided to ignore it.

"Either blue or green, something to inspire a calm and tranquil feeling. The total opposite to the den of iniquity."

"Honey, you do *not* want calm and tranquil for your bedroom, believe me."

"It's not my bedroom, it's Neil's and this is what he needs, something to help him decompress."

Leo wore a pained expression and I knew he was holding back a hell of a zinger. Ever since our tiff, he didn't tease me in quite the same way, as if he needed to atone for some egregious sin. "Out with it."

"I thought helping him *blow* off some steam was your *job*." Leo snickered like a prepubescent boy.

"You've been spending too much time with Marty," I informed him, ruining my chiding tone with a smile.

Leo plucked a swatch out of my hand. "Not that one, it's too, *Under the Sea*."

I snatched it back. "Then it's perfect." For my merman.

"What are you going to do about the furniture?" he asked as I ordered two gallons of my color.

Under my instruction, Marty and Leo had hauled every stick of furniture down to the curb where a veteran's group was more than happy to receive it for their charity. Once it was empty, I set to work tearing out the nasty old carpet and the ugly mirrored closet doors and dragged it all down the stairs for the trash. It was hard, intense labor but the result was rewarding.

Neil had sanctified my ring so I could use it again. I was going to do the same for his bedroom.

"Yard sales," I answered Leo as I rocked Kenny back and forth in the stroller. "I already ordered a new bed and I figured I could find some decent pieces to refinish." Thank God I had the truck because the prices some people charged for delivery were beyond obscene!

Leo narrowed his eyes at me. "Who is going to cart all this fab swag back to the room?"

I grinned at him. "Come on, I want to pick out a new ceiling fixture."

"You're really going all out on this?" Leo shook his head but followed me to where Marty chased Josh down the interior illumination aisle. Kenny gurgled from the stroller as if he was eager to join in. Both boys were totally back up to speed after their ordeal.

"Marty, catch him before he breaks something!" I cried as Marty scooped Josh up and tickled his stomach.

"Hey Scamp, you want Uncle Marty to take you to the garden center to look at the fountains?"

Josh nodded eagerly and Marty rolled his eyes at me but allowed Josh to pull him down the aisle.

"Your brother is good with kids," Leo observed.

"That's because he still is one." I craned my neck to study

the lights but they were all a big bright blur. "Anything catch your fancy?"

Leo scrunched his mouth and stared up. "If it were me, and I'm just saying, I'd put in a ceiling fan. That way you can lie there naked and let the breeze blow over you on hot summer nights."

"Oh, I like it." Or perhaps it was just the thought of Neil naked that got my blood pumping.

We picked out a sixty-inch ceiling fan which seemed massive to me but Leo insisted it would "fit the space well".

"You need anything else?" Leo asked after we'd secured the fan.

"Spackle. I noticed some divots in the sheetrock." And I didn't want to even guess how they got there. Probably Amber throwing shit in a tantrum, possibly at Neil. Though he'd never intimated as much I could picture the scene clearly.

"So, who's gonna install this bad Larry?" I asked as we carted our cache to the checkout.

"You could wait until Neil comes home, I'm sure he's got the skill set to do it."

"You're missing the point, Leo. It's a surprise for Neil. I'm not gonna make him work for it."

Leo snort laughed. "You will *always* make him work for it darling, it's your nature."

The memory of our late-night phone call skittered across my consciousness and heat scalded my cheeks. No way was I going to tell Leo how mistaken he was, I was a dirty talking easy piece, at least when it came to Neil.

Who hadn't called back since. Not once in two weeks.

The supplies took a hefty chunk out of my cash, but I felt justified. "So are you gonna hit the church rummage sales with me?"

"In November? Sugar dumpling, you are out of your mind."

"You'll do it, I know you will." We unloaded the cart into the truck and went back for Marty and Josh. "So, I hear you're taking my brother car shopping this afternoon?"

Leo nodded. "The insurance money came in pretty quick and someone has to keep you country bumpkins from being taken to the cleaners. What's on your agenda?"

"The men are coming to install the new carpet on Thursday so I have to patch today and paint tomorrow, give the room time to dry."

Leo shook his head. "I can't believe you turned down a car to do home improvement on someone else's house. Doesn't it worry you that you're totally dependent on him?"

It did, but I didn't have a choice. "I need to do this, for him, for me. For us."

He smiled and gave me a hug. "You're my hero, you know that? Come over later, I make a chocolate volcanic eruption cake you don't wanna miss."

"I don't know, Leo. Sounds awfully gay to me." I winked at him and he gave me a kiss on the forehead.

"Glad to have you back, love. It wouldn't be the same without you."

LATER THAT NIGHT, after I put Josh and Kenny to bed, I thought about Leo's words while I sanded the patches of spackle on the wall. Sure I was back, but for how long? As I worked to fix up the bedroom, I accepted the possibility he might come home and say thank you very much and then show me to the door. Everything had seemed so clear in the hospital when we'd been together, the last time we'd been together. Whoever said distance makes the heart grow fonder was totally full of shit.

He said he loved me and damn it all, I wanted to believe that. That it was really me and not just because I loved his children, was willing to wait at home for him.

"Hey, Maggs." Through the bedroom windows, which I'd opened to dispel the dust, my brother called out to me.

I slid the screen up. "What's doing, Sprout?"

He hefted a six-pack of beer. "Would have rung the bell but I didn't want to wake the kids. Come let me in."

Glad to take a break from my own company, I closed the lid to the spackle can and hurried downstairs.

"You want something to eat?" I asked as I shut the door behind him.

"What do you have?" He twisted a can of beer off the ring and handed it to me, condensation on the ice-cold can dripping to my paint speckled jeans.

"Everything." It was true, I'd been cooking up a storm. I led my brother into the kitchen and opened the fridge. "The lasagna is for the VA shelter down the road, I'm dropping it off in the morning but the baked ziti and the pot roast is fair game. Also raisin gem cookies and peanut butter blossoms—but leave some for Peter, those are his favorite."

"What's with the food orgy?" Marty asked as he scooped a heaping lump of ziti onto a plate.

I took a drink from my beer. "Well Josh is picky so I've been experimenting with different recipes, seeing what he'll eat other than chicken nuggets."

Marty watched me as his plate spun in the microwave. "That's all? You're not slaying the fatted calf in case the prodigal father returns?"

"He's working Marty, not carousing exotic whorehouses." Even as I said the words I fought to forget the dream from last night where he'd been doing exactly that.

My brother accepted my words with a nod and said nothing more as he tucked into his plate.

"So how's the new ride?"

He nodded, always ready to talk cars. "Great ride, excellent suspension, shitty gas mileage, just the way I like 'em."

I rolled my eyes. "Would it kill you to be practical every once in a while?

Marty thought it over as he chewed. "You know, I never tried it, but it just might."

Well, at least he hadn't answered with his mouth full.

Marty cleaned his plate and got up to fix another. At least the food wouldn't go to waste. Lately, my appetite had been flighty at best. I stared out the window into the night.

Where the hell was Neil?

I'M IN HELL. Three fucking days I'd been pinned down by these bastards, some of whom weren't much older than Peter and some sick bastard had placed a rifle in their hands and told them to go shoot the infidels or die trying.

To my left, J.T. peered over the dunes, using his night-vision goggles to scan for a possible location of the hostages. American tradesmen, who'd been down on their luck and decided to roll the dice and take contracting jobs overseas, in countries ending with stan. A classic case of wrong place, wrong time, and my team was responsible for locating their whereabouts.

Why couldn't we all just get along?

J.T flashed me a hand signal. *Hammer's on point.* I had the radio, it was part of my job to keep in contact with Roberts's team on the far side of the hill, let them know when we found something.

Though I'd been back out in the real world since being

diagnosed with PTSD, this was the first mission where lives were at stake, where a single fuck-up could result in a visit from the reaper coming to collect his due. At one time I'd lived for the rescue missions, I enjoyed playing God, at least until I discovered I was fallible, seeing a hostage die while under my protection, in front of her kid.

Shit, my hands were shaking like a fucking newbie. *Maggie, think about Maggie.*

I wondered what she was doing right now, on the other side of the world. Was she asleep yet or maybe up working on some project or another? Maybe Josh and Kenny were having nightmares, it was only too likely, after the kidnapping. God, how I wanted to hear her voice, to be sure she was still there.

"Jesus Christ, Neil, get your head in the game." J.T slithered over to reprimand me when he saw my mind wasn't where it needed to be.

Sucking in a fortifying breath and signaled him with an *I'm cool.*

You better be, because out here we don't get second chances. I don't want to have to explain to your girl that you fucked up and that's why you aren't going home to her.

He was right, this shit was going to get me or someone else killed. Being a cocky son of a bitch had been my M.O. before, I needed it back now.

The radio crackled to life in my ear. "Hostages located. We move in five. Get your team into position." The voice on the other end fed me coordinates I memorized to relay to my team. We were in a hot zone, the rag-tag militia for this area fanning out to find the Americans they knew were close by. Things were about to become furiously intense.

"Acknowledged," I said and got ready to do my job.

CHAPTER TWENTY-SIX

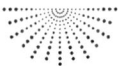

Damn AC unit just up and quit on me. The service tech I'd called to come fix it couldn't make it out until the next afternoon. Skippy. At least the room was complete. The dove gray carpet was soft and thick, playing nicely with the blue-green of the walls. The blanket chest I'd refinished with a cherry stain matched the two nightstands I'd totally scored on. On top of them stood the clear glass lamps I'd been slowly filling with seashells the boys and I had collected from our walks on the beach. Instead of the tacky closet doors, I'd hung a woven blanket sporting a picture of a waterfall on hooks like a shower curtain to be pulled aside to reveal Neil's walk-in closet.

My ring money was gone, as was the nest egg from Neil's father but this was so worth it. As I gazed around I could only wonder what Neil would think when he got home. If he came home. As I hung the rest of his clothes up in the closet, the question I'd buried for the last three weeks surfaced again.

Had he changed his mind?

Sweat trickled down between my breasts. It was

November, for crying out loud! Tomorrow was Veteran's day and it had to be at least 85 degrees. How did people survive before central air?

I took a cool shower, cleaning the sweat off and drying off before the humidity of the bathroom had me perspiring again. I'd brought a tank top and underwear in with me and pulled them on wearily. All of my stuff was still in the guest bedroom but the new Queen-size bed with fresh gray sheets and deep blue duvet looked awfully inviting. I'd wanted to share it with Neil for the very first time. Defiance seethed in my gut. I'd done all the work so I might as well reap the benes.

Even with my new feisty streak, I settled down with the phone inches from my hand.

Frickin' hell, it was warm. The open window to the bedroom and the hard-working ceiling fan Marty had installed did nothing to cool my fevered body. I kicked off the covers and stripped off the top as well before dozing lightly.

Warmth lapped at me, centering between my thighs. The heat was inside me, the familiar dull ache sharpened to a killer point. I groaned and tried to turn over but hands gripped my thighs, keeping me in place.

My eyes flew open just as my panties were pulled aside and his tongue dipped down for a real taste.

"Neil." I gasped and sat up, wanting to stop him so I could see his face, assure myself this wasn't a dream. The slutty part of me wanted to hold him in this position forever. I ran my hand across his back, tears springing to my eyes. The knowledge that he was home and safe, outweighed my sexual desires and I shimmied out of his grip. He growled like a dog who'd had his favorite chew toy snatched away and I shivered.

"Need you," he grunted, gripping my calves and dragging

me back down. His fingers hooked in the sides of my underwear, stripping them off me in one smooth move. He was raw and fresh from the field, not having showered or changed his clothes and there was a vacant look in his eyes.

My heart thundered against my rib cage as a new thought drifted to the forefront of my mind. The changes I'd worked on so tirelessly weren't evident in the dark and the new bed stood in the same space the old one had occupied. The only other time I'd seen him this mindless was when…"You know who I am, right?"

He stopped trying to shove my legs apart, his body stilling completely. "God, Maggie, *of course.*"

I grinned up at him, fully relieved. "Just needed to check."

He closed his eyes and I could see the tremor in his hands. Concerned welled in me. "Are you all right?"

Eyelids closed, he nodded and drew in a shaky breath. "It was…bad this time, what I had to do. The only thing that got me through it was thinking about coming home to you."

My heart melted into a mushy pool of goo and I reached up behind his neck to pull him down to me. Our lips met and white-hot sparks erupted across my nervous system. Our breath mingled, tongues tangling, mating in a frenzy. He was here, with me, finally!

I broke the kiss on a gasp, needing air. His hands roved over my electrified body, touching everywhere and his lips traveled down my neck. *"So soft,"* he rasped as callused fingertips grazed my skin.

With no thought other than to get his naked body on mine as soon as humanly possible, I pulled and yanked at his T-shirt until it came free of his pants. His deeply tanned skin was slick with sweat and I breathed in the scent of his hair, sucking his earlobe between my teeth.

He reared back and whipped the shirt over his head, tossing it over his shoulder. I sat up and licked a trail across his chest, enjoying the salt that made my taste buds sit up and sing for more.

When my tongue flicked over his nipple, he shuddered and then shook his head, as if trying to shake a thought loose.

"You sure you're okay?" His heart was hammering in his chest and I placed my palm above the rapid tattoo.

His sea-green eyes had gone molten with desire, the scruff of his beard oh so very GQ sexy. "Okay is not the word I'm thinking right now."

I curled a finger around a lock of his chest hair. "What are you thinking right now?"

"More Maggie." He pushed me back onto the pillows, one arm pinning both of mine above my head, forcing me to arch my back. His smile was pure wickedness as he used his free hand to brush back and forth across my breasts. He caressed the undersides, stroking up and down the valley between, intentionally ignoring how the peaks stood up to garner his attention. I shivered when I saw him studying my face intensely as if categorizing my reactions.

"Please," I begged, rubbing against him in my need. Never had I experienced lust like this, the intensity flowing in waves through my blood, lost in the grip of tides I couldn't see or hear but felt all too keenly. A woman could drown in pleasure like this.

Slowly, he lowered his head, his gaze still locked on mine as he took one nipple into his mouth. My lips parted on a wordless cry as his tongue swirled around the bud, and pulled, tugging lightly with his teeth. My breath came in shallow pants by the time he switched to the other side, his free hand continuing to torment the wet peak he'd abandoned.

Without conscious thought, my pelvis rocked up to him, wet with desire and burning with need.

He laved my nipple once more, pulling back, releasing my hands as I panted, aching for his touch.

"So many times," he murmured, running the backs of his fingers along the slopes of my breasts. "My imagination couldn't even begin to comprehend how incredible you would be, how passionate."

I stared up into his face, some unnamed emotion was warring with the desire he clearly felt. "I'd give anything to know what you are thinking right now."

"I'M THINKING that you are the most incredible woman I've ever seen." *And I don't deserve you, but damn it all, I'm going to keep you!*

Her passion was addictive, cheeks flushed, eyes bright, like someone had turned a light on inside her. Dark curls spilled across the pillows, her pale skin luminescent. She was the embodiment of desire like someone had reached into my mind and used what they'd found to construct a woman I would find completely irresistible. From her generous breasts to the soft curve of her belly and down to the sexy flare of her hips, even the dark thatch of curls which hid her sex from me.

Not for long.

My one taste of her hadn't been enough, would never be enough. I moved my fingers to caress the folds, watching as she gasped and wriggled, needing more. "Spread your legs for me."

She made a whimpering sound and did. The pink lips of her body glistened and my mouth watered to taste her even as my cock jumped, eager to delve inside her wetness. I was going to make her come first though, even if it killed me. I'd used her body once and even though she'd never said anything—never *would* say anything— I knew in my heart I hadn't brought her pleasure before.

I couldn't remember it and she shouldn't either. Set in my determination to do whatever it took to make this our first night together, I bent my head to kiss her thighs.

Her muscles tensed and then relaxed as I stroked her skin and she propped herself up on her elbows to watch.

"Remember what I said about spectator sports." I took one of her small hands, splayed her fingers, and positioned it so she held her outer lips open for me. From the way she sucked in a breath, I could tell I'd shocked her again. *Good,* I thought savagely. She needed to lose the idea of me as some sort of champion. It didn't seem to matter what I took from her, how I abused her trust, she still watched me through rose-colored lenses. What better way to shatter the prince charming fantasy than to attack her like a rutting beast?

Even as the notion crossed my mind, my body rebelled. Damn it, I *liked* that she saw me as the good guy. She deserved a real hero, not a broken one.

"Are you just gonna stare all night?" Her soft drawl curled around me, as warm and inviting as her body.

"I could," With the picture she made, nipples jutting, fingers holding herself open, she was the stuff of fantasy. "Too much talk and not enough action, is that what you're telling me? I'll be sure to put something else in my mouth to remedy the problem."

Shoving my hands under her ass, I lifted her to my mouth, tongue dragging slowly along the female flesh that tasted sweeter than anything I'd ever known. So warm, yielding to my every stroke, a liquid pleasure I swallowed with relish.

She cried out as I went deeper, slowly laving, giving attention to every tender bit of flesh. My cock ached and I couldn't help grinding it into the mattress, needing the friction.

"So sweet." I pulled back to look up at her, needing to see her face. Her lips were parted, gasping for breath, eyes heavy-lidded.

"Please, Neil," she begged. "I'm so close,"

Control broke and I fell on her again, needing to give her whatever she desired. So hot and slick, I licked her madly while my brain fell back into a primal mode of *must please the female.* Taking her clit between my teeth I lashed it with my tongue and she fell back on the bed, stuffing a fist in her mouth to stop a scream.

Mine. As her body convulsed I delved to taste her orgasm. Swirling mindless ecstasy, experiencing all that she was, my woman.

Distantly I realized she was pushing at my head, trying to pull back.

Not in this lifetime.

"NEIL...I...NEED A MINUTE...HERE." Holy hell, what was *that?* I'd had the freaking mothership of all orgasms and yet he gave me no time to assimilate, kept at me, every thrash of his tongue making my body jerk.

"More." The one word full of gravel and need and I yielded, letting my legs fall open completely, not having enough strength, or will, to stop him. The stubble on his chin was a soft scrape, reminding me that this had been the first thing on his mind, not sleep or a shower but tasting me. My fingers were still where he'd placed them, holding my sex open to his onslaught, baring me to him. This was so wicked, so freaking incredible.

Wetness slid against wetness, his eyes were shut as he

tasted me, his tongue circling the opening to my body before working up to lash my clitoris again. And back down to explore, tantalize…

He *worshiped* me with his mouth as if he wanted to find every little secret bit about me, would pull the knowledge into his body, one lick at a time.

The tightness was building again, the fire stoked to a fevered pitch. My back arched as he laved my flesh. "Oh, god, Neil, I'm going to—"

He slid two fingers inside as my body was racked in spasms. The hardness deep within shattered me, sent me even higher as my muscles clenched. Stuffing that fist back in my mouth was my only option as my body bowed off the bed, a scream trying to break free.

After, I drifted for what felt like an eternity, complete and at peace. Slowly, the world came back into view, the gorgeous man who rested his head on my stomach, watching me with those amazing green eyes.

My body twitched in aftershocks and he smiled, a totally male expression of pride stamped on his face. I reached out and ran a hand through his hair. His eyes closed in bliss.

I frowned, realizing that I had come twice and he still had his pants on. "Don't you need to…?"

Mischief glinted in his eyes. "Need to what, love?"

I blushed. He was gonna make me say it. "Come? Are you happy, you sick bastard who gets off on making innocent young girls talk dirty?"

"Yes, yes I am. Besides, you like it too, admit it." The Cheshire cat didn't sport a bigger grin.

"Well, don't you?"

I didn't think it was possible but his grin widened. "Already did. For an innocent young girl, you are one hot commodity."

CHAPTER TWENTY-SEVEN

Neil left me only long enough to "hit the rain locker". I snuggled under the covers, the air from the ceiling fan cooling my body. Barely lucid, I felt the mattress dip beneath his weight as he snuggled up behind me.

A million questions ran through my mind, not the least of which was, "so you wanna do it now"? I opened my mouth to ask but all that came out was a yawn.

He nuzzled my hair, pulling me tighter against his solid frame. "Sleep, love. I want you fully charged for tomorrow."

Spent and totally compliant I did as he bade, shutting my eyes and not opening them until sunlight spilled through the new curtains. A smile on my lips, I rolled over but the bed next to me was empty.

Damn, waking up alone was so old hat. I had a man now, he should be here. I stretched and yawned, realizing that no, maybe I didn't want him here, because it was morning I had nasty set-your-nostrils-on-fire breath and needed to use the bathroom. Scrambling out of bed, I scurried to use the facilities then turned the shower on while I brushed and flossed and rinsed with mouthwash. I stepped under the spray, lathering my hair and rinsing it clean when I looked down at my legs. Holy planet of the apes, Batman!

Inch long dark hair sprouted out from pasty white legs. Ick, Ick, Ick. All that was missing was the support hose and orthopedic shoes! Sheesh, under my arms, too! When had I become so slovenly with my personal upkeep? Sure, I'd been distracted lately but this was untenable!

Good thing Neil had been seriously hard up last night because under no normal circumstances was this a turn-on.

I turned the water off and lathered my underarms first, scraping the daisy razor along the skin, removing the evidence of my black-Irish ancestry.

I'd just turned the shower back on when the new curtain was pulled aside and I let out a yip.

"Was hoping to find you still in bed, but shower works, too." His hot green gaze roved over me, making my girl parts contract sharply. "Yeah, wet and naked totally works for me."

I swallowed, filled with regret at our crappy timing. "We can't, the boys will be up soon."

"They've been up for over an hour." He grinned at me and began stripping off his jeans. "Up and fed and happy as clams, over at Leo's house for the day."

I was so caught up in the floor show that his words didn't sink in at first. "Say what now?"

His pants and boxers pooled around his ankles and as he bent to step out of them I took my time slowly perusing his tan legs dusted with golden hair, the sculpted dips in his shoulders, arms, and back, enjoying the play of well-developed muscles as he moved. When he straightened, I couldn't help but stare at the massive erection, resisting the urge to lick my lips until his statement made its way home.

"The boys aren't here?" Just the two of us in an empty

house with no family to force us to check the wild current of animal lust that flowed between us. *Dear Penthouse....*

"I asked Leo a while ago if he would watch the kids so we could have a day to ourselves. Is there room enough in there for two?" He hesitated like he thought I might say no when it was all I could do not to attack him and possibly kill us both in my rabid fervor. I reached out both arms, a blatant invitation for him to fill them.

Naked, he stepped over the rim of the tub, and into my eager grasp. My back hit the wall as I allowed him the full extent of the spray, biting my lip as the water hit his perfect body.

"Can I wash you?"

Again with the hesitant tone. Was it possible the magnificent man actually feared *I* might reject *him*? I didn't have the heart to tell him I was already clean so I nodded and was instantly rewarded when he spun me around so my back was pressed against his front, his thick shaft nestled in the cleft of my ass cheeks. He didn't press the advantage though, just lathered his hands with the soap and set to washing me thoroughly.

The thought went down the drain as he explored every millimeter of my skin, starting at my neck and working slowly, methodically down.

Despite the heat of the spray, I was shivering by the time he reached my breasts. When he cupped them in his big hands, kneading the flesh in a way that exceeded basic hygiene, I rested my head against his shoulder.

"You're so incredibly beautiful," he rasped in my ear, pinching and tugging. The sensations spiraled downward, making me grow wet between my legs and I rocked against him, wanting a deeper kind of contact. He sucked in a sharp breath as our arousal filed the bathroom like steam. "So sensual."

Those were not words I'd ever thought would apply to me, but in his arms, they fit like a glove. He made me into this incredible fantasy woman, unleashed something fierce and needy, primal. I reached one arm behind my head, tunneling my fingers through the wet silk of his hair and he nuzzled the tendons in my neck. I tilted my head to allow him better access.

His hands traveled lower, over my soft belly, the rounded hips which I always hated, but seemed to delight him, as he used words like soft and delicious to describe what he touched and tasted. His hips had started to rock.

"Put your leg up on the tub." His voice had picked up that deeply sensual gravelly tone. It was an order but I wasn't about to obey, another thought in my mind.

Instead, I turned in his arms, standing on my tiptoes to kiss his mouth. His tongue plundered my mouth and I let him have this small victory, and leaned into him fully—breasts to chest, his erection pressed directly against my belly. The sensations were pure magic and I couldn't stop rubbing against him like a cat.

He didn't notice when I took the soap from him, only seemed glad to have use of both hands to clutch me to him. I could have gone on that way forever but he pulled back first, his breaths ragged. "Maggie, I need—"

I pressed a finger to his lips. "My turn." I soaped him up, not nearly as meticulous as he had been with me, but then again, he was already turned on, raring to go. The water from the showerhead rinsed the suds away and I followed up with kisses to his glistening skin.

As I sank to my knees, I smiled up at him, wondering if he knew what I was about to do. This time I gave in to the impulse to lick my lips and studied him up close. He swelled under my scrutiny, the head growing moist. Somehow taking all of him didn't seem likely but I was going to do whatever I could to please him. My hands slid up his thighs as I met his hot, green gaze again, telegraphing my intent. The angle was beautiful, he towered over me, yet his eyes pleaded, begged me to love him. He'd said on the phone this was what he'd fantasized about the first time, my mouth on him and I really wanted fantasy to be blown away by reality, so to speak.

Set on this course, my tongue darted out for a first taste.

"Maggie," I ground out as she took me fully into her mouth, her hands cupping my ass, holding me to her. As if I would ever try and get away from this? The powers that be broke the mold when they made her, I thought distantly as I watched her, blue eyes hypnotizing as she pleasured me.

The shower was still on, beating against my back in a rhythm that aided the sensual show she put on for me. Those lovely breasts swayed in time to her movements as she licked and sucked me deep. I reached down to cup her face, running my thumb along her cheekbone. Eyes like blue flames radiated a heat I never could have imagined but reveled in nonetheless. She enjoyed this, having this power over me. It turned her on like a light.

Her tongue swirled, stroking, adding more pleasure to an already incredible experience and my balls drew uptight.

"You're going to make me come," I panted, my hands fisting in her wet hair. Expecting her to pull away, I let out a strangled shout as she took me deeper. It was too much—sensation overloaded my brain as I pumped into her mouth, watching as if from a distance she swallowed what I gave her. I stumbled back as my knees gave out, sinking to the bottom of the tub.

"Jesus," I wheezed, my vision blurry, my cock still twitching as even the water falling from the showerhead was too much. As if she could read my mind, she reached up and shut off the water. Watching me warily, gauging my mood.

Shame coursed through me, a different kind of heat rushing beneath the surface of my skin than what I'd experienced moments ago. Here I'd gone and literally blown my wad in under two minutes. Could I do *nothing* right in terms of this woman? "Where the hell did you learn that?" I flung the question at her like an accusation and winced when I realized I didn't want to know the answer.

She drew back as if I struck her, hurt flaring in the blue depths of her eyes. "Sorry, I didn't learn anything, it was all instinct. I thought you liked it." Her tone held a defensive note, her face so passionate moments before had gone stone cold. I'd asked her to be honest with me and she had, brutally so, but I needed to return the favor.

Pulling her into my arms, I held her close. "I fucking loved it, don't think for a second I didn't. I'm just embarrassed."

She pulled back and tilted her head at that curious angle. "Why?"

Did she really not get it? "Men aren't supposed to come that fast."

She scowled at me, opened her mouth then snapped it shut again as if biting of the words before they escaped. Her eyes narrowed "That's the dumbest thing anyone has ever said to me."

With a chastising look, she scrambled out of the tub and swathed herself in a towel. Though my knees still shook, I stood up, only for her to toss another towel in my face. Her ire was evident as she drawled, "Neil, I think you need a timeout to gather your wits as they seem to be every which way. I'm gonna go rustle up some breakfast."

❄

CURSE all the ridiculous ego-driven bastards and their dangly bits! I pulled on a tank top and shorts, forgoing underwear in my haste to get out of the bedroom before he emerged. Neil had yet to say anything about my *weeks* of hard work. I doubted he'd even noticed.

Don't be stupid, my mother's voice hissed. *Straight men don't notice home décor.*

It's wasn't just about the room though, but the fact that he had some crazy agenda when it came to our love life, like a checklist in his head. One I'd apparently violated.

Well, excuse the hell outta me for not having read the playbook! How come it was okay for him to cross lines and test boundaries but when I did it—and he fricking enjoyed it — I'm accused of….well, I'm not sure what he'd been implying but I really didn't appreciate his tone.

And his explanation as to what had him acting like the jackass? That he was gone in sixty seconds—like the jackass! God save me, I'd almost said that out loud. Pretty sure he wouldn't have appreciated the comparison.

"Maggie, hold up a second," he called, tossing the towel on the floor.

My lips compressed into a Frau Hardass grimace as I glanced from the heap of wet fabric then pointedly back to him. With a muttered curse, he picked it up and returned to the bathroom where I was sure he would hang it up on the towel rack. My heart softened—he was trying, damn it. I rewarded him by not slamming the door as I minced down to the kitchen.

CHAPTER TWENTY-EIGHT

I had coffee perking and four eggs cracked in a bowl, whipped within an inch of their lives by the time Neil came down. Focused on my cooking I still noticed how absurdly glorious he was, and chastised myself for a fool for pushing him away. We needed a little breather though.

"I know you're mad—" he began but I shook my head and bent at the waist to retrieve the coffee creamer, answering only when I was fully upright again. "No, I'm hungry and hurt, not mad."

He heaved a huge breath, scrubbed a hand over his face and I noticed he'd taken the time to shave. "Shit, that's even worse."

I inhaled the glorious aroma of brewing coffee, sucking in the stamina the scent provided. Why could nothing ever be easy with us? Here we had a whole day to ourselves and we were at opposite sides of the kitchen, facing off like strangers.

In so many ways, we still *were* strangers, despite what we'd already been through together. The intensity of every moment was like a narcotic, addictive and confusing, fogging my mind when I needed to think clearly. I finished cooking breakfast and put it down in front of him. He studied the plate, refusing to meet my gaze.

"Neil, look at me."

He glanced up and I saw fear etched into the planes and angles of his handsome face. My throat closed up and I reached for his hand.

"I love you. That's not something that's going to change, got it?"

Relief shone in his eyes. A nod and his hand covered mine and he tried to pull me toward him. I resisted, tugging my hand back. Amber had really done a number on him. I hope she rotted in prison till the sun exploded. If I went easy on him now though, if I let him skate it would become a pattern and a habit and I wouldn't be doing either of us any favors.

"I love you," I repeated and held up a hand when he looked like he wanted to say something, needing to get this all out on the table. "But that isn't a magic wand to fix everything. Not every single aspect of our lives is going to be hunky-dory. Your job, for one, seriously sucks."

He opened his mouth and I rolled over him again. "Wait a second, let me have my say. I'm not asking you to make any changes, at all. I know being a SEAL is part of who you are and no way would I ask you to give up anything. This is a reality we're going to have to deal with."

He nodded. "Thank you."

"I'm not done." Another cup of coffee was in order. "Eat while it's still hot."

That wicked smile made a cameo. "Yes, ma'am."

Maybe it was way too Donna Reed of me, but I derived so much fulfillment from cooking for him, nourishing my man.

"Are you gonna eat that?" He pointed to my plate where I'd only nibbled on half a slice of wheat toast. I slid it towards him. "Have at it."

"So what else?" he asked as he made quick work of the remainder of my breakfast. I hopped up. "You still hungry I can make—"

He snagged my hand, pulling me toward him. "No, you wacky domestic goddess, I mean what else on the list of demands."

"Oh." What else was there? I'd considered so many things, mulled over every aspect, thought about all the stuff we needed to discuss. I only had one actual demand. "Well, I'd appreciate it if you wouldn't treat me like Amber."

His face closed up, there was no other way to describe it as all expression slid right off. "I don't."

I put a hand on his chest. "You're not at all worried I'm going to lose interest in you and the boys, run off to follow my bliss?" Turn into a money-grubbing ho-bag.

He searched my face, pushed the hair out of my eyes. "Not when I think reasonably about it, no."

My lips curved up. "And how often does that happen?"

"Not very," he admitted.

"See, I keep waiting for you to realize I'm not what *you* want and to toss me out on my can."

His eyebrows drew done in a deep v. "Why would you even consider that?"

"Because it's what happened to me before. My mama always said your life's experiences are what shape you and even if the situation is entirely different, you're already trained to react to what you knew before."

He nodded, accepting my statement. "I wish I'd met your folks, they sound like good people."

"They were good people, *boring* people, but salt-of-the-earth types." My smile grew. "Your mother would have had an aneurism if she met them."

"My mother isn't so bad—"

"Your mother is a bitch on wheels and could drive a nun to drink."

He leaned back, studying my face. "Is she a deal-breaker?"

"Nope." I shook my head. "Unconditional means I don't get to make exceptions or provisos. You have to put up with Marty though."

His groan was obviously theatrical. "I'd almost managed to forget about him."

I punched his arm, hard. He winced and made an exaggerated rubbing motion mouthing the word "ouch".

"Should I kiss it and make it better?" I offered.

"Only if you're ready to end this particular conversation with me tossing you over my shoulder and hauling you back to bed."

Giddy, I leaned down and brushed my lips against his arm, sitting back up, my eyes flashing a challenge.

He knocked the barstool out of the way and I gasped as he closed in on me. The split second I spent deciding whether to run or be caught was wasted as he literally scooped me off my feet. Reflexively my arms went around his neck. "I thought I was going over your shoulder?"

"Who knows what you'd do in that position. You're like the ocean—I can't turn my back on you."

He wasn't wheezing as he carried me upstairs and that plus the super sexy masculine fragrance of him was a total turn-on. I melted against him like butter.

"I like what you've done with the place," Neil commented as he sat me down on the bed.

A grinned split my face. "You noticed!"

He looked vaguely insulted. "Of course. It always looked a little like Satan's honeymoon suite decorated by a casino pit boss."

I threw my head back and laughed. "My sentiments exactly." Then a thought occurred to me, one which should have surfaced before I'd even started the project.

"You don't mind I took it upon myself—"

He leaned in, his lips claiming mine, whether to cut off the inane chit chat or answer my question. It was a gallows kiss as if the world was ending for one or both of us and this was the last time our mouths would fuse. The sheer intensity of it scared me a little. Fire this hot had to burn out eventually.

His tongue tangled with mine and I pulled him down on top of me, needing his weight on me, his heat warming me. His hands stoked the fire sliding up to my cheeks. I loved the way he cradled my face, as though I was precious to him. I lost myself in him, forgot my concerns and fears as all my attention focused on touching him, loving him.

He broke the kiss and rolled off of me, yanking up my tank top to tongue my nipples with fervor. My hand cupped him through his jeans, feeling the heat I wanted inside me so badly I ached for it. Every pull of his lips sent a fresh torrent of lust down until I was dizzy with desire.

He palmed the other breast, pinching my nipple while rocking into my hand. Delirious, I started working the zipper on his jeans needing to free him, knowing once I did he couldn't put off our joining any longer.

One of his hands found its way into my shorts and fingered the wetness there until I gasped for mercy.

He pulled out of my grip and yanked the shorts down. I kicked them off until my legs were free and then his hand was back, his green eyes bright as he fondled my sex.

"Is this how you like it?" he rasped as his thumb circled my clitoris.

I nodded but it wasn't enough for him. He took my hand, sucking my index finger into his mouth before placing it on my swollen nub. "Show me."

Though I desperately wanted to, I resisted as I asked, "This isn't one of your stupid checklist maneuvers is it?"

His eyebrows pulled down in a scowl. "What do you mean?"

"Toss the rule book, Neil, you don't need a formula with me."

Masculine lips twitched. "I didn't realize I was so transparent."

"Like a freshly washed window." I stared up honestly into the green depths of his eyes, willing to drown in them. "Haven't you figured out yet that we're not an average couple? We need to make up the rules as we go along because the regular ones don't apply."

He didn't say anything and I took advantage of it to knock him onto his back and straddle his waist.

He stared up at me with an expression that was pretty close to awe and I threaded my fingers through his and bent to brush my lips over his mouth, plunging my tongue in to mate with his, and grinding my naked sex onto him through the jeans. He pulled away, closing his eyes, the corded muscles of his neck straining, the embodiment of raw, masculine power.

I kissed a trail to his ear and hissed "No more agenda?"

"There's so much I want to do to you, with you."

"You will," I vowed. "We have time. What do you want right now, more than anything?"

I was sure he was going to say something about being inside me, my inner muscles clenched anticipating it me but he shocked me again.

"I want my mouth on you, so I can lick you until you come, begging me to fill you."

Something contracted sharply down there at his words. "You've put a lot of thought into this, haven't you?" Even as I said it, I slid up to align my sex with his face.

His eyes slid shut as he breathed in deep, nuzzling the flesh of my inner thigh, making me shiver. "This was what I thought about for weeks, loving you like this, tasting your pleasure."

Then he did, tongue parting the curls of my pubic hair to explore the flesh that was greedy for him. His fingers unlocked from mine so his hands roved up my body, cupping my breasts as his mouth worked thoroughly on my wetness.

Deeply tanned fingers played on my pale breasts, pinching my nipples while lips on lips, tongue swirling and teasing, coaxed me even higher. I covered his hands with my own, back arching to feel as much of him as I could. He lashed my clit, over and over, then gentled it with a slow, loving stroke. I couldn't help but squeeze my breasts as he thumbed the nipples. Sensations rocketed through me and I lost track of everything until his hands wound around my hips, positioning me higher so he could tongue the opening to my body.

"Neil," I panted, teetering on the brink. "I need you."

He tossed me onto my back, and I wanted to scream, frustration clawing at me until I realized he was fighting to free himself from his jeans. Somehow he understood I meant inside of me, now, before I came.

Jeans gone, he took that huge shaft in his hand, sheathing himself in a condom before running the head up and down my wetness, causing me to shiver in expectation.

"Please, Neil." I arched up, ready to feel him deep within me, needing his hardness to fill me while I climaxed.

The first push was tentative as if he didn't want to hurt me. I gyrated my hips, spreading my legs as far as they would go to make room for him. "More," I panted, clutching his shoulders to hold him down to me.

He thrust forward and I cried out, muscles spasming around him, pulling him deeper still.

"Maggie." His voice, filled with gravel held a note of strain as he kept himself very still.

Leaning up to claim his lips I kissed him softly looking into his eyes. "Let go, love me, it's all right."

With a shout he did, his hips surging like a piston, ramming me oh so deep, sending me off again. I held his gaze, let him see what he did to me, how much I loved him as my body milked his while he buried himself inside of me.

Another surge and I felt him go over the edge. His release intense as everything else, his gaze fixed on mine and it all came back to me, the love, the need, total and absolute connection. His breaths rasped and he shuddered, still rocking inside me well after he'd spent.

His lips claimed mine, even as aftershocks shook my body. In this position, he could feel everyone and he groaned aloud and buried his face in my hair.

"I love you, Maggie." My name on his lips was the best sound of my life, and I savored this moment. Nothing could make this better.

Hours may have passed before he let me go, slid out of me to prop himself up on his arms. "I've got something to tell you and it'll probably sound sort of…strange."

Our legs were intertwined and I caressed his face, staring into the hazel green depths which spoke more words to me than his lips ever did. "You can tell me anything at all. I'm not gonna guarantee a reaction, because in case you haven't noticed, I'm something of a loose cannon."

A grin split his face as he raised my knuckles to his lips. "I might have caught on to that one. Wait here."

I was treated to a prime view of him walking naked over to his seabag, where he, Lord have mercy, crouched down to dig through its contents. Perusing the expanse of golden skin I licked my lips and thought *Mine.* Would I ever get used to how perfectly male he was in every regard?

He turned and dove back for the bed, and a giggle escaped as my body bounced back into his arms, where his mouth hunkered down over mine as if he couldn't wait to reestablish contact with me fast enough.

I shivered, recognizing the sentiment.

Our mouths met, tongues tangling and I arched up against him while clutching him to me, legs wrapping around his waist.

"Maggie." His breathing was rough as he pulled back, heat in his gaze, but also determination. Plucking one of my greedy hands off his back he brought it back to his face and kissed the knuckles before sliding a ring on my fourth finger.

Though he didn't speak aloud, I heard the question clearly, it was written on his face. My attention turned to the ring, a princess cut diamond in a gold setting and my eyebrows knit together.

"Hey, that looks just like...where did you find this?"

"A pawn shop, down by the base."

I whipped my head to face him. "No freaking way."

He cleared his throat his expression somber. "I seem to be a metal detector for that particular ring. Can find it wherever it is, so I was hoping you'd always wear it so I can follow wherever you go."

There was no hesitation when I met his eyes, my own filled with tears. "Of course I will."

His lips descended on mine as he gave me that end of the world kiss and I let the tears fall freely, my ring glinting in the sunlight.

Just as I'd thought, it made some Navy sweetheart very happy.

Hooyah, how I loved being right.

"**F**or the love of Pete, Marty, we don't have all day!" I tapped my flip-flop shod foot on the blacktop, ready to be married already.

"Is my tire over the line?" Marty craned his neck out the window. "I don't want to get a ticket."

"Come on!" My future awaited me on the beach, a few hundred yards away. The plan was to be married at dawn, exactly ten weeks after we'd met. Blood tests were done, a J.P lined up and here I was in a whitish sundress and a tiara, waiting for divine intervention to light a fire under my brother's ass.

Finally satisfied that the tire was secure Marty, locked the truck and circled around to where I stood toe-tapping. "Are you sure you want to do this now, like this?"

"Everyone we love is here now. He's in the military, Marty. He can't screw around with dates. I'm sure, Neil is sure. Why wait?"

There were plenty of good reasons not to wait. His leave was up in two days and he'd probably be going back overseas. His parents were in town to stay with the boys, and he had a hotel reservation for tonight, room number 517. How I was so ready to debauch him in room 517. Well, for me any room would do but he insisted we needed to start our lives together with a clean slate.

Really was there any way to say no to him? Well, maybe if I were crazy and *wanted* to say no to him. Besides, how many guys would actually see the symbolism in that? The least I could do was cooperating and strip when told.

I glanced at the light on the horizon and picked up my pace, half dragging Marty. We dashed across the street and in between two hotels to get to the sand, where I kicked off my flip-flops.

"I always thought you'd do it up, you know, one of those big poofy girl weddings with swans and shit."

"Nope, no swans for me." There they were, down by the shore. Neil's back was to me, his attention on the horizon but still resplendent in his dress uniform.

Kenny squirmed in Ralph's arms and Josh held Peter's hand. We had to hurry up because he needed to be at school by eight-thirty.

Marty stopped and planted his heels. I was ready to deck him, manicure be damned, but he looked so forlorn I hesitated.

"What's wrong, Sprout?"

"You deserve better than this," my brother said so quietly I had to strain to hear him. "Taking care of us all this time, now you're going to marry some Navy guy who already has kids? When are you going to do something for yourself?"

Was it possible to be touched and livid at the same time? "Marty, you fool, that's what I'm *trying* to do. I want to be with him, to be a part of his family."

My brother didn't look convinced so I continued. "Ever since Mom and Dad died, we got by, but what I wanted was to be part of a real family again. You don't need me to take care of you anymore, Sprout, so stop pretending this is about me."

He wouldn't meet my gaze. "I don't know what I'm going to do."

"Well, you're going to get your behind in gear and walk me down to the beach and give me away. Then you are going to go stay with Leo and landscape some more lawns until you figure out your next move."

He shook his head. "You make it sound so simple."

"Marty please, I'm begging you, can we pretend today isn't all about you?"

He nodded. "Sorry, I'm just going to miss you."

"Thank you, Sprout. Now take me to my man!"

For once in my life, my brother actually listened, walking me across the sand to where Neil waited with a smile on his face. I'd forgone the bouquet because I didn't like to torture living things and instead laced my fingers through his as the sun rose over the ocean. It was a perfect day for a new beginning.

The End

MISADVENTURES OF THE
LAUNDRY HAG

**Want more Maggie and Neil? Join them in the zany
mystery series** *Misadventures of the Laundry Hag*

Book 1 Skeletons in the Closet

Maggie Phillips hasn't had it easy. As the wife of a retired
Navy SEAL, and the adoptive mother of two little hellions,
Maggie is constantly looking for ways to improve her family's financial situation. She accepts a cleaning position for
her new neighbors (who redefine the term 'eccentric'), never
imagining she will end up as the sole alibi for a man with a
fascination for medieval torture devices when he is brought
up on murder charges.

While Maggie struggles to prove the man's innocence, her
deadbeat brother arrives, determined to sell Maggie and Neil
on his next great scheme and to mooch with a vengeance. If
that isn't bad enough, her in-laws, (the cut-throat corporate
attorneys) descend on the house, armed with disapproval and

condemnation, for the family's annual Thanksgiving celebration.

As the police investigation intensifies, Maggie searches for the killer among the upper echelon of Hudson, Massachusetts in the only way she can— by scrubbing their thrones.

Of the porcelain variety, that is…

Now available on Audiobook Narrated by Suzanne Cerreta

IT'S NOT MY WORDS THAT COUNT. IT'S YOURS!

Please consider leaving an honest review for this book. Reviews help readers like you select the kind of books they like and help authors like me sell books to the right readers. I found one of my favorite series from a two star review.

Thank you for reading!

Jennifer L. Hart

ABOUT THE AUTHOR

USA Today bestselling author Jennifer L. Hart writes about characters that cuss, get naked, and often make poor but hilarious life choices. A native New Yorker, Jenn now lives in the mountains of North Carolina with her imaginary friends. Her works to date include the Damaged Goods mystery series and the Magical Midlife Misadventures.

Visit Jenn's website Hart's Hideout for more.

Want exclusive behind the scenes access to what Jenn is working on next? Become a Patron today!